I0741902

Dedicated to my Mexican Friends

Shafted

A Mexican Tale

Novel

T.S. Aguilar

1

DARKNESS, HEAT, HUMIDITY, and dust. The air thick with the bitter stench of rancid sweat and excrement. Men at work in a mine on the north-eastern edge of Mexico's silver belt. They labour six hundred meters below the *Sierra Madre Occidental*, the mountain ridge that runs from the border with the United States of America in the north all the way south to the state of Guadalajara.

A one-meter-high fissure, a gash at the base of a rock wall reveals a sump of slurry, rock shards, urine, and faeces. A slab of rock the size of a large suitcase pins a man by his left arm and shoulder into the stinking waste. Barely audible over the din of the clanking machinery rings out his scream for help.

It is I, Rigoberto Pereira Cervantes, who is screaming for help! I am drowning!

My foreman, Miguel Patín turns, sees my predicament, gets down on his knees, and shouts orders to the other miners. One man props up my head. Everyone else shovels the watery, slimy sediment and razor-sharp rock shards with their calloused hands from the bottom of the sump. Blood mixes into the slime as their hands are cut.

Desperately, they try to keep the liquid level below my nostrils and save me from becoming another statistic. But the slurry keeps on flowing back as quickly as these men dredge the pool. It washes over my face. Fear of my imminent death chases away any hope for survival.

Beams of yellow light from the miners' grimy helmet lamps stab into the darkness and reflect off the surface of the sump. Eerie circles and shadows dance on the jagged roof of the fissure. It looks as if the dreaded mountain spirits have come to claim their dues at last!

Miguel grapples with the slimy edge of the rock. He tries to move the slab, but his hands slip up. Swiftly, he moves into the crevice. Bent low, he places his feet to the left and right of my head. He gets a good grip on the heavy slab to raise it. His taurine bellow and the miners' shouts of encouragement echo off the walls as he squats down low to lift the rock in an effort of superhuman strength.

The ripping of cloth is heard when his overall splits wide open. His bare arse hits me square in the face and dunks me deep into the sludge the moment he heaves the rock away and frees my arm and shoulder.

How's that for brown-nosing your boss?

Moments later, the mechanic Vicente and our face-man Javier place me with great care on a makeshift stretcher. They carry me to the cage in the main shaft to get me out of the mine and to the medical station. In pulsating pain, I glance back at Miguel and want to thank him for saving my life. But he has already turned and walks away back to his task of digging for silver bearing ore.

As soon as I have been hauled out of the dark back into daylight, two security guards put me on a proper stretcher and carry me into the medical station.

Nurse Mireilla, a small woman of supple frame, and a pretty, almond shaped face, stoically watches them dropping me off like a bag of meat.

The stretcher clunks on the tiled floor. I cry out in pain. The guards bitch about some specks of slurry on their neat, brown uniforms and spit polished boots.

"Who's that?" asks the nurse.

"Number 2733," answers one of the guards.

"And what's his name?"

"Don't know. Who cares?"

"Cut the crap," is the nurse's sharp response. "I want his name."

The guards poke into their breast pockets and extract folded sheets of paper. They check the lists of workers' numbers and names and one of them mumbles, "Rigoberto Pereira Cervantes."

"What was that?"

"Rigoberto Pereira Cervantes."

2

"Thank you." The nurse gives them a stern look and continues, "And now get out!"

She points to the door, and I note with some surprise how the guards follow the direction of her stubby finger like a couple of lambs. Certain to be in capable hands with her, I decide that now is a good time to faint.

Stripped of my boots, overall, and underwear, nurse Mireilla brings me back from the land of coma by hosing me down with lukewarm water in the bathroom of the medical station.

A moment later I am subjected to x-rays, put on the operating table, and processed by Doctor Gomez as if on an assembly line. He shows no mercy and scowls when I scream out in pain. To shut me up, he gives me a painkilling injection before he straightens my fractured bones and puts on a cast.

Gomez is a member of the board of directors and had to be dragged out of a meeting. He is upset but not about having to attend to yet another accident victim. I am the fifth one of the day with one fatality already recorded as I read later on a whiteboard in his office. No, the good doctor is livid, as he loudly proclaims, on account of his director's vote having to be cast by proxy in an all-important decision on further cost cutting measures of the mine. To add to his outrage, "that recalcitrant scumbag", as he refers to me in front of the nurse, has the nerve to waste more of his valuable time by demanding a medical report.

Mireilla dresses me in a neon orange "mine property" overall she cuts open at the left sleeve all the way up to the shoulder to fit over the extensive plaster cast. Then she seats me in a "mine property" wheelchair and pushes me into the doctor's sanctum, a luxuriously furnished office separate from the surgery and consulting room.

"What could you possibly want with a medical report?" Doctor Gomez asks. "Can you even read? Are you literate at all?"

A permanent grin seems to be etched onto his round face. His eyes, however, show no sign of humour. Angrily they pierce me from behind his gold-rimmed spectacles. It is my heartfelt wish to wipe away his grin and match his facial to his ocular expression. Drowsy from the massive dose of painkilling injections, it takes me a moment to formulate a response.

"Yes, I can read," I mumble. "Anyway, the medical report is not for me."

"Indeed?" he says in a voice thick with sarcasm. "Then who might be the ultimate benefactor of such a report?"

"Whoever, uh…"

"Whoever? That's not specific enough to waste time with paperwork of little consequence, wouldn't you agree?"

"No, I wouldn't agree," I mutter and strain to gather my thoughts. Haltingly I continue, "From your comments to the nurse about my x-rays, the plaster cast was put on, and I quote, to allow the fractured clavicle, humerus, radius, and ulna to heal. I also heard you say that you wouldn't assess any possible damage to ligaments and cartilages. Therefore, I'm sure you agree, I may require further medical attention, or I could suffer a long-term disability as a result of your incomplete treatment of my injuries. Hence, I will have to have a medical report of my accident to inform any one of your esteemed colleagues entrusted with treating me at some future date about the origin of my condition. Otherwise, he or she might think my ligaments and cartilages are busted from jerking off too much, wouldn't you agree?"

Doctor Gomez is speechless. I have succeeded in wiping the grin off his face. He gapes at me with the expression of an insulted carp while rocking to and fro in his high-back leather chair that must have cost the mining company the equivalent of my annual wages. He reaches into his pocket and takes out a golden lighter and a pack of American cigarettes. He lights one of the coffin nails, inhales deeply, blows the smoke in my face, and leans back.

"All right," he says suddenly, jerks forward and slaps a pad of medical report forms on his desk. "Of course, the report will be limited to the extent of your injuries. What's your name?"

2

IN CASE you were wondering, I'm not a miner. Actually, I'm a copywriter. I had run away from an overly stressful situation in my, I should say, "previous life" I couldn't handle any longer. I got stuck in the god-forsaken mining town of Tepetapa with a busted car and totally broke. I took a job underground at the *Minas de Plata Tepetapa S.A.* for five pesos an hour mucking out a stope, that is, I was shovelling muck, the broken ore, out of a stope and down an ore chute. No other job was to be had. But making hardly any money is better than making no money at all.

The first time I went down the main shaft into the humid, evil smelling, thick air in the rattling cage together with some forty miners was the beginning of my new life. The sounds, the smells, the language used, even the camaraderie among the miners was in every respect unlike anything I had ever experienced, heard, or seen. The speed of the lift's descent from level to level caused my ears to pop, and the further down we went, the more I wondered if I had made the right decision.

But there was no turning back. For one, I was already in hock to the tune of over six hundred pesos at the company store for overall, helmet, and boots. For another, a big, calloused hand rested on my shoulder and held me back every time the cage stopped, and I wanted to get out. The hand also guided me out of the cage on level six and, I was certain, would have prevented me from turning on my heel and running away. That hand almost the size of a toilet lid belonged to Miguel Patín, my foreman.

A powerfully built and broad-shouldered *castizo*, Miguel towers at least a head above everyone else at over one meter ninety and about ninety-five kilograms of muscle. He leads thirty miners, his tough crew of *cholos*, *lobos*, *moriscos*, *coyotes*, *harnizos*, and me, a *mestizo*.

I should explain what these names mean. Contrary to some other countries, in Mexico they are not racist definitions. They define our origins and assign us to a group functioning like an extended family. In my case, being a *mestizo*, it means that my parents are of European and Native origin. Miguel being a *castizo*, his parents are a *mestizo* and someone of European origin while a *cholo* and *coyote* are of *mestizo* and Native origin, depending on the father or mother being a Native. A *harnizo* is of European and *coyote* parentage. *Lobos* and *moriscos* are the offspring of Native and African parents depending again on the mother or the father being African. It looks to outsiders confusing but it is crucial to remember that it is not a racial classification. It is simply proof of Mexicans having no prejudice when it comes to falling in love and producing offspring.

So that is our tough crew of Mexicans. We have the back-breaking task of digging for silver-bearing ore on level six under the guidance of Miguel. He is a no-nonsense kind of guy. He knows his stuff. He is respected. And when he raises his booming voice, people will listen.

Well, when I say people will listen, I have to qualify that. Peers and subordinates listen and follow his instructions. But the directors of the mine, North Americans of European descent with Doctor Gomez, the one token Tex-Mex among them, are a different kettle of fish. They have their own agenda and don't listen to their serfs. Miguel, experienced and of sound judgement in all matters pertaining to the underground operation of the mine, might as well have talked to a rock wall on the many occasions he presented his concerns or suggestions for improving the work conditions until the day Miguel made the directors listen, follow his instructions, and obey his demands. And did they ever. And didn't we, and all of Mexico, have a belly laugh. But I'm getting ahead of myself.

Underground, Miguel is a man of few words. Every man of his crew is admonished not to waste time with small talk or complaints. The noise level makes a conversation impossible anyway.

On my first day in the pit, Miguel put me through my paces without exchanging as much as two words. He showed me how to set up and operate the eighty-kilogram jackleg drill for horizontal drilling and how to connect the slurry pump and hoses. I learned how to insert and wire up explosive charges, and got hands-on experience with the scaling, placing reinforcements, as well as removing broken ore with a hydraulic gathering arm. Once I had seen it all and had done it to Miguel's satisfaction, I was left to my job of chute-man mucking out the stope.

Yet after work, over a beer at the cantina, Miguel became quite talkative. I learned from him all there is to learn about mining for a novice. First thing he hammered into me was that there are no horizontal shafts. The main shaft, the ventilation shafts, the ore chutes, waste passes, winzes, raises and the ore bin are vertical. The horizontal openings are levels, drifts, and stopes, he said.

The levels link the main shaft to other shafts or raises. A horizontal opening driven towards the ore body is called a drift. Stopes provide access to the ore body where the drilling and blasting and the actual extraction of the ore take place. The blasted rock is the muck, which is scraped into a hole in the ground, the ore chute from where it drops into the ore bin at the bottom of the main shaft. At the lower end of the ore bin is the skip filling station. The skip carries the ore up the main shaft to the mill above ground.

Beyond the basics of a mine's structure, Miguel enlightened me about various tasks such as scaling, the process of removing loose rock from the face, roof, and walls of the levels, drifts, and the stope. It is done to detect faults and cracks that call for reinforcements to make the workplace safe.

The reinforcements used in Tepetapa are expansion bolts with steel plates and sprayed concrete. But scaling and installing reinforcements are time consuming, material intensive, and cut into the mine's profit.

Weighing profit against safety, the board of directors decided in favour of profit and ordered cutbacks to basic mining safety measures to improve the profitability of the mine. Barely two weeks after my arrival, scaling of levels, drifts and stopes as well as placing reinforcements were cut back to practically nothing. It reflected on the one hand the directors' relative short-term commitment to the mine and on the other, their dastardly attitude towards us, the mineworkers.

Miguel bitches every day to the mine inspector about the safety cutbacks. As the foreman of our crew, he is responsible not only for following the ore body but also for assuring the drilling and blasting advances according to the daily quota, and every man's safe return to the surface. But management doesn't give a damn about mine safety or equipment maintenance and won't reverse its decision. Consequently, my accident hasn't come as a surprise to anyone.

It is only due to Miguel's foresight and prudence that his team hasn't experienced any loss of life or limb. Everybody fears a collapse, an avalanche of loose rock burying everyone at any moment. The miners expect it every time the awful sound of crunching rock is heard, or shards fall on their helmets. Rock falls have regularly killed miners of the other eleven crews working underground in Tepetapa.

The moment before my accident happened, the claw of the hydraulic gathering arm I used had snapped off and slid into the sump at the bottom of the horizontal fissure. I scrambled after it and slithered into the ooze on my back. A crunch was heard, the slab of rock slammed down, and it pinned me by arm and shoulder into the crevice. I had enough breath left in me to scream before my mouth filled up. It was pure luck Miguel stood nearby watching Vicente fix the slurry-pump. He saw I was drowning and immediately jumped to my rescue.

Thinking about my accident and how narrowly I escaped death, I am looking out of the large window of Doctor Gomez's office. It provides a broad view of the mine compound's gate and the town.

The gate, guarded twenty-four hours a day by a heavily armed security force, is to my knowledge the only breach in the three-meter-high chain link fence topped by coiled razor wire that surrounds the entire complex of mine, mill, and smelter.

The big, dusty plaza in front of the gate is the town's hub of activity with a few commercial structures on the perimeter.

A grey mass of concrete slab hovels covered with rusty corrugated iron sheets stretches to the south. They are the workers' living quarters.

The town is watched over by a little white church on a plateau in the western flank of the valley.

Directly opposite the mine gate, stands the architectural oddity of Tepetapa, an old, three-storey brick building. Built as a private residence by one of the mine's previous owners in the year 1928, as a legend above its front portal informs the many visitors, it now serves the community as the whorehouse.

The structure looks completely out of place with its ascetic, straight lines broken up by Jugendstil windows, swooping curves of a Gaudiesque balcony and a broad, Italian marble stair leading up to the entrance, a solid steel door with a spyhole.

8

Squat, one-storey adobe structures flank the house to the left and right, respectively. It is the cantina, the local watering hole, and a pawnshop, the local financial institution. In my opinion, they are the most appropriate neighbours of the whorehouse.

At a right angle to the cantina stands the wooden structure of the company store where almost anything money can buy is obtainable. Food and medicine, textiles and shoes, household goods, furniture and basic tools fill the shelves. However, not a single radio or television set can be purchased. The valley of Tepetapa is cut off from any public communication with the outside world. Neither a telephone is accessible, nor newspapers are sold. The only way to communicate with the rest of the world is by mail. But to the best of my knowledge, nobody has ever received a response to a letter mailed to friends or family.

The view of the town from the doctor's office is partially blocked by a watchtower and the guardhouse to the right of the mine gate. The low pay-office building to the left is patrolled by guards armed with rifles, handguns, and truncheons.

It is payday. Mothers with children in tow and female prostitutes and their male peers called *maricas* mingle in the heat and dust of the plaza. They are waiting for the miners from the early shift to collect their pay and dispense their hard-earned "riches".

Workers wearing tattered overalls, heavy boots and safety helmets, the grime of the day's work on their faces, stroll one by one through a narrow opening in front of the pay-office. They register their presence by shouting their employee numbers into one of the small windows.

The scene is reminiscent of a high security prison, and the mineworkers are indeed prisoners of the mine, the town, and the narrow, claustrophobic valley not more than a kilometre wide.

A few minutes after the siren wails to sound the change of shifts, long lines of exhausted looking men form at four of the five pay-office windows. One after another, each worker shouts his number into one of the windows and a piece of white paper with his number and the current date at the top is presented. In return for applying a thumbprint, a small manila envelope with the employee number and the week's earnings handwritten near the upper edge is pushed out. The men rip open their envelopes and count the wages while remaining at the window.

It is the mineworkers' responsibility to assure their pay corresponds to the amount written on the envelope. They have to put aside a ten per cent cut of their pay for the security guards. It is a company-enforced graft if they want to keep working.

How's that for job security?

No document such as a payslip changes hands. No name is ever mentioned. Every man is only known and addressed by what he is to the directors and the guards - a number.

Doctor Gomez finishes writing the report. He hands it across the desk and says, "Here's your report. Now let me give you a word of advice, Number 2-7-3-3. You've turned out to be not only a recalcitrant scumbag but a semi-literate dimwit as well. People like you are not held in high regard around here. I'll make sure security keeps an eye on you. One wrong move or rebellious word out of you and you're gone. You understand? You're just another member of the nameless, unwashed masses, replaceable at any time."

I pick up my bottle of pills, get up out of the wheelchair, nod to him, and mutter, "Yes, just like you, doctor."

My remark stops him from lighting another cigarette. He jumps up, leans forward, and shouts something in English, part of his baggage from Texas, his place of origin. Although I speak English quite well, I don't understand one word of his wild curse.

Left arm raised to eye-level by the support cast, I walk into the waiting room. I pick up my bundle of overall, work boots, and helmet, nicely baked together with dried slurry for easy carrying, and join a queue of the nameless and unwashed colleagues shuffling up to the pay-office windows.

3

SLOWLY Miguel walks away from the pay-office window. His strong-featured face, grimy with dust, sweat, and slurry, is distorted in anger. Anybody within earshot can hear him grumble and curse. He holds the small manila envelope with the meagre earnings in his left hand. In his right, he crumples and rolls a few banknotes and coins into a ball. It is the cut of his earnings for the security guards.

He snorts sucking up snot from his deepest inner crevice and spits a blackish-greenish wad, big enough to extinguish a small fire, onto the ball, thus making the money instantly unrecognisable as legal tender. He walks up to the guard at the gate and drops the spitball into the Brownshirt's hand. The guard tosses the sticky mess with an expression of disgust through the open fifth window of the pay-office and shouts, "Filthy swine!"

A mad scream and curse are the immediate response from the office to Miguel's form of graft payment. The guard looks to the window. He expects to receive an order to take action and holds onto the steel post of the fence.

Unperturbed by the scream, Miguel steps out through the narrow opening and shuts the sliding gate with a quick, strong pull.

The guard howls, his fingers jammed between gate and post.

The commanding officer of the security guards bursts out of the office. Still adjusting his holster, he shouts, "You! Number 1-8-0-3! Come back here!"

Miguel ignores the order and its shrill repetition and walks towards his wife Laura and their three children Gabriel, Pilar, and Benito who are waiting for him. The metallic clicks of the release of gun safety catches are heard. Unfazed by the threat of catching a bullet in his back, Miguel smiles at Gabriel, his oldest son aged five, and ruffles his hair. Then he hugs his wife and his four-year old daughter Pilar and gives them pecks on the cheek. And at last, he picks up Benito, the youngest of the siblings at age two, who squeals with delight when his dad lifts him high above the crowd and has him settling on his left arm.

Miguel turns around with Laura by his side and Gabriel and Pilar in front of him to face the officer. Six guards, four on the ground and two on the watchtower, aim their assault rifles at Miguel and his family.

Benito begins to bawl facing the rabid officer who shouts at the family just a few steps away. Miguel tries to calm Benito, gently patting his back and laughing at him. It is to no avail. Benito just takes another deep breath and howls louder than the officer.

The bedlam gives some of the miners standing nearby reason to stop dickering with their families, friends, or prostitutes, turn towards the gate and advance a few steps. Suddenly confronted by a hostile crowd headed by a vociferous two-year-old blaring at full throttle, the officer gives up. He orders his men to withdraw but not before he shakes his fist at Miguel and spits out before him.

Miguel shrugs and walks with his family through the crowd towards the cantina. They pass miners and mill and smelter workers who hand over the week's wages to their spouses and firmly demand without much success to keep a few pesos for a drink or two. Some arguments are loud and come close to the exchange of blows. Others amount to no more than expressions of resignation as the women plead their cases for the money they need to buy food and clothing and pay utilities. A few of the men even attempt to escape the looming confrontation with spouse and children. Keeping their heads low, they take a roundabout way through the crowd to the cantina. But all of them are caught. Their women have spread out the kids in a crude form of dragnet nobody can escape. Despite the occasional laughter there is not one happy face in the crowd. And why should there be an expression of happiness when there is no reason to rejoice? Every family lives from hand to mouth, is always in debt to the company store and never can make ends meet despite all their efforts and hard work.

Resting his head on Miguel's shoulder, Benito has fallen asleep. Gabriel holds his father's right hand and tries to keep in step with him. Pilar, a shy, little beauty, walks between mother and father and hides her face in the folds of her mother's long, dark skirt whenever somebody looks at her.

Laura, a petite, shapely woman wearing a headscarf tied in the neck, glances back at the mine when they are a few steps away from the cantina. She looks up at Miguel with her big, dark eyes in a sort of reprimand.

12

"Is this ever going to end?" she asks.

Miguel stops and solemnly shakes his head. "No, my love, not until I stop the corruption."

"How do you think you'll ever do that?" she asks him.

Miguel looks at the people around them and a devilish grin lights up his face. "Oh, next week I'm going to eat the money, squat on the guardhouse desk and pay the graft in digested form to raise a bit of a stink among the leeches. If every miner followed my example, we'd stop the corruption in a day."

Gabriel laughs. Pilar looks baffled as if trying to picture her huge dad trampling with his big feet all over the desk of the small guardhouse office and taking a dump. Laura slaps Miguel's arm and snickers. "That's disgusting."

Miguel puts Benito at his feet on the dusty plaza, straightens up, and looks at Laura with a bitter expression. "Yes, my love," he mutters in his gravelly, basso profundo voice. "I agree. Taking a dump on a desk is disgusting. But what's even more disgusting is that I get paid hardly enough for seventy hours of hard labour to put food on the table for you and the children, and that these useless bastards," he raises his left arm and points at the guards, "with the backing of the gringo directors, can demand and receive a cut of our starvation wages so we can keep our jobs. That's truly disgusting!"

Laura looks at her husband and touches his arm trying to calm him when she sees his helpless rage. She hugs him and says, "I know, *cariño*, I know. It's just… I'm so afraid."

Miguel rubs her shoulder and proceeds to take his wages out of the manila envelope.

He gives Gabriel, Pilar, and Benito a coin each for the purchase of a treat, folds the remaining change into a fifty-peso note, and hands the rest of the money to his wife.

It takes Laura only a wink to count it - three hundred thirty pesos. She looks a little aghast and counts the money again. It hasn't become more. Dejected she drops her arms by her side and says, "It's barely enough to pay our debts at the store."

Miguel raises his hands in despair. Seeing tears well up in her eyes, he looks up to the sky, reaches for Laura, holds her close, and mumbles, "It'll get better once we're paid our bonus."

He bends down to tuck the small amount of money he kept for himself into the shaft of his boot.

An ear-splitting shriek of excitement, envy, and arousal coming from behind puts him back in the upright with a jolt. Miguel turns on his heel and faces a tall transvestite by the name of Juanita, who wears a bright floral dress, heavy make-up, a blonde, curly wig, and white platform boots. It is Miguel's turn to let out a muffled shriek at the sight of the *marica.*

Juanita clasps a white-gloved hand over his mouth and stares at Miguel's baggy overall. He adjusts his wig a bit and says with a giggle rising from his throat, "Mother of God! You intend to go into my line of business?"

"Are you crazy?" blurts Miguel with some hostility. "Whatever gives you that idea?"

"Well," snorts Juanita and winks coquettishly, "the way you exposed your assets just now, I thought I'd be forced into early retirement. I could never stand up to your kind of competition, darling."

Miguel hears Laura say, "You have a fresh air vent in the back of your overalls. Very practical."

Juanita cackles and hoots before he says, "I'll say!" He enhances his statement with a wave of his hand.

Already irritated by Juanita's remarks and Laura's and Gabriel's snickering, Miguel does a clumsy pirouette when Pilar sticks a hand into the ripped overall and reassuringly pats her dad's bare behind.

Torn between anger, embarrassment, and amusement, Miguel thunders, "Bugger off, the lot of you! I have to settle my bill at the cantina!"

14

4

A SMALL wooden table on spindly legs and two matching chairs stand just inside the cantina's broad, open entrance. It stands out from the rest of the bar's sturdy furnishings. It is "my" table since I claimed it as my permanent eating and drinking location shortly after my arrival in Tepetapa. Seated there, I am under the illusion of not belonging to the clientele of mine workers while still being part of the crowd, which reflects my ambiguous view of my presence in the valley.

I have a beer, rest my plaster cast on the backrest of the other chair, and watch the hustle and bustle of the shift change on payday. Nothing has changed since the first depressing impression I have had of the atmosphere of desolation of the town centre, the town itself, and the valley.

The "lifelines" of Tepetapa, the road in and out of the valley, the overland power cable and water pipeline, snake their way down the mountainous terrain from the south.

The valley's precipitous, rocky, barren flanks to the east and west form the natural town limits never allowing anyone to see the sun rise or set. The valley tapers off to the north into a narrow gap offering a view of yet more desolate rocky strata all the way to the horizon.

Crammed into this narrow, forbidding fold of the earth's crust is the town with its cheek-by-jowl setting of low concrete hovels in a crisscross of winding alleys. The road is the dividing line between the housing and the mining compound, which is dominated by the headframe, a huge slagheap, and a gleaming white administration building.

The skeletal tower of the headframe with its huge and constantly spinning wheels at the top stands tall above the mine's main shaft. It serves to raise and lower the cage to carry miners, tools, and machinery and drive the skip that brings the broken ore up from the bottom of the shaft. But more than just a service unit, the headframe also symbolises life and death of this town. It represents life, however minimal and miserable, to about nine hundred miners as long as its wheels keep spinning. It will symbolise death of the mine and the end to the livelihood of the mineworkers once its wheels come to a permanent halt.

The mill, smelter, drab ventilation house, transformer-station, warehouse and machine shop, a rusting water tower and the low pay-office building make up the rest of the productive sector of Tepetapa. The mill is connected to the skip station of the headframe by conveyer belts. Adjacent to the mill is the smelter where the crushed ore is separated into its components lead, copper, antimony, silver, gold, and platinum. Cast into pellets and bars, the metals are shipped out by truck never to be seen again by the booted and helmeted moles that extract it from the belly of Mother Earth.

The gleaming white, three-storey office building with big windows and a patch of lawn and shrubs in front of it sits in stark contrast to the dirt and dust of the rest of the compound. It houses air-conditioned offices, a laboratory, the medical station and such amenities as squash court, swimming pool and the director's bar and dining room, which are off-limits to hoi polloi and riff-raff, as the workers are referred to as a mass by the directors. None of the miners has ever become aware of the existence of such luxurious amenities in Tepetapa.

The directors' cars and two sixty-passenger shuttle buses for the guards and office employees are parked in an underground garage accessible at the back of the building.

Office employees and guards don't live in Tepetapa and aren't permitted to socialise with the labourers. Not that anybody per se "lives" in Tepetapa or that there is the opportunity or the specific wish expressed by either group to mingle with the other. It is just another facet of the mine directors' mysterious grander scheme of things.

No facilities are provided in the mining compound for mine workers to take a shower or change clothes. We have to come to work in standard overall, safety-boots and helmet that have to be purchased at the company store, black for miners, green for mill workers and grey for smelter operators. And although we pay for the gear, it remains the mine's property.

The overalls don't have any pockets, and nobody is permitted to carry personal belongings, not even a bottle of water or a sandwich, into the mine. Refried black beans, tortillas, and water are served three times per shift, and the "meals" have to be

16

consumed during the three ten-minute breaks granted for such purpose.

The refried beans give everybody gas. Small wonder the fresh air requirement underground is on the rise as the shift wears on. The methane content is at times so thick, one could carry it out of the mine in the helmet, which would still stink of digested beans by the time it hits daylight.

My laconic remark one day about the president having ordered the capture of the methane gas at the exit vent to bottle it and sell it back to the miners as fuel for cooking at home caused quite the uproar. Miguel accepted it as a joke, just a joke, but to claim the miners had to pay for their own farts when buying fuel to cook their dinner was not a laughing matter for my colleagues. They are hard-working and good-hearted but simple people he said sternly to my face.

As he walked away, I could hear him chuckle. And the crew's roar of laughter washing back out of the stope was proof of him having managed to explain the funny side of the vicious cycle my remark implied.

Washing down my painkillers with a beer, I sit at my table and watch the colourful crowd on the plaza. And I am not the only observer. The rabid officer's screams penetrated the sedate environs of the boardroom in the administration building.

At the height of Miguel's confrontation, a big office window is crowded with rubbernecking directors. Several of these gringos even use binoculars to have a closer look at what they must have considered a real knee-slapper. Highly amused and engaged in animated conversation, they watch the guards level assault rifles at the defenceless family, wave money about as they place bets on the outcome, and cheer or jeer their wins or losses, once the confrontation is over.

It is truly remarkable to think that these gringos are the descendants of migrants who more often than not had to escape situations of oppression, despair, and poverty. In other words, it had taken their forebears, who frequently had to live in mud holes as their first taste of freedom, only a few generations to raise a brood of bastards who in many ways behaved worse than those their ancestors had to suffer and escape.

All of Tepetapa is on its feet and mingles on the open town square during the evening shift change, except the men of the night shift going down into the mine. In all some four hundred and fifty workers enter the mining compound for the late shift while the same number of men quit the early shift and collect their weekly wages. At the peak there are more than a thousand men, women and children raising dust in the square.

The women and children trundle off home or go to the company store in search of some soda pop or water to wash down the dust. But the workers and male and female prostitutes, so it appears, want to wet their parched throats in the cantina - all at the same time. There is already quite a crowd gathered in the cavernous watering hole by the time Miguel's shadow darkens its threshold.

He had been one of the last men to leave the pit and I watched him since he stepped away from the pay-office window when his frustrations and subdued rage came to the fore. Exasperated I saw him face the guns of the armed guards with little Benito on his arm. I suppose the reaction of any other person, and I include myself, would have been a protective stance in front of children and spouse - but not Miguel. He seemed to have sensed that the guards, who have the reputation of not being able to hit a barn door with a howitzer at six paces, wouldn't dare to cause a bloodbath over what? A few coins and banknotes covered in snot?

Miguel saw right through the guards' bluster and challenged them to live up to their posturing. But who knows what else had moved him to take the risk? It might have been his despair best summarised in a statement such as, "If you are going to shoot and kill me, then kill my wife and children, too. Because without a breadwinner, they don't stand an ice-cube's chance in hell to survive."

The only thing keeping me from jumping up and screaming was my deep-down conviction that Miguel knew what he was doing. And his strategy worked, didn't it?

With these thoughts still stirring in my mind, I greet Miguel and we shake hands. He looks at my raised left arm in the huge plaster cast, pulls a face, points at my bottle of beer with a chuckle, and says, "Washing down all the good stuff you swallowed in the pit?"

"Yes, good stuff," I mutter and smile in agony.

He bends down towards me and whispers in a sombre tone, "Was this the last we've seen of you in the mine?"

18

When I shrug my right shoulder in a non-committal response, he shakes his head solemnly and says, "No, Rigo, let there be no doubt. You must insist on wanting to return to work as soon as possible. Otherwise, you'll be cut off from any sick pay and you're a goner. Understand?"

I hadn't been aware of these terms of employment and nod in tentative agreement, although it isn't my intention to go underground ever again. I had my fill of muck, slurry, dust, and second-hand air. I would be happy to forget about my busted car and leave town with my week's pay and the two hundred pesos I had managed to save. Instead, I agree with Miguel, and while I am nodding, he says something that makes me want to get up and run away.

"You got a medical report? Yes? It is an invaluable document we can use to nail the directors to the cross. It will play a significant part in our next demand for better pay and safe work conditions!"

He pats my back, straightens up, swaggers to the bar, disappears in the crowd, and leaves me behind in tatters.

I don't want to get involved in a strike! Despite all the help and support I received from my colleagues over the past three months, I still don't consider myself one of "them"! I am not a miner!

I am a screwed-up copywriter from the city of Mexico! I ran away from a life of pretence and credit cards that collapsed around me when my wife had run off with a door-to-door vacuum cleaner salesman!

It is my only wish to get back to my "normal" life of *tacos*, *enchiladas*, *burritos*, and pizza delivered to my door and watching football games on TV!

That is my life! The comfortable, shallow life I had come to appreciate so much since fate had forced me to see the other side of the coin of Mexico's much-touted economic miracle by joining their two northern "amigos" in a free trade agreement. I am sick and tired of the brutal reality slapping me around the head in Tepetapa every day!

Yes, I recognise the injustice and exploitation suffered at the hands of Mexico's "amigos" and something inside of me rebels against it, but only to the degree of confirming the prejudice I have held against the gringos all along. And that is sufficient, isn't it? Any grievance the miners have is "their" grievance, not mine!

I look down at myself, see the orange "mine property" overall, my bare feet, my calloused right hand with the broken fingernails still showing traces of slurry and mining dust. I look around at the faces, some on the verge of drunken stupor, some looking lecherously at the wares and promises the prostitutes have to offer.

The scene reminds me of a crude rhyme a friend had learned on a visit to Germany. He taught me a couple of lines I never forgot. It goes like this:

"Des kleinen Mannes Glück allein
ist ficken und besoffen sein."

Roughly translated it means, "The average Joe finds happiness only in fucking and being drunk."

It describes me to a T!

Oh, it is hard to admit the truth, especially the truth about yourself to yourself! I was one of "them", just another average Joe!

I raise a fluttering hand to order one more beer and a shot of something stronger.

I knock back the tequila put down in front of me by the waiter trying to wash away the horrible image floating around in my mushy brain. It is the image of Miguel pushing me ahead into the guards' gun barrels shouting all the while, "Follow me! I'm right behind you!"

5

WHAT HAPPENS NEXT is a bit hazy - officially, at least - on account of my consumption of painkillers, beer, and tequila. At an advanced stage of pickling my brains, I witness a dramatic sequence of events.

It starts with Laura, little Benito on her arm and Gabriel and Pilar hanging on to her skirt, rushing out of the company store. She is upset and wipes away tears when she pushes her way into the cantina in search of Miguel. Locating him is only a matter of following the direction of his booming voice.

Silence spreads in circles until even I stop muttering to myself while Laura relates her story in fits and starts. She tells, in a nutshell, that the money Miguel had given her doesn't cover her debts at the store due to the rate of interest the shopkeepers have raised to fifteen percent a week. Consequently, she can't purchase any food. One has to pay one's debts entirely including the arbitrarily calculated interest before one is given any further credit.

The soft clink of glasses washed at the bar is the only sound punctuating Laura's quiet sobbing. It is the silence before the storm.

Miguel jumps up and bellows, "*¡Carajo!* That's scandalous! Bloody outrageous!" His fist slams down on the table. The glasses and bottles dance a little jig. Addressing nobody in particular, he shouts, nay, he roars, "Fifteen percent interest? A week? The bastards!"

He gathers his breath and, waving his arm, he shouts at the men around him, "Follow me!"

Five members of his underground crew, Hector, the moustached, grizzled old man whose age nobody knows, Benigno, the long-haired, brainy explosives expert, Felipe, the bearded actor who had fallen on hard times, Vicente, the rotund, balding machinist, and Javier, as broad-shouldered and outspoken as our foreman, all of them get up. They storm after Miguel out of the saloon and march in a tight formation up the steps and into the company store.

Miguel's booming voice flows and ebbs across the plaza to the rhythm of the store's swinging door as clumps of women and children leave the establishment in haste.

Choice insults can be heard leaving no doubt about the six miners' intense dislike of the grocers and their rip-off scheme of raising interest rates at will.

Laura and her children come to stand next to my table. At the first sound of a crash that signals the start of the altercation, she ushers the frightened boys and girl into my arm and runs towards the store. A shop window explodes, and Laura gets almost hit by a cash register sailing in a neat arc towards her. It lands with a thud at her feet, bursts open, and spills its contents and inner parts.

Laura leaps aside, falls to the ground, and looks anxiously back. It is the signal for the miners who are still in the grogshop to stop gawking and join their colleagues in the company store. Most of them are so intoxicated they only manage to lurch and arrive just in time to see the entire storefront collapse and two massive barrels of molasses roll towards them. They hurry to get out the way but for one who gets flattened by a barrel.

Thanks to the removal of the storefront, I have a clear view at last of what is going on, and Laura's children can watch their daddy at work.

Miguel, Vicente, and Javier give the three security guards in the store a sound thrashing. The guards try to flee the scene, are pummelled, subdued, and fettered with their own handcuffs.

Hector climbs over the long counter and wrests a shotgun out of a shopkeeper's clutches. He hands it to Felipe who is already smashing the security guards' rifles to smithereens by hitting them against a vertical support beam. It leaves the wooden beam in a sad shape, and it breaks in half.

Benigno is lifting and pushing the plywood counter out of its moorings. He tries to shift it out of the store. Quickly, a few of the miners storm in to lend him a hand. Another cash register is flung into the square. The counter follows, and the total destruction of the store is under way.

While Miguel and his musketeers still chase shopkeepers in the expanse of the warehouse-style aisles, some of the follow-up crew wave to the women who are watching the brawl from the sideline. They encourage them to help themselves to whatever they need. It turns into a looting party, and the women of Tepetapa participate in the bargain hunt once they have been attracted by the noise or are informed by friends and neighbours about the free-for-all.

A short time later the trays of the busted cash registers are empty, the wares on the store-shelves have been pilfered, the women carry home the loot, and the roof of the store is collapsing with a sick moan.

By the time the security guards in the mining compound cotton on to the realpolitik of the hour, the miners are back in the watering hole celebrating their "victory" with a drink.

The festive mood is rudely brought to an end by the security guards storming the boozer. Immediately an area is cleared. Guns in one hand, truncheons in the other, the guards assemble just inside the doorway.

The patrons withdraw to the side opposite the bar and the back of the capacious establishment.

That gives me a seat of front row centre.

The officer strolls forward slapping the thick end of a truncheon into his hand. He looks from face to face and says, "I have good reason to arrest every one of you!"

Ismelda, the local barber, amateur dentist, and part-time whore in a steel-blue satin dress, a two-hundred-pound battle-axe with porcine facial features steps forward. She chortles at the officer's utterance and asks in her shrill voice, "You think, we'll let you?"

The officer ignores the question and the ensuing snickering of the men behind her and continues, "But I'm only interested in the instigator of this, uh, this wanton destruction of company property."

He points his truncheon in the general direction of the ruin formerly known as store. He pulls his revolver from the holster and spins its barrel with his thumb.

"We don't want to use force, but we will, unless the instigator comes forward and gives himself up. We know who it is."

Ismelda takes another step towards the officer. Handbag swinging by her side, she stands with her fists placed where one assumes her hips to be.

"Listen, you brown dog turd," she pipes up, "you have your flunkies raise one stick or fire a single shot and I personally will beat the crap out of you."

The officer pulls back his head and tucks in his chin. He doesn't know what to say. Ismelda takes off one shoe. Holding the stiletto heel at shoulder height she limps yet another step forward and sneers in a threatening manner.

Male and female prostitutes step out of the crowd and join her, handbags swinging. Now the miners and mill and smelter workers pick up their courage and shuffle forward with clenched fists.

It is an intriguing impasse of riot-truncheons, high-powered rifles, and revolvers against handbags, a stiletto heel, and bare fists.

After a ten-second eternity without the exchange of another word, the security guards withdraw from the cantina upon the officer's signal.

There is no whooping, no jeering, just uneasy silence from the cantina's patrons as the guards are marching away across the plaza. It is a shallow victory. The guards will get their man some other way, some other day.

6

STILL FEELING GROGGY on account of my pill and alcohol consumption I am forcibly dragged out of bed by two guards early in the morning. They march me at gunpoint to the administration building and into the wood-panelled, marble-tiled boardroom that has been converted to a makeshift courtroom. The large table serves as a judicial bench fronted by rows of chairs.

I am led to a seat in the second row on the left. Three patched up guards and six bruised grocers are seated to my right. All of us face the thirteen clean-shaven, nondescript, pudgy, pasty gringo faces of the directors roosting behind the bench. Their lack of truly distinguishing characteristics is in all likelihood the reason for having placed white cardboard nameplates in front of them. How else could they possibly tell each other apart?

Dumas, Gomez, Blaskiewicz, Cameron, O'Hara, McCaw, Callaghan, Peterson, Arbuckle, Hnatiuck, Lord, Romanov, and Henderson are the names.

Surely, they don't expect the accused, the witnesses, or the guards to be able to read, let alone pronounce those names except for the name Gomez. Or have they changed their minds about their chattel being illiterate ignoramuses?

The dramatic entry of my eye-catching plaster cast and neon-orange overall causes a few gasps and I hear Callaghan, the man in the centre of the panel mumble in English to nobody in particular, "My gawd! Look at what the brute did to that guy, eh?"

I have no idea why my presence is required and feel highly uncomfortable. All the booze and painkillers have played havoc with my brain and vision. Additionally, the room's murky light is the reason why at first sight I mistake the directors in their dark, fifteen-hundred-dollar silk suits for a gathering of giant Teflon-coated cockroaches.

Miguel was apprehended upon his return to work and is dragged into the kangaroo court by a detail of four security guards. They occupy the front row and the proceedings begin.

The fine gentlemen of the "court" sit in judgement over an atrocity committed by an ungrateful, subhuman creature of the worst kind, states Callaghan in his opening salvo. He continues with a litany of accusations of Number 1-8-0-3 having done extensive material damage to company property and irreparable damage to the spirit of community, co-operation, and friendly co-existence. Out of wholesale frustration resulting from his and his wife's inability to get by on the generous wages paid to him, he had gone on a rampage with the aim of enriching himself and his cohorts by obtaining goods and money illegally.

The "generous wages" cited by Callaghan are a laugh. It is a sure sign the plaintiffs-cum-prosecutors in expensive threads never had to feed and raise a family of five on an income of less than forty dollars a week. Neither is any one of them versed in the finer points of jurisprudence to the best of my knowledge.

Untrammelled by such minor imperfections, they assume the air of prosecutor, judge, jury, and executioner. The pseudo-legal proceedings are supposed to lend their court an aura of legitimacy, despite having denied any form of counsel to Miguel.

Presumably, the prosecutors want to do their finger pointing uninterrupted by supercilious arguments of cause and effect in defence of a desperate husband and father's reaction to the shopkeepers' cutthroat schemes of raising prices and interest rates at will with the directors' support.

It would have been of little solace to Miguel to recognise that every time these guys point a finger at him, they point three fingers right back at themselves. He is far too realistic to let this kind of observation distort or improve the picture because it wouldn't.

Gomez presents an abridged Spanish version of the accusations for the benefit of all present. After he is finished, he casts suspicious looks in my direction and mutters something in a low voice to the men seated next to him while pulling an index finger horizontally across his throat. The two men nod in agreement and raise objections when I am called upon as the first witness.

Callaghan doesn't listen to them, points a pencil in my direction, and says, "I want to hear that guy's story. Tell him I want to know every gory detail of what happened to him."

According to his wish, I begin by listing the extent of my injuries. Quickly it becomes evident that Henderson, seated on the far right, and Gomez, seated second from the left, are the only self-appointed judges with a sufficient command of Spanish to act as interpreters. Every few words, I am interrupted in mid-sentence and the two give summaries in English.

Their translations vary greatly. The result is confusion. Heads turn from left to right and back again. Clarifications are demanded as to what I had said. Amused I watch their increasing perplexity.

I draw Callaghan's attention by waving my right hand and saying with a smile, "I can repeat in English what I just said."

Consternation is the response. Heads are put together in whispered exchanges. A miner who speaks English? Who is this guy? What's his name?

Callaghan taps his pencil on the table, raises a hand in my direction, and says, "Please… carry on then."

Encouraged, I launch in my colourful English into a brief outline of what had happened to me.

I continue with the argument that the destruction of the store will be nothing in comparison to the destruction of the whole town disappearing in the ground. Massive sinkholes will open up due to the cutbacks in scaling and reinforcement as well as other basic mine safety measures of the levels, drifts, and stopes and result in the collapse of the mine.

Unimpressed Callaghan waves a hand and urges me to finally get to the point of what the accused had done to me.

"I am getting to that," I say, point my right hand at Miguel and continue, "This man saved my life. He pulled me out from under the collapsing rock. If it weren't for him, I'd be dead, and you would have had two corpses on your hands yesterday! My injuries are the result of your stupid cost cutting, the cutbacks of safety measures, and your greed! And greed is the shopkeepers' sole reason to commit extortion with your blessings, which was the root cause of the rebellion against the store."

Bedlam ensues behind the bench. "What is this crap, eh?" and "What's he mean, two corpses?" and "Belly-aching bastard!" and "Irrelevant! Irrelevant!" is heard. Gomez shouts above the din, "I told you this guy is a muckraker! Throw him out!"

Callaghan demands the bench to be quiet, points his pencil at Miguel, turns to me, and asks, "If your injuries are not a result of this man beating you up, what the hell are you doing here?"

"Good question," I respond. "Evidently you ordered me to be here and now that I speak in defence of the accused, you are getting pissed off with me."

It finally dawns on Callaghan to have called me as a witness on the assumption that I had been one of Miguel's victims.

I point at the two guards. "They dragged me out of my bed and brought me here at gunpoint. Would you resist a couple of rabid guards holding a loaded gun to your head?" After a brief pause, I conclude, "Does that answer your question?"

A moment of stunned silence is followed by another round of indignant denials. Gomez consults Callaghan pointing out his mistake.

Without losing a beat, Callaghan stabs his pencil in my direction and barks, "Just stick to what's at issue here! Did you or did you not see the destruction of the store, the fighting and the looting?"

I shrug my right shoulder. "Of course not. Doctor Gomez, your company quack, hadn't told me that his medication didn't mix with alcohol. So, I was practically blind after a couple of pills washed down with the first bottle of beer and a shot of tequila."

That statement brings the requirement of my presence to an expeditious end. The guards follow Gomez's enraged order to "throw the bum out" and hustle me out of the "courtroom", to the gate, and onto the sun-drenched plaza.

An hour later, while I am having breakfast in the cantina, three of the bruised shopkeepers settle down at a table nearby and discuss at length the rest of the proceedings.

Instead of lynching the bastard, they whine, Miguel had been given a chance to pay off his "debt to society". He would work only twelve-hour night shifts for the bit of extra pay it provided and have every week two hundred pesos deducted from his wages until the damages were settled.

In their opinion, Miguel had got off too lightly with his sentence. Neither their bruises nor those of the three security guards had been taken into consideration in the calculation of damages incurred. The shopkeepers are incensed and swear to give not a peso of credit to Laura. Never again! Ever!

On the other hand, perhaps they should, one of them voices his objection. After all, if they won't let her buy stuff on credit, they can't charge her interest. That wouldn't do, another one agrees. It is a lucrative bit of extra income they shouldn't have to forego. But charging her interest might again incense her husband and could lead to another thrashing at his hands, says the third.

28

Glumly the other two nod and in unison they declare they are not to be envied. A shopkeeper's lot is the toughest lot of them all, they sigh.

They reach the consensus of not giving Laura any credit for a while, at least until Miguel's sassy spirit has been broken and he came to them begging on his knees.

Satisfied with themselves at last, they revel in the image swishing around in their tiny grocers' minds of Miguel grovelling at their feet.

7

THE FOLLOWING WEEKS not only a keen observer could see Miguel go to the dogs and watch his family getting pushed to the brink of disintegration. As the days wear on, a once proud man, who used to swagger, shoulders squared, across the plaza to the cantina after work, is slouching past in the early hours of the morning on his way home. Unshaven for days and his thick, black hair growing long, he looks the part of an outcast. Every day, so it seems, his posture becomes slightly more stooped. His consumption of beer is cut back to one brew a week, his talk with colleagues reduced to empty chatter. But worse yet, one could see the condition of his children deteriorate. Soon they don't wear shoes any more, and their carefully patched up clothes are but rags.

Laura has to bear the brunt of things getting worse by the day. She faces her children's cry for food and their need for clothes every waking hour. She watches Miguel, exhausted and hungry as he is from work, refrain from nibbling more than a dry tortilla so he wouldn't take any food away from his family. Laura herself starts to look haggard with dark circles under her sad eyes. She loses weight and where her face had once expressed cautious optimism there is now just a look of resignation and despair.

At first, she had bartered the family's few possessions for additional food with friends and neighbours. But soon there were no more goods to be bartered. Their friends proved to be good weather friends. The neighbours turn their backs on them and won't even consider providing the least bit of assistance. It reflects the underlying spirit of "Serves them right!" It is a sentiment expressed especially by those families who benefited most from the looting rampage and try to cover their feelings of guilt with pompous self-righteousness.

Six weeks into Miguel's sentence, coinciding with the removal of my plaster cast, the situation becomes unbearable for Laura when little Benito falls ill with a high fever. Shortly after six o'clock in the morning on my way to the cantina, I watch Laura on the empty plaza where she confronts Miguel with the news of the sick child. She needs money to buy medicine. A loud argument ensues. It comes to the point of Laura yelling insults and accusations in a hysterically shrill voice and once actually raising her hand against Miguel.

I rush over to them and interrupt the embarrassing face-off. Against Miguel's objection - his damned pride still won't allow him to accept alms - I press fifty pesos into Laura's hand. She hurries off to the store to get the needed medication. Miguel simply crumbles, totters to the corner of the cantina, and hides his face in his big hands. His twitching shoulders tell me that this tree of a man is crying, crying tears of shame, rage, and frustration. After a while, he slouches away without looking back, a man of broken spirit.

Laura comes out of the store, stops, looks at me from a distance for a brief, pensive moment, and gives a timid wave of thanks. I raise a clenched fist as a sign of encouragement to her. She understands, nods, turns into the alley leading to her home and quickly disappears from view.

I enter the cantina, sit down at my table, and order some breakfast. Mireilla had removed my cast a few days earlier and my freak-show is over.

It is time to regain my strength. I have to do daily exercises to rebuild muscle and assure the full range of movement of arm and shoulder. As my sick pay is but a pittance of one hundred pesos a week, I have taken on a janitorial job in the whorehouse. I figure swinging a broom, handling the heavy floor polisher, and taking out buckets of garbage is sufficient exercise and I get paid for it to boot. And in return for little favours such as writing letters for some of the women, I make out like a bandit on certain fringe benefits.

I have just finished a bowl of *huevos rancheros*, eggs in a spicy vegetable soup, when suddenly Laura stands in front of me. She smiles painfully and drops money, a bill and coins on the table with the words, "Thank you very much for your help, Rigo. The medicine was only thirty-four pesos fifty. Here is your change."

Caught in the process of getting up, I almost lose my balance. Dumbfounded, I can only mutter, "Are you crazy? Keep the change, for God's sake."

She shakes her head and close to tears she whimpers, "Miguel won't let me."

"Ahh, Miguel, Miguel!" I scoff and take a step away from the table without touching the money. "His damned pride won't let him do a lot of things."

"No, it isn't that at all," she says. "But we don't even know if we can ever repay you the money for the medicine."

She picks up the change and holds it out to me. "Please…"

Something inside of me snaps seeing Laura cower when she has no reason to do so. I see her face framed by the black cloud of my fury. I grab her by the arm and pull her out of the cantina away from the hear-all, see-all, gossipy barmen and waiters.

Out of earshot, in front of the whorehouse at the bottom of the marble stairs, I bark at her in a low voice, "You are crazy! Your children have nothing to eat, and you worry about paying back a measly sum of thirty-four pesos fifty? Your damned pride forbids you, too, to ask for help? A lot of men in Tepetapa owe your husband one hell of a lot! I am one of them, you understand? If it weren't for Miguel, I'd be dead! You hear? Dead!"

Laura shrinks away from me and raises a hand in front of her face as if she feared I was going to hit her. Instead, I reach for her wrist and tug it gently.

Feeling the soft skin of her lower arm, suddenly unexpected warmth gushes through my veins. I am overcome by the desire to wrap Laura into my arms and hug her in a gentle embrace. I want to show her how I feel. And I might have done something really stupid like showering her with kisses right there on the open plaza, if it hadn't been for her big, dark eyes that must have read my mind and condemned me to inaction. For a moment we just look at each other. She seems to recognise my absence of ill will towards her, relaxes, and turns her head a bit to scrutinise me out of the corner of her eyes.

I have lost track of what else I had wanted to say and let go of her wrist. But she doesn't let go of my hand. She looks at me and says softly, "You are a good man, Rigo. One day you will meet a woman who deserves you."

My inside wants to explode with derisive laughter at that remark. I would meet a woman who deserves me? What kind of woman deserves someone whose calling in life is thinking of clever advertising one-liners to entice the public at large to buy tampons and toilet-bowl cleaner and wasn't very good at it? But I don't laugh out loud. I just hold her hand that in its softness feels capable of alleviating all pain and in its firmness rejects all advances beyond the point of kindness towards each other. I hear myself say, "Yes, Laura. For sure."

I reach into my trouser pocket for some money and ask, "How much is a bag of black beans and a big can corned beef?"

While I am peeling some of the bills off my scarce reserves, she shakes her head vehemently and says, "No, you mustn't."

Ignoring her, I put a hundred pesos into her hand and gently but firmly wrap her fingers around the money.

"I hope it's enough," I say. "Now go, buy what you can and make a meal of it. See that Benito gets better soon."

She starts to cry. Tears stream down her face. She wraps her arms around my neck and gives me a hug and a peck on the cheek. Putting my hands on her hips, her warmth engulfs me as she ever so tenderly leans against me. She hugs me briefly a little firmer yet and presses herself against my body.

We stand apart, she smiles impishly, and chuckles while wiping away her tears. It is the chuckle of a woman who knows, oh yes, who knows what she has just done to me. I can only guess she is thinking as well that her hug has been the best bit of love I never have had.

She puts the money into one hand and holds up the fist. "This will be more than enough for a good meal. You are invited. Will you come? Tomorrow morning?"

I nod, grin, and wink at her. Her cheeks flush with colour giving her face some radiance. Looking back at her, I walk up the steps to the whorehouse door.

Laura's smile vanishes. Casting me a guilty look, she whispers, "What are you doing? You're going in there? You mustn't do that, Rigo, not at this hour of the morning."

I flash a smile at her and say, "But I must, Laura. The women and men are waiting for me desperate for my gentle yet thorough touch. They crave my service."

The colour drains from Laura's face. She whispers, "They are desperate? For you? But they are…"

"Yes, Laura, the women are whores and the men *maricas*. They don't mind being called whores and *maricas*. All of them have been called far worse names."

Laura shrinks away and presses her hands to her stomach. "Then you are… you are a *marica*?"

My laughter in response to her question irritates her profoundly. I let her hang out to dry for a moment before I spread my arms wide in a dramatic pose and say, "No, Laura, I am the garbage man! I mop the floors, refill the Vaseline jars, and take out used condoms by the bucket full!"

She shrieks with laughter and clamps a hand over her mouth. Still chuckling, she whispers, "How can you work here? This... this is the whorehouse!"

I nod in agreement with her. "Yes, Laura, it is, and it needs cleaning like every other house. You have to drop your prejudice to work here, look at the residents as people like all other people and they'll accept you. And you get paid for your work, too."

I ring the doorbell and look back at Laura. Although we are a good distance apart by now, I see her eyes light up. But I wasn't sure if it is a sudden flash of inspiration or just the reflection of her being amused.

The door is opened, and I step into the whorehouse.

8

IN THE STILL EARLY MORNING HOURS of the new day the herbal smell of simmering stew wafts through the alley and conceals the stench of urine and garbage normally encountered in the narrow passageways of Tepetapa.

Miguel and I, we look at each other, eyebrows raised, and follow the delicious scent with flared nostrils all the way to the door of his dreary looking dwelling. Faintly, the sweet sound of Laura singing the old and ever popular tune *"Amor del Alma"* can be heard. Miguel pushes the door open and bids me to step inside ahead of him.

Unadorned, austere, and rectangular, the hovel is a bit larger than my bachelor abode, but in every other respect, it is as drab as every other one I have seen.

A dining table with chairs and a wardrobe fills the space at the right front. A ceiling to floor curtain at the back pretends to create some privacy for the matrimonial bed. Behind a dividing wall on the left are the shower and the toilet as well as a small storage room, which serves as the sleeping-quarter for the children. Along the wall beneath wall-mounted shelves stands a two-burner, gas-fired stove next to a deep precast concrete sink. The unpainted walls are bare save for a daguerreotype portrait in sepia tone of a stern looking man in uniform. It hangs over the dining table near the front window. The back door leads to a small, square open space, where laundry hangs out to dry on a line. A whiff of smoke curls past the open door into the early morning sky. Gabriel and Pilar's voices can be heard. Laura is busy at the stove cooking our meal.

"Good morning, Laura," I greet her and doff my tatty sombrero with a flourish. "Whatever it is you're cooking, it smells heavenly."

Laura nods to us, smiles and keeps on singing while stirring a dark, thick stew with a wooden spoon in a cast-iron cauldron. Baffled about her response, I look to Miguel. He is amused and points to a chair at the table. I sit down. Quietly, he waltzes past Laura to the rhythm of the song and stops at the sink. His hand on the tap, he waits for Laura to finish the song before turning on the water to wash his face and hands.

Laura withdraws the wooden spoon from the stew, blows on it, and samples the beans.

"Mmmh, perfect!" is her verdict. "Good morning, Rigo. You are in for a treat," she says with a happy smile.

"That's wonderful," I answer still a bit baffled.

Miguel dries his face and hands, sees my expression, and says with a grin, "I guess you don't do much traditional cooking, do you, Rigo?"

"Traditional cooking? I don't cook at all," I mumble. "What makes you say that?"

"Your face."

"My face?"

"Yes, it's one big question mark."

"My singing threw you off, didn't it?" asks Laura. "If you knew traditional cooking, then you would know that you have to sing to the black beans to soften them just right. But you must sing the song to its very end. And you mustn't cry or let water run lest the beans mistake the drops for tears. It would turn them as hard as gravel."

"Uh-huh," I respond and ask innocently, "Does the same trick work for boiling eggs?"

Infectious laughter reverberates off the walls while Miguel changes out of his overalls behind the curtain and Laura goes to sneak a look outside.

She waves to me to come to the back door. I peer over her shoulder at a picture book sight of Pilar and Gabriel squatting to the side of a makeshift hotplate, a large flat stone supported by rocks with embers glowing underneath.

Pilar dips her hand into a bowl, scoops up a ball of dough, and forms a perfectly round cornmeal flatbread, a tortilla with the skill of a seasoned baker. She passes it to Gabriel who lays it onto the hotplate. He turns over three others with a serious look, tests the firmness, and puts one onto a pile on a dinner plate next to him. Benito sits against the wall testing their wares stuffing his mouth with bits of tortilla.

"How are you coming along?" Laura asks.

Pilar peeks into the bowl and without looking up she says, "Three more and a small one for Benito."

A short while later the family and I are seated at the table. I see shiny eyes and happy faces at the sight of the hearty, yet simple meal Laura serves.

It is a thick black bean and corned beef stew with home-made tortillas and side-dishes of fresh tomatoes, pickled eggs and *chiles rellenos*, broad chillies stuffed with a crumbly, flaky, light-yellow *Queso Manchego*, a cheese made from sheep's milk. It is a real treat and tastes delicious.

What little money I had given Laura had been put to outstanding use and I feel profoundly happy about the help I had been able to provide.

The circles under Laura's eyes have almost vanished overnight. Benito looks quite healthy again though he is still recuperating from whatever ailed him. The conversation is lively and concerns mainly the food and other light topics until I point to the portrait hanging on the wall and inquire about the man it depicts. I mention to have noticed a certain resemblance of his and Miguel's striking facial features. Laura and the children listen attentively when Miguel speaks.

"That's my ancestor, General Juan Nepomuceno Almonte," says Miguel casting a pensive look at the picture. "He was a hero of Mexico's war of independence leading a brigade at age 12 in the year 1805. He was also the youngest diplomatic emissary in Mexican history. At age 19 he was dispatched to London, England, where he successfully negotiated a commercial treaty on behalf of his country barely a year after independence. He was known to be a man of principle guided by his sense of justice and fairness. He fought for land distribution to natives and people like you and me. But when he condemned the government for its stupid policy of granting huge tracts of land and mining concessions to American individuals and companies for pennies in what is now Texas and California, he was declared a rebel and a traitor."

He pauses to munch on a *chile relleno* before he continues, "As you know, Rigo, in Mexico you are judged not by what you are or what you can do but by your origins and heritage. And the memory of the thousand or so upper-class families goes way back to the Spanish conquistadores, Aztecs and beyond. In short, to those in power I am not Miguel Nepomuceno Patín, able-bodied Mexican citizen and miner. I am the descendant of a traitor. That's the cross

I have to bear. I bear it with pride, and I share the values in which the old man believed."

He raises his glass of lemonade to the picture in a salute to General Almonte. Laura, Gabriel, and I follow suit by raising our glasses as well.

During a moment of silence, I look from Miguel up to the picture. The resemblance has come alive, now that I am aware of the spirit shared by Miguel and his ancestor. I break the silence by saying that I have never heard of a General Almonte.

"Of course not," says Miguel. "His deeds, the many good ones and those considered bad, were erased from our history books."

"Without a trace?"

"Without a trace."

"Not even a street, a plaza or a one-dog village has been named after him?"

"No," says Miguel and a sly smile begins to play around the corners of his mouth before he continues, "At least, not in Mexico. But talking of a one-dog village, in 1859 while he was still alive, a village in Canada was named after him."

"In Canada? Was he held in high regard there?"

"Not to my knowledge. But evidently, when two villages separated by a river merged into one after building a bridge, the good people there had to come up with a new name for their community. They picked one out of a newspaper by counting their shirt buttons, I suppose. Juan's latest exploits were featured, and they must have thought of themselves as courageous as Juan for having the guts to scrape out a living in the mud-hole in which they were stuck."

"Oh well," I declare, "that's better than nothing."

"Better than nothing?" protests Miguel. "Have you ever seen a recent picture of that town?"

"No, of course not."

"Well, I have," says Miguel. "If that town has any appealing sights or redeeming qualities then the town's elders have no talent for presenting them. In the picture of a newspaper article, I saw some years ago, it looks worse than Tepetapa."

He leans back, clicks his tongue, and pats Laura's hand in appreciation of the meal. He looks amused. "Believe me, it's a questionable honour to have a town like that named after you. Small wonder, Juan's ghost seems to haunt the town of Almonte."

38

"The town is haunted?" I ask surprised.

"Maybe not the whole town," says Miguel and shrugs. "The newspaper article reported the people of Almonte celebrating the anniversary of naming the town. In their blessed ignorance about Juan's status in Mexico, they invited the Mexican ambassador to the feast. He obliged and had barely finished enlightening the local dignitaries about Juan Almonte's status of lousy dog here in Mexico, when the horse-drawn carriage used to cart him around slipped off the road, flipped, and dumped the ambassador in a ditch."

We roar with laughter and cheer General Almonte's ghost, wherever it may roam.

Soon after the meal the strain of Miguel's nightly twelve-hour stretch of hard labour begins to show. He yawns and apologises, "You must excuse me, but I'm stretched to the limit from work. I'll have to go to bed soon." He yawns once more and adds, "But thanks to this wonderful meal I shall sleep soundly and have a good rest. Thank you, Laura, Gabriel, Pilar, and Benito for all your work. And thank you, Rigo, for your kind help."

Modestly I accept his words of gratitude by saying, "I wish I could do more."

He props up his head in his hands and mumbles, "You can and you will, Rigo. I have plans to present our demands for better pay and a safe workplace. We'll have to talk about it when I'm not so tired…"

His voice tails off and a moment later he snores. He has fallen asleep sitting at the table.

I whisper my thanks and a good-bye to Laura, Gabriel, Pilar, and Benito and tiptoe out of the house.

9

ABSORBED IN THOUGHT, I stroll down the alley away from Miguel and Laura's abode on my way to work. I am acquainted now with their private side and home environment, where I saw Miguel not as my superior but as a loving and devout family man. And I must say, Miguel Patín, the private person, had impressed me even more than the foreman working underground.

He seems to have overcome the humiliating experience of Laura berating him in public and accepting money from me, who is essentially a stranger to his family nucleus. His spirit is on the mend as far as I can tell. He laughed and joked and was quite the entertaining storyteller on any subject, which excluded the mine, work, or money.

Laura steered our table conversation clear of these sensitive topics with a watchful eye on Miguel. No question, she wanted the meal to be the happy affair it turned out to be.

Miguel seemed to regain his strength of old with every bite he ate. As well, the children, despite their threadbare clothes, looked much better. Voraciously eating their food to the last morsel, Gabriel, Pilar, and Benito gave Laura plenty of reasons to smile. But she rarely smiled. And when her face lit up with a smile, her eyes weren't the windows to her soul showing an inner happiness. Something big weighed on her mind. I could see it every time she looked at me, and I saw her being very uncomfortable about me recognising her mixture of fear, anxiety, and guilt.

At first, I put the way she looked at me down to our encounter the previous day, when, for all to brief a moment, she had shown herself to me not as the cool and somewhat distant wife of my superior, worried mother of three children, but as a sensuous wench.

But in view of her actions and reactions at the dinner table, I am convinced of an ulterior motive to the looks she gave me. She has something cooking, and it isn't another tasty bean-stew.

She knows how little money it took to purchase the ingredients for the wonderful meal she prepared. She also knows that the boost the meal has given her family would be short-lived unless she unearthed other sources of income. All she needs is a handful of pesos to assure the return of cautious optimism to her home.

Who knows what goes through the mind of a wife and mother who wants to see her family healthy, well fed, and properly clothed? The human mind scans thousands of facets in the process of finding a way out of a dilemma. It can come up with solutions to let one rise to unexpected heights or lead one down dark and slippery pathways one would not even contemplate to tread under different circumstances.

To what lengths is Laura prepared to go for her children and especially for Miguel? She wants him to be his old self again, the man of mental capacity and physical strength who provides for his family and intrepidly stands up for fairness and justice.

What is there for her to do to support him and augment the family income? There are no jobs for the women of Tepetapa, neither in the mine nor the cantina, pawnshop, or company store. And the wives of mineworkers would never be employed by the company for work in the administration.

The mineworker's wives can't contribute to the financial wellbeing of their families. They are limited to household chores of cooking, washing, scrubbing, and nursing. The wives and mothers in Tepetapa are condemned to be mere appendages of their men.

I can't see a way out of the dilemma for Laura and Miguel. Without her help, he faces the almost Sisyphean task of just maintaining his dignity. Miguel has shown himself to be a smart man whose central values in life are ideals beyond amassing material wealth, which, ironically, is the root cause of the deck being stacked against him.

I know from professional contacts with business executives in the city of Mexico that a man like him is always considered dangerous. People who worship at the altar of Mammon, whose church is the stock exchange, whose leitmotiv is personal enrichment and unabashed greed, regard a man of Miguel's integrity as a threat.

Was it possible of the local congregation subscribing to that faith, the directors of the mine seeing him as such a threat? Was it feasible they tried to work him to utter exhaustion, even death?

The directors had gained insights into the volatile mood that prevailed among the miners, and they had been able to trace every outburst of renitence back to its source, which is Miguel's firebrand oratory, his sharp vision, and readiness to take action. They had seen the danger he poses. They had probably seen as well that there is nobody else in this town quite capable of taking his place. Wouldn't it therefore be a logical step for them to try to silence him and prevent him from providing leadership to the masses of average Joes?

Miguel's singular outburst of rage as well as his punishment did not result in the improvement of the miners' income or work safety. On the contrary, it led to the directors enforcing further cutbacks to safety measures, reducing wages by fifteen percent, and raising the daily drill and blast advance quota. They didn't get to hear as much as one word of protest. Miguel had been effectively withdrawn from circulation.

The miners know they are getting shafted. But in view of the armed guards, threats of severe repercussions and several mutinous miners having disappeared overnight without a trace, including Javier, the face-man, and his entire family, nobody dares to rebel against it. Not even Miguel voices any protest. He is simply too exhausted from twelve hours of work a night seven days a week to contemplate a call to arms.

Before my time in Tepetapa, the nation's miners attempted to organise and go on a strike for better pay and improved work conditions. Their actions were brutally squashed. Not only had the national mine workers union ignored a call for help, but also the federal government appeared to have sided with the mine directors by deploying a battalion of the *Fuerzas Especiales*, the Special Forces of the Motorised Cavalry, who maimed and killed striking miners and covered up the bloodshed.

These memories linger and the miners have relinquished rebellion. In the absence of Miguel's keen sense of cutting to the heart of the matter and shedding light on the cause of their debacle with a few well-chosen words, they don't know any longer what is what. They bitch and complain on payday and let their anger and frustration out in tirades of abuse on spouses, families, friends, and anybody within earshot. Instead of channelling their rage and making the source of their misery their target, they help the directors to destroy whatever communal fibre is left by striking out in every direction and alienating even the last people well-disposed to them. In many ways, so do I, and worse yet, I have a clear picture of what is being done to us and I have no idea what to do about it.

The miners' reduced earnings due to the cutback in wages and bonus payments have serious consequences for Tepetapa. While the pawnshop and the company store experience an economic boom charging excessive interest rates, the few other forms of free enterprise permitted in Tepetapa totter on the verge of bankruptcy. The cantina's business is down and the repair shop, where my car is parked and anything from an alarm clock to a diesel engine can be put right again, has reduced its open hours to one day a week. The mechanics work in the mine the other six days. The barbershop in the basement of the whorehouse is mostly empty except for the emergency extraction of a tooth or a desperately needed haircut. Ismelda has returned to selling sexual favours and services. But even the "girls and boys", as Lucy, the madam, refers to her charges, feel the pinch as fewer men can afford to frequent the whorehouse.

What can we do, the working people of Tepetapa, to break the stranglehold, I ask myself as I walk across the plaza. We are outmanoeuvred, overpowered, and cornered by a well-armed, brutal force of security guards under the orders of sinister, calculating minds. I have no answer, simply no answer.

10

The coldest and darkest hour of the day
is the hour before dawn.

UNDER NORMAL CIRCUMSTANCES when employer and employees strive towards the common goal of success for the company and cooperate, work conditions improve, wages rise, and a sense of satisfaction prevails.

But in Tepetapa the exact opposite is the case. Over the past few weeks, things have gone from bad to worse, even for the whorehouse business.

Lucy, the madam in charge, is a seasoned professional. Like the personified iron fist in a velvet glove, she runs a tight ship. Although she rarely leaves her confines, everybody in town knows her shock of bleached hair and fears the probing stare of her eyes so dark one couldn't tell the difference between iris and pupil.

But as tough and demanding as Lucy is, she has a kind streak and provides help to people in need. She assists unconditionally if her help is welcome, and the recipients respect her.

Miguel, whose family is in dire need of assistance, never receives as much as a friendly nod from her. He is known to barely tolerate the presence of the whorehouse in Tepetapa and has been overheard of decrying Lucy and her ilk as maggots of society.

I, on the other hand, have developed a cordial relationship with Lucy and her charges. After my plaster cast had been removed and I ran out of money, Lucy offered to help me by suggesting I could earn a living with cleaning and polishing the floors of her establishment. I accepted the offer, became a daily fixture in the whorehouse, and got to know and like Lucy as a stern but fair boss. I improved my lot even more when I found out that most of her "girls" are barely literate and hadn't been in touch with family and friends for long stretches of time. So, I offered to write letters for them and convey whatever they desired to say. My service had been received with open arms, uplifted the spirits of the women, and I gained fringe benefits as their "man of letters".

In her late forties, Lucy keeps herself in superb physical shape. In front of her "girls and boys" and within the limits of her house, she isn't shy about showing off her assets. Occasionally she struts around clad only in a frilly, light-blue robe, lacy thong-panties and her trademark plume decorated, high-heeled slippers. This raw form of presenting herself helps to underscore the demand she puts on her protégées to stay clean, stay healthy and don't be shy to flaunt your assets.

In other words, she is leading by example and a mild form of intimidation, a management method that works. She applies it without inhibition whenever she deems it necessary as I found out myself one day.

That morning I had had a couple of beers for breakfast and, according to Lucy, wasn't fit to do my janitorial job. She loathed people who drank on the job or, worse, showed up inebriated. She had noticed the telltale smell on my breath and was furious. During the severe tongue lashing that followed, she gesticulated wildly to underline each word and make it stick. Inadvertently, I suppose, her robe fell open.

Believe me, there is nothing more threatening to the strength of a man's backbone then a voluptuous and to all intents and purposes naked woman who takes on the stance and tone of a furious drill sergeant and yells, "Look at me when I'm talking to you!"

My psyche couldn't handle the role reversal of her female attributes from warm, welcoming and enticing to looming and threatening. It forced me to avert my eyes, which was, of course, the exact opposite of what she demanded. My head was spinning as my eyes flitted up and down. Her tone became more cutting and her stare icier and more reproachful. In no time at all she turned me from a happy-go-lucky, slightly tipsy young man to a shrivelled-up wimp with the spinal qualities of an overcooked noodle. And that was just a sampling of her firm rule.

Besides her flamboyance and great physical shape, Lucy was also an astute businesswoman. Whenever her fortunes took a turn for the worse, she came up with a plan or an idea to get her over the hump.

For example, when the directors, that is, her business partners and sponsors if not to say pimps, decided one day to demand a bigger cut of her gross income, she gave the appearance of nonchalant agreement. A week later, on Mexico's Independence Day, she held a lavish reception for the directors that turned into an orgy of bacchanalian proportions. She recorded all the activities and forwarded a videotape of the proceedings to the next board meeting with a list of the names and private addresses of each board member's spouse. A small note attached to the package suggested Lucy should pay a reduced rate of half the old charge. The board acquiesced to her suggestion after a partial review of the video.

Now Lucy faces another hump because her business slowed to a crawl due to the miners' reduced income.

It got so bad that Vanessa and Jauvita, her top-grossing female and male charges respectively, want to pack their bundles and leave for greener pastures. Lucy has to do something to salvage her business.

And out of nowhere appears "Lola", a woman of mystery who provides her services only to clients who agree to be blindfolded, have their hands tied and let her do a "top job". On pain of a severe beating and being banished from the whorehouse forever, her clients are admonished not even to think of lifting the blindfold to catch a glimpse of "Lola" in the raw. Consequently, her reputation soars and some nights there is a line-up of men willing to pay a premium for her services.

Wild rumours concerning "Lola's" identity begin to circulate and stories about her sheer unbelievable performances are exchanged at the cantina. The men are happy, have something to talk about, a distraction from the daily tedium. Their wives on the other hand are infuriated. They often have to make do with even less of the already scarce financial resources as more and more men withhold bigger and bigger portions of their wages and spend it on "Lola". Whichever way you look at it, the woman of mystery is the talk of the town and Lucy has a hit.

How much of the stories I overhear at the cantina are true is hard to say. It is also of little interest to me. I listen in on some of the boisterous accounts in the hope of hearing a detail or two that would give me a clue about "Lola's" identity. The screen of secrecy thrown up around her really intrigues me. Although I am a trusted worker holding down the janitorial job in the whorehouse and talk to the "girls and boys" every day, nobody gives the tiniest snippet of information away.

My questions are simply waved off even by those women who confide their most personal and intimate details to include in the letters I write for them. They provide their service with a smile in exchange for my penmanship and keep their mouth shut as soon as I mention "Lola". After a lot of poking around in the dark and getting nowhere, I am convinced "Lola" is one of Lucy's charges role-playing in a charade, a hoax to stimulate business. But it is vehemently denied by anyone who cares to listen to my speculative inquiries. I leave it at that because the whole matter of "Lola" has become a bit of a bore and it is also none of my business.

It is on the day Nurse Mireilla gives me a clean bill of health, about ten weeks after my accident, and declares me fit for a return to work, when to my great surprise Miguel turns up at the cantina. It is at an hour when he should be down in the mine. He looks much better since the time I had seen him last during the meal with his family. He wears a brand-new overall, had a haircut and is clean shaven although his face and hands are grimy, proof he got a shift release after only a couple of hours of work. He gives me a slap on the shoulder and asks me to join him in a corner at the back of the saloon.

While I trot after him, I ask, "What are you doing here? Aren't you working today?"

Over his shoulder he replies, "There was another death. My crew. Level eight. I took the rest of the shift off."

"Another death?" I ask incredulously.

"Second one this week," he says casually. "Conditions are so bad, the big collapse isn't too far off. Believe me."

We sit down. He orders drinks for us, digs a small stash of cash out of the shaft of his boot, pays for the beer, and puts hundred and fifty pesos, three crisp fifty-peso bills, on the table in front of me. "Here's the money I owe you, Rigo."

Surprised he wants to settle a debt I never regarded as one, I push the banknotes back. "You don't owe me any money, Miguel. If anything, I owe you for saving my life."

He chuckles and squints at me. "Don't be silly. I didn't save your life, Rigo. I saved the life of a colleague. It could have been anybody. Take your money and shut up."

That is an order I stubbornly refuse to obey. "It's yours, Miguel. If you don't want it, then spend it on your family. Buy a present for your children or Laura."

Upon the mention of Laura's name, Miguel falls silent. He picks at the label of the beer bottle and tears off little shreds. He takes a big gulp of the amber liquid before he finally speaks. Staring at the bottle in his hand, he mutters, "Laura... I hardly know any more what she looks like."

"What do you mean? You're not separated, are you?"

"Separated? No. But we might as well be with my twelve hours of work every night. And when I sleep, she's awake. Now that things have picked up a little with the bonus payments I get, she's started to neglect me. She won't even talk to me."

"*Hombre*," I say and clamp my hand on his shoulder. "Then this is your big chance! Why don't you go home? Talk to her. Do all that, you know, a man and a woman do."

He takes a swig and puts the bottle down with a bang. "Don't be stupid! You've been married, Rigo. You know there are times when your woman doesn't want to have anything to do with you. Laura holds me responsible for the misery we are in and... Oh shit, she's right. Besides, I wouldn't know what to say to her."

Glumly I look at him. "The kids? Are they alright?"

He nods. "Yes, they're fine. Laura bought shoes and clothes for the children." He pauses and adds, "On credit. At the store. I could hardly object seeing what state they were in. They look good now. Laura's a good mother."

In the silence that follows, Miguel listens to some miners mouthing off about "Lola". Bemused he turns to me and tilts his head in the direction of the whorehouse. "You still work there?"

"Today was my last day. I'll be back at work tomorrow morning, early shift, level six."

"Good... Uh, you know anything about this, uh, Lola?"

"No, nobody does, except Lucy and her girls and boys. And they keep mum, won't say a word about Lola, even to me. If you want my opinion, I think Lola's a hoax. You know, every night another one of the girls pretends to be Lola. How could anybody tell? Nobody's ever seen her."

48

Miguel laughs. "Yes, possible, but I don't think so. Everybody in the pit is talking about Lola. And it sounds as if all the men talk about one and the same woman."

I shrug. "So what?"

After a pause he mumbles to himself, "Man, I haven't had a woman in ten weeks." He looks at me, puts his hand on the hundred and fifty pesos and says, "You sure, you don't want the money? I know someone who will."

Before I can answer, he swipes the banknotes, chuckles, and gets up. Leaning towards me, he whispers in a confidential tone of voice, "I bet one of my kidneys that in a couple of hours I'll know who this Lola woman is."

He tips his forehead and goes to wash his face and hands at the sink next to the door of the urinal. A minute later he swaggers out of the cantina and takes a sharp right turn to the whorehouse.

I have to laugh in anticipation of Miguel getting bounced. Lucy enforces the strict dress code: No shirt? No shoes? No service! I return to my rickety table at the doorway to watch the comings and goings on the plaza and order a plate of hot and spicy *enchiladas*.

11

NIGHT HAS FALLEN and the plaza is dipped into the murky spill of the lights from the mine, the company store, the cantina, the pawnshop, and the whorehouse.

I just about settle down to enjoy my plate of enchiladas when I see Miguel hasten past, an irritated look on his face. He whistles to Hector and Vicente who come out of the company store. He talks to them, or better, pleads with them and for a while I am treated to a scene from the pages of the theatre of the absurd. Three grown men gyrate around each other lifting their legs, bumping their hips, and pressing chests together as they try to compare the measurements of their feet, legs, hips, and shoulders. They come to some form of agreement and leave together.

The enchiladas are good! I really enjoy my meal and hardly look up. That's why I get only a brief glimpse of a shapely woman in a long skirt, blouse and *rebozo*, a crocheted dark shawl draped over head and shoulders that doesn't permit a glimpse of her face. She walks past the mine gate into the dark beyond the pawnshop. There is only one place to go: the repair shop with its yard. What would a woman want at the closed repair shop at this time of night, I wonder and take another peek, but the woman has disappeared.

I have just about finished my meal when Miguel passes by again. It looks quite comical the way he walks in shoes one size too small, baggy pants too short to cover his ankles and a tightly fitting white shirt barely containing his deep chest and broad shoulders.

I get up and step out of the cantina to watch Miguel hobble up the stairs and ring the doorbell of the whorehouse. He is permitted to enter after Lucy's amused examination. It is rare to see her laugh, but this time she is on the verge of busting a gut after getting an eyeful of his ill-fitting shirt, slacks, and shoes. The steel door slams shut.

I order one more beer, relax, stretch my legs under the table and contemplate going home but decide to wait for Miguel's reappearance. Less than an hour has passed when I hear a ruckus erupting in the whorehouse.

A lot of jabbering and screaming is followed by the squeal of the steel door being opened. Miguel staggers out dressed only in the ridiculous slacks. The shoes and shirt are flung after him and the door slams shut.

I am shocked to see Miguel's face distorted in a grimace of pain and rage as he storms past and runs barefoot up the road leading out of the valley. Wondering what in the devil's name has happened, I see Juanita peek around the corner. He waves a hand for me to come outside.

Despite the dim light in the narrow alley between cantina and whorehouse, I see bruises on Juanita's face beneath his smudged mascara. He is upset and close to a breakdown.

He wipes away tears and sniffles, "Is Miguel your friend?"

"Well, uh, I suppose… yes. Why?"

"Something terrible has happened."

"What? What happened?"

Juanita seems to writhe in pain wrapping his arms around his midriff. He gathers himself and gushes, "He found out Lola's identity."

Yes, that had been his intention. He had obviously succeeded and been thrown out as promised. So why is Juanita so upset? Had he been assigned to give Miguel a beating? No way. Miguel would have laughed about that, I conclude and ask, "And…?"

"Don't you know?" he blabbers.

"Know what? Tell me!" I urge him.

"Lola…"

"What about her?"

"She is Laura, his wife!" Juanita bursts into tears and bites the knuckles of his fist.

Do you know this feeling, when unexpectedly something hits you in the head, a blow of a fist, a thrown object? There is this secondary rush of a charge emanating from the centre of the immediate pain. It is like an electric shock striking you not so much physically as it hurts you emotionally. That's what I feel at exactly that moment. I am stunned and reach out to comfort Juanita as much as myself with the embrace of a human being.

Juanita pushes me away and wails, "Don't coddle me, Rigo, I'm just an old fag."

He sobs and tears stream down his face when he pleads in a barely audible voice, "Find Miguel. You must watch him and keep him away, if he's your friend. He might do something stupid. Laura… the children…Oh, my God, what if he…" He leaves the thought unfinished and adds, "Help him. Please!"

He pushes me into the plaza, turns, and runs along the alley to the back of the whorehouse. I stare into the empty space after he has turned the corner. I am vacillating. I am not quite sure where Miguel might have gone, and I should start looking for him. Hector's voice rips me out of my stupor.

"Heh! These are my shoes," he cries and picks up his dusty brothel creepers. "What the hell happened here?"

"I have no idea," I mutter and set out on a long jog down the road where I saw Miguel disappear.

12

THE PALE LIGHT of the thin sickle of a waning moon casts a silvery-grey pall over the road and valley. The hovels of Tepetapa are more than a kilometre behind me and still the hum, drone, crunch and hiss of the mine, mill and smelter dominate the soundscape. The rhythmic chirping love songs of cicadas as well as the occasional rustle of unseen furry or scaly creatures living among the dry *jarales*, a kind of tumbleweed, and cacti also claim airtime.

My jog slows to a rapid walk, a slow walk, and a hesitant step-by-step forward motion until I finally stop. I look around. Boulders and jagged rocks, reminding me of sleeping giants, are scattered among the sparse vegetation.

Clouds move across the night sky, conceal the moon, and dip the landscape into almost total darkness.

Miguel is nowhere to be seen. I hold my breath. I listen. After a few seconds, I can hear my blood pumping. It is no use. I might as well turn back.

Miguel has probably gone home. As I turn around, I am stopped dead in my tracks by something dark flitting across the road. It is the size of a dog with short legs. I can also hear a whimpering sound.

An ice-cold hand seems to touch my skin. Gooseflesh spreads out over scalp, torso, arms, and legs. Chest and shoulder muscles become petrified. My throat swells up. I can't breathe!

Rabies, I think, whatever flitted across the road and whimpered is probably rabid and ready to attack me!

I force myself to exhale, want to take a deep breath and make a mad dash for home on the count of three when the next whimper, this time clearer and nearer, turns my legs into some rubbery substance. Now I can't move!

I look down. The dark colour of my slacks and shoes blends perfectly with the black tarmac of the road. I have ceased to exist from the waist down it seems.

Paralysed by fear and panic, I deliver myself to fate. I await the rabid beast to come dashing at me out of the bushes and slash my throat with its fangs any second. I am as good as dead. Close to tears I give up all hope for survival and relax.

I relax a bit too much and the urine running down my left leg soaks my shoe. It is a most convincing fact I am still very much alive and exist from the waist down.

No rabid dog is around that could have mistaken me for a fire hydrant. I am flooding my basement all by myself!

In the re-emerging moonlight, I look around cautiously for prying eyes smirking at my predicament. But the giant boulders are fast asleep. I take the first squelching step on the long way home only to be stopped immediately from taking a second step by yet another whimper, this time a short throaty sound followed by a long moan. What comes next might as well have been the clang of the bells of the *Catedral Metropolitana* in the city of Mexico exploding in my ears. It is a drawn out, basso profundo version of "*¡Puta!*" belting me around the head.

I have located Miguel!

He sits about ten meters west of the road on a sandy patch between two boulders. Presenting a pitiful sight, he sobs with his chin on his chest. His arms stretched forward between his knees he holds onto his ankles. Suddenly, his head snaps back, and he roars once more, "*¡Puta!*"

I stand not more than two meters away from him, but he doesn't see me. I call his name. A handful of gravel and sand thrown in my face is his reply. While I am spitting and hollering, he shouts, "Go away! Leave me alone!"

I don't follow his order and sit down next to him. Beyond that I don't know what to do. In my experience, when a woman cries, it is a cry for consolation, and a gesture, a gentle hug or holding her hand, will be welcome to alleviate her pain. But when a man cries…? Any gesture is too much and too little at once. A man wants others to feel the pain he suffers, and something like a slap on the shoulder can have explosive consequences. So, I just sit there drawing lines in the sand with a finger and lifting the sticky cloth of my slacks away from my left leg.

Suddenly Miguel asks with a shaky voice, "Did you know?"

It is obvious what he wants to know, and I say, "No, Miguel, nobody outside the house knew."

"But you…?" he asks and breaks off wiping snot from his nose with the length of his forearm.

54

"Well… I know it now. Juanita told me before he chased me after you to make sure you're okay."

"Juanita?" he asks quietly. "Is he all right?"

"He is shaken up and a bit bruised but otherwise okay."

"*¡Puta!*" mumbles Miguel. He presents an image of self-doubt and humiliation. He reminds me a lot of myself during my worst times not too long ago.

When I came home one day, a gossipy neighbour informed me that my wife had run off with the door-to-door vacuum cleaner salesman. All the vows, the promises, the hopes, the plans I had shared with her had vanished into thin air that very moment and tossed me into an emotional vacuum.

The realisation of my dreams having been betrayed left me feeling drained and empty in an empty house. It is an emptiness that craves to be filled. It is a huge vacuum sucking in everything and posing the biggest danger of self-destruction. Any distraction is better than none, I had thought at the time, stormed out of the house, emptied my bank account, and departed on the journey that had ended in Tepetapa.

Miguel has very few options to fill his vacuum. No money and no way out of Tepetapa, he has only his family as an outlet.

I must do something to channel his anticipated rage into a positive direction. Furiously I rummage for the appropriate words to say to snap him out of his brooding gloominess.

All I can think of saying is, "Come on, Miguel, time to go home."

His rejection of that notion is immediate and forceful. "I'll never go back there!"

"Of course, you will!" I bark back just as forcefully. "What about Gabriel? And Pilar? What about Benito?"

"I don't know," he whimpers. "I just don't know what to do…"

"And what about Laura?"

"That *puta*?" he yells. "I'll tear a strip off her if ever I lay eyes on her again!"

"Good!" I shout.

"Good? What the hell do you mean, good?"

"Listen!" I shout and get up. "Back at the cantina you told me you wouldn't know what to say to her! Now you want to tear a strip off her, meaning you have plenty to say to her! So, get up! Move your ass! Let's go!"

"I can't talk to a *puta*!" he insists.

"Is that so?" Angrily I jump back and kick some sand and gravel. "You really piss me off, Miguel! It's all right for you to go to the whorehouse and not just talk to a whore! Oh no! You go as far as committing adultery with the mysterious Lola because you can't talk to your wife! And in the process, you find out Lola is your wife, you've committed adultery with your own wife! And now you feel guilty! For creep's sake! Not even the pope would condemn you for committing adultery with your wife!"

Miguel watches my rant and listens slack-jawed to my twisted argument. It must look quite comical to him the way I underscore my tirade with grand, sweeping gestures while dancing about. Do I hear him snicker? I don't know if he does, but his voice has regained some firmness when he speaks.

"That's not the point," he says. "Laura's a whore. And everybody knows!"

"You're wrong, Miguel," I say emphatically. "Nobody knows!"

"You do!" is his sulky reply.

"Right! And I know a few other things, too!"

He gets up, takes a step in my direction, and glares down at me. "Oh, yes? And what might that be?"

Frightened by his sudden move, I step back to maintain a safe distance between my jaw and his ham-sized fists. I fear the worst.

"You've had good meals the past four weeks. Right? Your children are well-nourished, healthy, and dressed in new clothes and shoes. Correct? You have a new overall and money to spend on drinks and food. Right? Well, guess what? Laura still doesn't get a penny of credit at the store."

"What are you saying?" cries Miguel.

"Isn't it obvious?" I shout and lean back against a boulder as he reaches for my collar. "Laura subjects herself to the greatest indignity a wife and mother can endure so you and your children can maintain their dignity in a town that doesn't give a monkey's wet fart about…"

A sudden explosion of sparks and the sound of crunching bones in my ears cut me short and prevent me from finishing my sentence. Miguel's fist has prevented me from registering what happens during the next couple of hours.

13

THE PORTRAIT on the wall looks familiar but I can't make up my mind if the stern looking man in uniform is my father or my uncle. As if to tease me, he floats in and out of focus and disappears out of my field of vision when a soft, yet firm pair of hands turns my head. In the cold glare of a light bulb dangling from the ceiling I see the smiling face of Laura. I watch her lips move but can't hear a word she says. Certain she is declaring her undying love for me I slip back into my coma-like state.

When I regain consciousness, I notice that I am lying in the dark on a hard wooden plate. I have a pulsating headache. My head rests on a pillow. I lift a hand to assess the extent of the storm damage to my belfry. I can feel sticky bandages on my face and the right side and back of my head.

A wave of nausea rises from the pit of my stomach. Quickly, I take a deep breath, clutch the edges of my resting place, and stretch my neck to prevent me from throwing up. I stare straight up to stop my head from spinning. I look at the night sky through a window above my head. The nausea subsides and I notice the faint hue of orangy-pink mixing into the ultramarine of the starry firmament. Seeing the first signs of the looming dawn it suddenly hits me that I must report for work, the early shift starting at six o'clock. Panic grips me. I don't know what time it is. I try to raise my head and look at my watch. Another wave of nausea forces me back into a full stretch. I swallow hard and try to relax.

During the moment of enforced calm, I realise that I am lying on a table. A dim light flickers behind a curtain and I hear Miguel's and Laura's familiar voices mumbling in the background. Not being able to get up, I have no choice but to listen to the closing exchange of what I can only presume must have been a long conversation.

"Have you ever heard any of the women or men talk about each other or their clients?" whispers Laura.

After a brief pause, she adds, "Of course not. They don't. And they won't talk about me either. They are discreet. It is the basis of their business. They live in a world very different from ours."

"They sure do," agrees Miguel. "Scum of the Earth."

An ominous silence follows his remark. I imagine Miguel cringing under the reprimand of Laura's resentful look so familiar to me. I would smile at the thought if it didn't hurt so much.

"They are only made out to be scum," continues Laura. "Lucy told me about ancient times when whores were revered and worshipped. And in a way we continue this tradition with our admiration for Aphrodite and Venus. They were whores, and even a planet was named after Venus."

"That may be so," says Miguel, "but it doesn't change the standing of prostitutes in today's society. Look, Laura, if word gets out that you were Lola then I'll be the laughingstock of Tepetapa. We can't rely on Lucy not spreading the word. She has no obligations to be discreet. She is in cahoots with the gringos who let her carry on her business only as long as she pays them a share of her profits. If I call for a strike for better pay, she may try to please her pimps with a public announcement of Lola's identity. And once everybody knows that Lola is my wife, the miners won't give a damn about your motives for what you did. They will see only the obvious of you cuckolding me, and that you did it as a whore with anybody willing to pay the price. And then nobody will listen to a call for a strike, a walk-out."

"Strike! Walk-out!" interjects Laura heatedly. "Don't you remember what happened the last time a strike was called? The same is bound to happen again! The gringos will pay the military another huge bribe to beat down the strike, shoot, kill and maim, and cover up the bloodshed!"

After a moment of silence, Laura says with a tired voice, "Condemn me all you want, Miguel, but I wanted only to make enough money to get us out of here and start over somewhere else where we can live and work in dignity."

"Dignity!" says Miguel in a sarcastic tone of voice. "You know as well as I there is no place somewhere else to work and live in dignity. The other mines from Guanajuato to Chihuahua are not much better. And neither is that the point. The point is it won't help to turn your back on Tepetapa in the hope of finding a promised land somewhere else. We have to stay and fight for better conditions, fair wages, and our dignity. And here is the gist! Your rash action has put my plans in jeopardy. I wanted to wait for the next big accident that can happen any moment under the

58

present unsafe conditions to have a sound reason to call a strike. You have forced my hand. Now I'll have to act on the spur of the moment before word gets out about your whorehouse caper. Don't show your face ever again near that place. You understand?"

The long silence that follows tells me that their conversation is over. I get up slowly, stealthily, slip my feet into my shoes that stand under the table and sneak softly, softly out of the house without disturbing anyone.

As quickly as my condition permits, I hurry to my abode and change into my overall and boots.

All the while a premonition slows me down. I ask myself, why I am changing and rushing off to work? I am strangely certain that I am not going to go to work.

How absolutely correct my premonition is, I should find out a few minutes later.

14

FROM THE DISTANCE one could have mistaken the small crowd of men in front of the pawnshop for commuters waiting for a bus. The sun hadn't risen yet above the eastern mountain ridge and the town is still steeped into the valley's shadow of dawn. Some of the men stare and point at me as I come out of the alley leading to my hovel. I head straight for the mine gate. When I see it closed without any security guards in sight, I change my direction and walk towards the men to inquire if they know what is going on. They shuffle aside to form a narrow passage.

A yellowish rock the size of a large pumpkin lies on the ground. Stretched out from it is the prostrate figure of a man. He wears a white shirt, navy-blue silk trousers, and elegant leather shoes. His shirt is heavily stained with dark matter. At first sight I take it to be grease or engine oil. Only when I stand over the body, do I recognise the stains to be dried blood. His head, or what remains of it, is under the rock. It must have been smashed to a pulp. Taking a closer look, I see smudges of brain and fragments of skull with tufts of hair stuck to the rock.

Shocked I look from face to face of the men gathered around the corpse and notice a pronounced hostility not only towards me but also amongst the men towards each other. The atmosphere is charged with subdued rage and mistrust.

Who is the dead man? He isn't one of us, that is, a miner and mill or smelter worker. His expensive clothes give that away.

More and more men join the crowd. Hector is staring at me, and I ask him, "What happened here? Who is this man?"

He squints at me and says, "We don't know. We thought you could tell us!"

Horrified at the suggestion of my involvement in this crime or accident, I stare back at him. "Tell you what? What do you mean? I came here straight from home."

"That's a lie," he replies sharply. "I was at your place ten minutes ago and you weren't there. Where were you?"

Stunned by the accusation of being a liar and overcome by a strange feeling of guilt, I become tongue-tied and can't even think of what to say in response. The men shuffle forward, and the circle tightens.

Most of them I don't know by name. Besides Hector, I know only Raúl, a nasty bit of business with slits for eyes and mouth and an aquiline nose. Raúl grabs my right hand, inspects it, and stretches out my arm with a triumphant grin. Hector looks at the scrapes and a cut and detects traces of sand under my fingernails.

"Pretty rough hands for somebody who worked in the whorehouse swinging a broom and getting a stinky finger," he says underlining his words with a suggestive hand gesture.

"Yes! And look at the bandages on his face," adds Raúl. "Looks like he was in a fight! Maybe right here in front of the pawnshop! Maybe with this man!"

Raúl's voice becomes louder as he turns while trying to address everybody in the still growing crowd. "Maybe he was losing a fair fight, grabbed this rock, and smashed the man's head!"

Why doesn't anybody burst out laughing at his assertion? As if I could lift a rock of well over a hundred pounds, let alone holding it up with one hand while keeping down a man twice my weight with the other.

Ridiculous! But nobody laughs at the absurdity of the suggestion.

And so Raúl continues unchallenged working himself into a lather. "Maybe he is the murderer the guards asked us to bring in before they'll let anyone of us go to work!"

That is quite enough! I try to tear my arm out of Raúl's talon grip and shout, "Are you insane? I was nowhere near the plaza! Let go of me, you bastard!"

But as soon as I begin to struggle and try to punch Raúl with my weaker left arm, other men grab me and start to punch me in the head, my shoulders, and arms.

The crowd begins to shift, and I see some of the men trample on the corpse in their eagerness to lay hands on me.

Mob rule breaks out and a chorus of "Murderer! Murderer!" drowns out my screams of protest.

Raúl holds me by my arms twisted behind my back and pushes me bent forward through the crowd. I am scared of falling and getting trampled to death. Marched along in that awkward position, my head provides an easy target for eager fists. My helmet is knocked off and bandages, so carefully put on by Laura, are punched away and fall into the dirt. Blood is dripping from my mouth, nose and a laceration on the cheek torn open afresh.

Raúl rams me a couple of times into the wire mesh of the gate and shouts, "Heh! Open up! We've got your man! Open up already!"

I can barely lift my head. With my right eye rapidly closing as a result of a direct hit, I see with my left eye only a few mill and smelter workers of the night shift on the other side of the gate. Some of them pull back at the sight of my bloodied head, others are pushed aside by two security guards coming towards us. I recognise the officer. He signals Raúl to put me in the upright. Someone pulls back my head. The officer looks me over, full of doubt.

"That guy? Are you sure?" he asks. "He couldn't win a wrestling match with a wet dishrag."

"Of course, we are sure," says Raúl and adds with a tilting voice, "He practically confessed!"

The officer scratches his ear. "Practically, you say? What do you mean by practically? Did he confess or didn't he?"

I hear Raúl mutter to somebody. Hector comes into my field of vision and inspects my face. Do I see a trace of pity in his old eyes? Does he have a twinge of conscience and will tell the truth to get me out of here? I give him what I hope will come across as a pleading look. But Hector just nods, spits on the ground and says with a firm voice, "Yes, he confessed, the son of a bitch!"

My legs buckle. I want to scream out my disgust and spit him in the eye. I can't believe what a two-faced bastard Hector turns out to be.

This old man had been a father figure to me. During my first days in the mine, he took me under his wing and showed me a few tricks of getting more work done with less effort. In turn, I had done his work for him on many occasions when the air underground became too foul, and he was too exhausted to carry on. What compels him now to call me a murderer? I am so outraged, I begin to cry hot tears.

The gate is pushed open. A security guard steps out, puts me in handcuffs, and drags me into the mining compound. My helmet is flung after me and the gate snaps shut.

I hear Hector's voice when he addresses the officer, "Heh, officer, what's the matter now? We delivered what you asked for.

Where's our reward? You promised us five thousand pesos. And we want to go to work, too!"

Reward? So that is the direction from where the wind is blowing. Old Hector has sold his brother for a dish of lentils!

I rear up against my shackles, but the guard quickly suppresses any thought of rebellion with a vicious twist of the handcuffs. My faith in humanity is shattered. Night might as well have fallen so black is my outlook.

"Patience, old man," says the officer. "The directors will pay your reward. And you will go to work as soon as a small problem has been fixed. On what level do you work?"

"Level eight."

The officer laughs. "Level eight? Then you might as well go home, old man. Take the day off and enjoy yourself. Level eight is shut down for a major clean-up. It will take the whole day."

Howls of protest are heard from Hector and several other men. The guard lets go of me and I turn around to watch him. He pulls his truncheon from its holster and raps it against the gate. The scene that follows this pathetic "show of force" deserves nothing but contempt.

Hector, Raúl and three other men fall to their knees, clutch the wire mesh, get their fingers rapped, and thank the guard for reminding them not to hold onto the gate. They skid back a step as ordered by the officer. Hector pokes a finger into the shaft of his boot and gets out some money. Pleading for mercy and consideration, he pushes forty pesos through the wire mesh. The officer grabs the money, pockets it, and signals the guard to let Hector into the compound.

I can't believe his stupidity! He pays forty pesos to earn sixty pesos with twelve hours of backbreaking labour!

Other level eight crewmen follow his example. They pass the gate after paying a bribe and gather nearby to chat. Their smug expression of superiority over those colleagues who don't have the money to bribe the guards speaks for itself.

Hector and his cohorts have lost all sense of human decency and are living proof of the directors having succeeded in splitting the workforce not only into competing groups but totally selfish individuals. Each one of them doesn't give a damn any longer about the next man without whom he is less than a speck of fly-shit on the map of industrial productivity.

And the men of the other crews are just as bad. They fight to get in line according to level and crew numbers shouted by the officer.

Brutally they shove and push each other. Their lack of cohesion, the absence of a sense of belonging together in a workforce proves they have been successfully conditioned to forget that without them the directors wouldn't be worth a bucket of excrement.

I am utterly disgusted, lick some blood off my upper lip, aim, and spit the glob onto Hector's boot as a sign of my contempt. I expect him to jump me and beat me up, but he and the other men only turn away and walk over to the pay-office window to shout their numbers and register their arrival.

As nobody pays attention to me, I follow them and shout my number into the tiny window. "2-7-3-3!"

I figure if I was going to be beaten up by the guards, interrogated and "sentenced" for something I hadn't done, then I should at least get paid for it in the form of an entertainment levy.

Standing aside when the siren wails, I watch the men of the night shift leave the mine to go home and the mad rush of miners and mill and smelter workers of the early shift on their way to the cage of the headframe or the mill and smelter. Nobody deigns to look at me. Probably they forgot the incident on the plaza already or, more than likely, most of them hadn't even realised what the mad scramble had been about.

Soon I am alone and watch the officer and guard. They stand by the gate splitting their loot. His trouser pockets bulging with crumpled banknotes, the officer turns to the guardhouse and retrieves four metal rods, a steel mallet, and some yellow plastic ribbon. He points to the corpse, hands all the gear to the guard, and tells him to do some fencing in front of the pawnshop.

I look around and up at the watchtower. There is not another guard in sight. The officer is the sole representative of the security force inside the compound. That is highly unusual. Normally at least fifty of the layabouts make a general pain in the butt of themselves.

The officer seems to have remembered me. He strolls over kicking my helmet along. He points a thumb over his shoulder and asks with a smirk, "Why did you kill that guy?"

"I didn't kill him! I don't even know who that is, uh, was."

64

"Arbuckle," says the officer, "the director in charge of operations. Couldn't have wished to meet a nicer guy."

I scoff. "If he was such a nice guy, why was he killed?"

"You tell me!" is his response. "You killed him!"

"I didn't kill him!"

The officer shakes with laughter, "Then you shouldn't have confessed it to the knuckleheads, you knucklehead!"

"But I didn't," I shout. "I didn't confess anything."

"Doesn't matter," says the officer. "Somebody killed Arbuckle and it might as well have been you. We'll get a confession out of you, yet. Signed in blood."

If the handcuffs hadn't restrained me, I would have strangled the officer. What an ignorant sod! And what a promise of things to come! I cringe at the thought of having more pain inflicted and being lambasted with claims of guilt. It is a hopeless situation.

The bus with administrative employees on board rolls up to the gate. The officer pushes the gate open.

The bus drives slowly past and comes to a gentle stop. Office employees spill out and rush into the administration building. Mireilla, the nurse, is among them. She looks back, hesitates, and then struts towards me. She grabs me by the arm to pull me away when she notices the manacles. Without a word she turns and approaches the officer.

I can't hear a word of their exchange. Mireilla speaks very softly. But whatever she says must be very convincing. The officer protests meekly pointing to Arbuckle's remains now neatly framed by the yellow ribbon fluttering in a southern breeze. With a resigned look, he hands her the keys to the handcuffs.

Mireilla removes my restraints and lets them fall to the ground. She picks up my helmet and pulls me towards the entrance of the medical station.

We step into the waiting room and are taken aback by the sight of six severely injured miners sitting on the chairs or lying on the floor among blood-stained paper towels. Going from man to man, Mireilla does a quick assessment of the injuries before she unlocks the door to the surgery and consulting room where she sets up the medical equipment. She asks me to help her carry one of the men lying on the floor into the surgery and onto the steel table. She tells me to wait outside and gets down to work. Wondering how she alone will be able to cope, I leave for the waiting room and sit down next to a haggard looking old guy who presses a crumpled paper-towel against his right shoulder.

He scrutinises my face and says, "I didn't see you on level eight. They dragged you out just now?"

I shake my head and ask his name. We introduce us to each other. His name is Francisco. He is a recent arrival from Coahuila and a member of the crew working the late shift on level eight. I tell him briefly about the mob, the accusation of having killed somebody and my arrest.

He is shocked. With a dejected look, he curses, "Shit underground! Shit above ground! Shit! Why did I ever leave Coahuila?"

"I don't know," I say. "Why did you?"

"A handful of cash and a barrel full of promises."

It is a familiar story. Other newcomers to Tepetapa had told me the same thing over a beer at the cantina. Recruiters travel the country and hand out cash to those men who believe the promises, sign on, and are willing to relocate to Tepetapa the same day. Every week new arrivals are seen in town, but I have never seen a miner leave, only women and children.

"What happened on level eight?" I inquire.

"It collapsed," is Francisco's brief reply.

"Your level collapsed?"

"Eventually."

"Eventually? What do you mean? Come on, tell me what happened," I urge him.

Francisco sighs and his lips quiver. He must have had a traumatic experience and is in pains to talk about it.

He begins hesitantly, "About two hours into the late shift last night, the stope seemed to heave. A crunch was heard coming from all directions. The whole crew ran like hell to get out. We made it, except... one young kid was buried alive by falling rock. Dead on the spot. They said his name was Hernan Godoy. Did you know him?"

I shake my head. "No, I didn't."

"A fine boy he was, a *cuarterón* almost as big as Miguel Patín. You know Miguel?"

I nod. "Yes, I know him well."

"Then you know what a short fuse he has."

"Yes. What about it?"

66

"He blew up in the face of one of the directors and was fired. Had he been allowed to stay… He knows this pit like nobody else and…" Francisco doesn't finish the sentence.

"Miguel was fired?" I ask surprised.

"Yes. We had barely dug Hernan's body out of the rubble, when the mine inspector was wheezing down our necks."

"The fat guy?"

"Yes, Arturo, the fat guy. He had come to inspect the cause of Hernan's death and the safety of the stope. Although Arturo knows little about mine safety, he hesitated to declare the stope safe after looking around the mess. That's when Arbuckle, the director of operations, turns up and starts yelling at Arturo in English. He pressures him and Arturo is scared. Miguel watches the two guys arguing for a moment and steps in. I think he had understood little if anything of what had been said, just like the rest of us. But he must have had a pretty good guess, 'cause all of a sudden he roars at Arturo to tell Arbuckle if the stope was declared safe then he, Miguel, would feed Arbuckle's balls to the dogs. Arturo refuses to translate that. So, Miguel lifts him by the overall and bangs him with his helmet into the roof. And wouldn't you know it, a slab of rock comes down. It almost hits Arbuckle who turns as pale as a ghost. Miguel repeats his threat. There was no more need for Arturo to translate. Arbuckle had understood. He fires Miguel on the spot and adds, as Arturo translates, he would be blacklisted and never get another job in any mine in Mexico. Miguel laughs, turns on his heel, and walks out. That's when Arbuckle declares the level safe and forces Arturo to sign the inspection certificate."

Francisco checks the wound on his shoulder and says in a low voice, "Looks to me Miguel has something up his sleeve. He knows Arbuckle can't follow up on his threat."

Francisco looks at the blood-soaked paper towel and quickly presses it back against the shoulder. His wound, a deep gash won't stop bleeding.

I remember having seen stacks of white linen towels in Doctor Gomez's office. I get up and try the door. Finding it locked, I give the doorknob a well-aimed kick. The door springs open. I rush in, rip open a cabinet, and grab a pile of towels.

Back in the waiting room, I hand the towels to the grateful men and apply a compress to Francisco's shoulder.

Working feverishly, I wonder how I mustered the courage to kick in the door. Had that been me? Breaking and entering? Stealing towels? Yes, I had jumped over my own shadow for the first time in my life and I feel good about it.

I sit down again next to Francisco and want to hear the rest of the disaster on level eight. The implication of Miguel having a motive for killing Arbuckle has aroused my curiosity.

"What happened next, Francisco?" I ask with more than a trace of impatience.

"We carried on as best we could, but without Miguel the going was tough. None of us can handle the drill the way he does. We slugged it out at the face and had sat the explosive charges ready for a blast. We were on the way out of the stope to let it rip when the roof collapsed."

"The stope collapsed?" I almost yell in anguish. "Was anybody killed?"

"Look around, we are the remains of a crew of forty. Some men may still be alive in a pocket where the rock structure was stable. The stope caved in exactly where Miguel had predicted its collapse. They're still digging."

"They? Who are 'they'?"

"Security guards."

"What? I don't believe it."

Our conversation is interrupted when Mireilla looks in from the surgery. She is astonished to see the men with their wounds wrapped in snow-white linen towels and crooks an index finger commanding me to enter the consulting room where she comes right to the point.

"Where did you get the towels?"

"The doctor's office."

"The door was not locked?"

"No, but I, uh, opened it."

She nods slowly and says sternly, "I can just imagine how. You know, Rigo, you don't belong here, this town, this company. You have immense talent, that is, talent to get into trouble. I will help you once more and then... I never want to see you again in the medical station. Sit down."

She wipes away the blood on my face and neck and cleans and clamps the lacerations. She applies cold compresses to the swollen half of my face and wraps my head with bandages to leave only

68

my left eye, mouth, and nostrils uncovered. Then she asks my number and writes a note to certify that I have suffered a work injury that requires one week to heal.

"Now get out, Rigo, and hurry up! Doctor Gomez will be here any minute," she says pressing the note into my hand.

I do as I am told. Mireilla has a way of persuading even the most stubborn blockhead with few words.

15

THE DIRECTORS have arrived and parked their limousines in a row near the remains of their colleague. Some of the men are in shirtsleeves others are dressed in their regalia of dark three-piece suit despite the already sweltering heat. Holding their chins or patting down their hair, they move around the rectangle of yellow plastic ribbon with measured steps, a picture of dignified perplexity.

The rare sight of twelve shiny luxury cars and the directors gathered around the corpse let my curiosity get the better of me. I decide to hang around for a moment. Two directors dash towards me and growl as I pass between two limousines. Looking fiercely protective, they stand by their cars and watch me walk by. What the hell were they thinking I was going to do? Steal a wheel? Suck gas out of their tanks? Perhaps it is just the mummy-disguise of my bandaged head that scares the living daylights out of them.

Stopping to look at the corpse, I listen to the directors' conversation. But they aren't concerned with their colleague's demise, only with the safety of their cars. Imagine that! Twelve worldly men take the opportunity of being gathered at a colleague's place of death to rehash prejudices about Mexicans and their devious ways of getting at the gringos' material possessions.

"Keep your eyes on the little wetbacks," I overhear Cameron say to Romanov. "They are a real menace. Crawl under your car, take out the plug from the sump, drain the oil, and - phoom! - there goes the engine in the middle of nowhere. Can cost you more than a new engine, I'll tell you!"

"Oh yes," echoes Romanov the sentiment. "I've been forewarned by others. In a special compartment, I carry always and wherever I go a loaded gun."

"In your car?" asks Cameron.

"Where else would I have a special compartment?" Romanov asks with an indignant look and scratches his fat behind.

Two of the directors duck under the yellow ribbon and try their hand at moving the rock.

After a few grunts and groans, Callaghan tells them to stop and suggests calling the security guards. Henderson takes a cell-phone from his trouser pocket and dials a number. The telephone in the guardhouse rings.

The officer reaches through the open window and answers the call. In disbelief he looks back through the wire mesh of the gate at the wonders of high technology. Henderson uses a tiny gadget that had cost hundreds of millions of dollars to develop to send a brief instruction over hundreds of kilometres up to a multi-million-dollar satellite and back to earth so he wouldn't have to walk the roughly thirty meters and talk to the recipient of his message in person.

How's that for progress?

Waiting for something to happen, after Henderson has snapped his cell-phone shut, I move to the side of the small crowd and stand on the invisible dividing line between the directors and the women and children who gathered nearby. They watch the men and listen to the gringos' droning drawl from a respectful distance.

It is great entertainment for the Mexican women and children to hear the directors speak English.

North Americans, of course, are oblivious to their speech pattern of chewed, mangled, and swallowed vowels and consonants sounding off kilter to non-Anglophones. A couple of boys stuff marbles into their mouth and provide speech imitations. They earn amused looks and laughter for their near-perfect copy of the sounds wafting across the corpse.

The display of cheerfulness irritates the directors to no end. Suspecting the women and children are taking the piss, they look for something suitable to demonstrate their authority. The appropriate subject is found in the guy with the mummy disguise standing aside.

Callaghan points a finger at me and asks Gomez, "What's that guy doing here, eh? What's happened to him? Go ask him what happened to him."

Standing close by, Gomez turns to me and repeats the questions in Spanish.

Hoping he wouldn't recognise me, I hold up Mireilla's note with a finger over my number, lower my voice and mutter in chopped phrases, "Accident... down in the mine... heard of dead man... express my sympathy."

Gomez peers into my visible eye, tilts his head and asks, "Don't I know you? What's your name?"

I am thinking, quick, quick, what's my name, what's my name? I nod slowly and say, "I'm Raúl, Sir… at your service, Sir… pleasure to meet you, Sir."

Gomez rubs his chin. "Raúl, you say. Hmm…"

Callaghan calls, "What's the matter? What's he say?"

Without letting me out of his sight, Gomez answers, "I can hardly make out what he says. He's one of the few guys who got away on level eight. From what I gather, they already know about Arbuckle down there. He says he's here to express his sympathies."

Callaghan belts out a laugh. "Sympathies? From level eight? For Arbuckle? I don't believe it!"

A wave of raucous laughter spreads through the ranks. Disparaging remarks are voiced about Arbuckle and his jackboot methods of maltreating miners and ignoring mining safety.

I shudder. These men are not the ignorant gringos they are thought to be. They know exactly what they are doing. Every single one of their actions is calculated.

Dumas, a podgy nonentity with pig's eyes, thinning, cropped hair and carefully trimmed stubble around his snout, sums it up when he says, "Who's going to go in the pit and kick ass now? I mean, we can't let the rabble think for one minute they got room to breathe. Right?"

Gomez grins and says to him, "Why don't you go and kick ass? You have a pretty mean streak, don't you, Rob?"

"No can do, man! Not me!" says Dumas and cackles. "That's not within the scope of my defined activities."

"We'll discuss it later," interjects Callaghan when the officer and his sidekick guard appear with a stretcher. "Listen, Gomez, make the officer understand this was an accident. Arbuckle stood to close to a truck loaded with mining waste or something like that. You'll need a signed testimony from him to that effect. It must support the autopsy report you'll have to write. Grease his wheel a bit if he starts to squeal. Okay? We don't want the cops to come here and snoop around. That's the last thing we need now."

"No problem," says Gomez. He turns to the officer and instructs him to remove the corpse and take it to the medical station for an autopsy. Then the subordinate guard will have to clean and rake the spot on the plaza and remove any traces of the "accident" before noon.

Those men make me sick. I feel a sudden urge to get away and want to find answers to the questions turning over in my mind.

Why does Callaghan arbitrarily declare Arbuckle's death an accident, yet by a rock falling off a truck, the least of the probable causes? Why does he tell Gomez to fake an autopsy report supported by testimony amounting to perjury? Why does he mention specifically that he doesn't want the police to come and investigate Arbuckle's death? What does he mean by saying a snooping cop was the last thing they need now? The cops had never come here before to look into the fatalities occurring almost every day. Why would they come now? Because Arbuckle was a director, because he was a gringo?

It suddenly occurs to me that I have never seen a hearse or an ambulance in Tepetapa. What happens to the corpses of the miners killed on the job? There is no cemetery in this town except the final place of rest of two priests in a sepulchre behind the church, and these two clerics had passed away a long time ago. The killed miners' remains have to be put somewhere. But where? And what happens to the bereaved?

It begins to dawn on me how little I know about the operation of this company town as I meander away from the dusty plaza, the suffocating alleys, and low hovels. I take the path leading up into the western flank of the valley. I follow it in the hope of some fresh, clean air to help me clear my mind.

16

DEEP IN THOUGHT I stand on the very edge of the cliff. The view down the precipice with a sheer drop of over a hundred metres evokes a feeling of having scaled a massive prison wall. That impression is underscored by the sight of a new guardhouse and gate on the road about three kilometres out of town. A tall fence has been put up right across the valley. Tepetapa is a real prison.

Beyond the flanks of the valley is open terrain without guards, surveillance cameras, or chain link fences. There is nothing physical to hold anyone back from just walking away, unhindered and unobserved. The valley, its drama and petulance, bickering and misery, life and death feels far away from up here, as distant as a faint memory. A warm, gentle breeze out of the south, a mere whiff not strong enough to raise a whirl of dust or move a tumbleweed is conducive to an atmosphere of peace and calm.

The open terrain is a plateau, a barren plain with barely any vegetation. It stretches out to the west as far as the eye can see. Its forbidding openness dares the beholder to take the first step of a journey out of prison. But for the uncertainty of what lies beyond the plateau, behind a jagged mountain ridge on the far horizon, it could be a gateway to freedom.

Tracks of boots and bare feet venturing out and returning to the spot where I stand seem to attest to the attempts of people facing the challenge lying ahead and submitting to the fear of the unknown. The hostility of the vast open space had probably immobilised their legs. It presents an invisible yet insurmountable barrier. The certainty of the next meal back in the prison of the valley below did the rest. Weighing intangibles such as freedom and human dignity against hunger and thirst, it is normally the stomach's argument that wins the day.

Everything looks so tranquil from the edge of the cliff, so orderly and neat, it leaves no room for doubt of the valley having to be the way it is.

From where I stand, the mine with its rectangular layout looks like a toy, a neat little toy with wheels spinning, conveyor belts conveying and the tall smokestack belching grey smoke into the azure sky. The steady ripple of grey plumes is interspersed at intervals of three to four minutes by puffs of brilliant-white clouds followed by a thin black trail lasting not more than a minute each. Tepetapa is a picture of productive industriousness.

Across the plaza and along the alleys people scurry back and forth like ants. Is that how the directors see us, I wonder, ants crawling in and out of the ground? Does it matter to them more than it matters to a three-year old who smashes bugs with a stone when one of those ants was squashed? Probably not.

A large group of women and children appear to be busy and purposeful loading bundles and parcels onto four trucks standing in line next to the company store along the road. Under the watchful eyes of some guards, they get onto the tarpaulin-covered backs of the trucks. The convoy leaves the valley.

The rocky path is more difficult to negotiate on the way down than it had been on the way up. My lack of visual perception depth due to one bandaged eye doesn't help either. Every few steps I have to stop to assure a firm hold for hands and feet along the narrow ledge. A slip-up is the guarantee of certain death.

The danger gives pause to think of the fragility of the human body. Made up of bones, tissue, gristle, fat, and sinews, it is nevertheless over seventy percent water.

Water? Yes, water, and there is no water used in the smelting process of separating the metals that are dug up down in the mine. But the brilliant-white clouds emitted by the smokestack isn't smoke, it is steam, hence water. Where did the steam that is blown into the atmosphere originate? And what is the source of the pitch-black trail that follows the brilliant-white clouds? What leaves black residues when it burns? Organic fuels, such as oil or fat, certainly produce black smoke, which consists of soot particles that escape the intense heat. Could it be the smelter is used as a makeshift crematorium for the bodies of the miners that were killed on level eight?

What a sinister thought, I think and move on.

About halfway down, where the narrow ledge widens to a walkway, two security guards block my path. Enquiring where I have been, I tell them that I took a walk for a breath of fresh air to help me recover from my accident. Apparently satisfied with my answer, they let me pass and follow me at a distance.

Near the end of the path, about a hundred meters from the church and hidden in a narrow recess stands a dark-brown metal box on a tubular leg. It emits a faint beeping sound as I pass. Moving back a couple of steps, it beeps again. It beeps every time I lean forward or back when passing it with my torso. Still wondering what could cause the signal, as I have no metal on me, except some small parts on my helmet like rivets and the lamp, the guards rush up behind me and tell me in no uncertain terms to move on. The box doesn't beep when they pass it hot on my heels.

Wanting to get rid of my escorts, I stop in front of the church as if contemplating to enter. They tip the peaks of their caps and walk on.

I study the church's Gothic arch entrance. The light-brown wooden door is a fine specimen of traditional Mexican joinery. Made of thick planks, it is held together by black, round-headed, forged iron bolts. The doorhandle is crafted of wrought iron rods elaborately twisted into the smooth shape of a mango. I am not much of a churchgoer and have no intention of entering the church, but the doorhandle is so inviting to touch, I can't resist putting my hand on it. I depress it and pull the door. Silently it swings open.

"Aarghhh!" I belt out as the priest standing right behind the door unexpectedly confronts me. He looks scary in his cassock, stiff collar, balding pate, ascetic face, and goatee. Judging by the face he pulls and his hands white knuckling a broomstick, he must feel the same about my unexpected presence. Evidently, he was sweeping the floor of the church.

We stand, we stare, at last relax, and manage one and a half sheepish smiles between us. He addresses me as "son" and, I suspect, expects me to address him as "father". He points to a sign inside the door informing the visitor that confession is heard from one to three o'clock in the afternoon.

"I didn't come here for confession," I say and add, "I have nothing to confess."

The priest gives me a morose look. "What is it then, my son? What seems to trouble you?"

"I have a headache," I mutter unable to think of anything else to say for the moment.

Miffed he stares at my bandaged head and grumbles, "You don't say. As if I couldn't have guessed as much."

He seems to wait for me to do something or go away. He fidgets with the broom.

He pushes the door open wide and waves a hand towards the altar. "Would you like to pray?"

"No, thanks. I don't feel like praying this millennium," I say.

He gives me a wide-eyed stare and starts to pull the door shut. I remember what I wanted to ask him and raise a hand. He stops and peers through the crack.

"Do you give last rites?" I ask.

The door opens up again. "Of course," he replies sharply, "I am the resident priest of this parish. Why do you ask?"

"I imagine that it must keep you quite busy."

"Busy?"

"Yes, at least twice a week."

"Twice a week?"

"Yes, on average. And about thirty times today. You should be working overtime. What are you doing up here anyway? You should be down in the mine right now."

"What nonsense is this, my son?" barks the priest. "There was no need to give last rites in over a year. And I will certainly not go down into the mine, unless I am requested to do so. I shall go wherever the patrons say my services are needed."

"Patrons? You mean the directors?"

"Yes! Of course!"

"Interesting… What does that make the workers in your eyes? Pawns on a chessboard to be pushed around and used and sacrificed at the pleasure of the patrons?"

The priest's face flushes red with anger. He gnashes his teeth and says heatedly, "Listen, son, I have had quite enough of your inquisition!"

"Inquisition?" I chuckle. "Yes, you should know all about that, shouldn't you? But this is hardly an inquisition and neither do I intend to use thumbscrews, hammer and tongs to press a confession out of you."

"Shut up, you… you blasphemer!"

"Blasphemer? Oh no! You got that quite wrong! I'm a muckraker in the opinion of your friends the patrons."

"I couldn't imagine why!" is his sarcastic reply.

In response I raise a hand as a kind of forewarning that I was about to wake his rooster. "One last question. If a miner comes to you with a request for last rites for a colleague, do you comply or do you tell him to go to hell?"

"I am not going to honour such an insolent question with a reply!" he barks. "There have been no deaths and consequently no requests for last rites! *¡Basta!*"

Black smoke belches again from the smelter's smokestack. A gentle breeze blows some of it in our direction carrying with it an unidentifiable acrid smell.

"Smell that?" I ask the priest. "That isn't the smell of molten metal. That's the smell of death. The bodies of thirty miners killed last night on level eight are being cremated. Without last rites. Without a Christian burial."

The priest must see in me the devil incarnate the way he runs his eyes over me.

He thunders, "How dare you level such outrageous accusation against the very people who provide the likes of you and other riff-raff with a living! The patrons risk everything so you can live in comfort and enjoy luxuries otherwise unknown to you! I should report you immediately to the authorities! Repent, my son, repent, or you shall go down in flames!"

"No, I won't."

"Won't what?"

"Repent or go down in flames. That would be against the very principles of a muckraker. I'd prefer you to report me to the authorities. Immediately!"

"I will!" he shouts. "Oh yes, I will!"

I begin to walk away but turn around after a couple of steps. Fury has taken a hold of me. Staring at the priest, I spit out, "While you're doing the reporting, why don't you ask your friends what happened to the bodies of the thirty miners that were killed last night! Watch their reaction! You might learn something!"

For a second it looks as if the priest is going to come after me and sweep me down the mountain. But he only tosses the broom aside, reaches for the doorhandle, slams the door shut and stands in front of his church. Arms crossed and chin jutting out, he impersonates the avenging archangel refusing Beelzebub access to his place of worship.

Agitated, I kick up some dust and hurry down the widening path. The confrontation with the priest has given me a clearer picture of how this town is run.

Respectfully or out of fear, people step aside as they see me rushing towards them. My clenched fists give every indication that I am not in a hospitable mood. Muttering to myself, I am so involved formulating the words to put the picture I have in my mind across to the listener in every detail and devastating clarity that I walk right by the house I want to visit. Realising I had overshot my goal, I turn back with curses on my lips.

People don't step aside any longer. They jump out of the way of a raging bull. And that is fine by me. I want them to jump. I want to agitate those bleating sheep, those subservient slackers, shake them up and out of their sullen attitudes towards each other, and unite them once more.

Fortunately, I am blessed with a strong streak of realism, a trait I inherited from my father, that tells me not to commit myself to do something I haven't had a chance to practice. Otherwise, I might have jumped onto a soapbox in my overheated condition and given an impromptu speech resulting in being laughed out of town.

Somebody else is more adept at talking to the people, not past them or over their heads. That somebody I have in mind is Miguel at whose door I have arrived.

17

WITHOUT APPREHENSION I barge into the house and holler, "Miguel, are you at home? I have to talk to you."

The room is hot and smells musty. Dirty dishes are piled into the sink. On the table are a jug of water, a couple of beakers, and a plate of tortillas under a clear plastic hood. The children's beds are empty. The room has the atmosphere of a deserted shell. The material things, furniture, utensils, sparse decorations, are all there, but the spirit that gives them significance, makes them useful, appears to be absent.

After the door has snapped shut behind me, there is a deep middle-of-the-night silence although it is almost noon. Some movement behind the curtains precedes Laura's sleepy voice. "Who is it?"

"It's me! Rigo," I say in a harsh tone of voice. "Is Miguel with you? I must talk to him."

Attracted by the noise, Gabriel peers in through the back doorway, stares with big eyes at my bandaged head, turns away and yells, "The bogeyman is here!"

A second later and simultaneously with Laura peeking out from behind the curtain, Gabriel, Pilar, and Benito cautiously peep around the doorpost. Pandemonium breaks loose. The kids scream and withdraw from the door. Laura disappears behind the curtain and wakes Miguel.

"Wake up, Miguel, wake up!" she shouts. "Rigo is here! Just look at him! Look at what you did to him! Wake up!"

Miguel takes a moment before he sticks his head out and gives me a bleary-eyed look. I want to say something, but Miguel pushes the curtain aside, exposes Laura in the raw, and staggers naked out of bed towards me scratching his nuts and matted pubic hair. The sight leaves me quite speechless.

Miguel grimaces and sucks air through his teeth reflecting the pain he must think I have suffered at his hands. He wraps his arms around me and presses me to his chest. He takes my head into his huge hands and looks at my bandaged face with tears appearing in his eyes.

"Rigo, my friend! Can you ever forgive me?" he asks. "I know you only tried to help."

Sobbing quietly, he doesn't give me a chance to speak. He squeezes the last breath out of me with another bear hug. Looking over his shoulder, I see Laura climb out of bed. She struggles with a faded bathrobe and tries to put it on. The old garment is inside out. It takes her a bit of tugging and pulling to straighten it. Staring at her legs, the curve of her buttocks and hips, her softly rounded shoulders covered by long strands of shiny black hair and glimpsing her white breasts with erect nipples like rosebuds, I feel my left eye is going to pop out of my head.

Confused by her sight, I am on the verge of forgetting the reason for my visit. Quickly I wriggle out of Miguel's embrace and turn to stare at the window. I want to pinch the bridge of my nose to help me refocus. But the bandages buffer the tweak of thumb and index finger perfectly.

"You don't understand!" I shout.

"But I do, Rigo," insists Miguel.

"No, you don't," I say, "this is not about me, Miguel, it is about you."

"Yes, of course," he sniffs. "I have to make amends. I will do whatever you ask."

"No!" I say gruffly and wave my hands about in helpless exasperation. "That's not what it's about! Take a shower! Get dressed! You must clear your mind! I have to talk to you about something very serious."

Silence follows my words. Looking surprised, Miguel does as he is told and goes to take a shower. Laura, dressed in the bathrobe, puts a big kettle of water on the stove, prepares to wash the dishes, and make a pot of coffee.

She avoids looking at me and doesn't say a word. Gabriel and Pilar's voices can be heard from the back of the house. They are having an argument. Benito is crying. Laura steps outside to talk to her children and calm them down. I take off my helmet and grope the bandages. They are bothering me more than they help. It is also a good idea not to show myself again in public as a mummy after my run-in with the priest and telling Gomez that my name was Raúl. My fingers find a strip of medical tape holding the end of the bandage in place. I take a seat and tear off the adhesive. Unwrapping my head, I collect the bandage in my lap.

Laura comes back into the room, sees what I am doing and probably thinks I have taken leave of my senses. She rushes up to me and gets a hold of my wrists.

"Don't do that," she pleads. "You don't have to show me. I gave you first aid last night."

Twisting out of her firm grip I say, "I know. Why don't you make us some coffee, Laura? The water is almost boiling."

I continue taking off the bandage. It is of no use trying to explain to her the reason for my visit. It is a matter to be discussed between employees of the mine. I have to tell Miguel the facts of the latest development in Tepetapa and leave it up to him to explain it to her.

Soon the aroma of Laura's coffee spreads throughout the room. She washes the dishes when Miguel joins me at the table. He is dressed in jeans and shirt. His hair is still dripping wet but combed. He pulls up a chair, pours coffee into two mugs, and grabs a tortilla. Greedily he bites off big chunks and washes them down with small sips of the hot brew. With an inquisitive look he watches me finish rolling up the bandage. I put it into my helmet with the compresses when Laura sits down with us and pours herself a cup of coffee. Silently I look from Miguel to Laura. They are used to the sight of my badly bruised face and wait for me to say something.

"Don't you want to freshen up a bit, too?" I ask Laura.

Her dark eyes probe into mine. She holds her coffee cup, finger crooked through the handle, thumb rubbing the rim, while she reads my mind. Her looks convey a message to me, a message that says, 'Go ahead, talk, but decisions won't be made without me.'

Laura puts the cup down, gets up with a sigh, puts a hand on Miguel's shoulder, and whispers a few words in his ear. There is a sudden and very noticeable change in his eyes as if a huge weight has been taken off his back. He reaches for Laura, but she turns away and steps into the shower. Miguel stares into his cup.

A smile plays around the corners of his mouth when he asks, "What did you want to talk about?"

"Did you kill Arbuckle?" I ask him bluntly.

That question shakes him up. Whatever he expected me to say, it hasn't been the implied accusation of being a murderer. He gives me a wide-eyed stare, clutches his cup with both hands, and doesn't answer my question.

"Do you know Arbuckle is dead?" I ask.

He shakes his head and shrugs, giving the impression not to give two hoots about Arbuckle's untimely demise.

"You expected him to get killed?"

He sits perfectly still and again doesn't respond. No answer is also an answer, I think and continue, "Did Arbuckle fire you last night and threaten to blacklist you to never get another job in Mexico?"

He stares into his cup again. After a while he looks up, shrugs and nods.

"That could be interpreted as a motive to kill Arbuckle and would make you the prime suspect, if the directors decide…" I don't finish the sentence and wait for Miguel to show some reaction.

His eyes and ears seem to crawl across the table as he leans forward and asks, "What…? Decide what?"

His anxiety surprises me. I am stumped. The Miguel of old merely would have shrugged at the mention of the directors. He would have laughed at the conjecture of being the prime suspect of a bloody deed such as murder. But there he sits cowering, anxious, afraid of his own shadow. He is frozen in fear and in no condition to talk to the miners as I had hoped. He is more likely to be the first one to turn his back on anybody who mentions the word strike.

I look up at the picture of General Almonte and see the determined look in the eyes, the firm chin, and the hard and yet humane facial lines of suffering seen and experienced. The face exudes a raw edge of willpower. I lower my sight at Miguel and study his face. It is similar to the general's but without the raw edge of willpower or a look of determination in the eyes. It is the face of a man prepared to run, not to stand up and fight.

Before entering the house, I had a vision. It had been the vision of Miguel getting fired up by the facts and observations I would present, a vision of Miguel talking to the miners, rallying the troops with a few well-chosen words, and leading a force of men that stood up to the directors' schemes and intrigues and struck them down. That vision has disappeared into thin air.

So much for the reliability of visions.

I know that Miguel is fully capable of fighting, of standing up and leading people when it counts. On the other hand, he is also a family man whose first concern has to be wife and children. He has the right to do whatever he deems best for his family. If that doesn't include fighting for a better Tepetapa, so be it. Who am I to interfere with his life, his happiness?

Weighing the options of rekindling Miguel's fire within and letting things slide, I am prepared to opt for the latter.

"Never mind, Miguel, they won't do anything," I say, "not under the present circumstances."

"What circumstances?" he asks perking up. "What is this about? You said you must talk to me. Speak up. Don't give me this question and answer game. Okay?"

"Okay... But I must ask you one more question."

He opens a hand indicating that I should go ahead and ask.

"Did you tell safety inspector Mendez that the level eight stope was going to collapse?"

Miguel looks baffled. "How come you know what I said to Mendez?"

"Did you tell him or didn't you?"

"Yes, I did, and to my great surprise he agreed with me."

"Right, but Arbuckle pressured him to declare it safe. You in turn threatened Arbuckle to feed his balls to wild dogs and he fired you."

"Who told you that?"

"Francisco."

"Francisco? The old guy from Coahuila? Haggard face? How come? Why would he tell you?"

"Because your prediction came true with devastating accuracy and consequences."

That statement puts Miguel back on his heels. With stiff arms he presses his hands against the table's edge and looks stony-faced for the time it takes him to grasp and digest what I just said. With a jolt he gets up and asks, "You mean, my stope, level eight collapsed? And...?"

"Last thing I heard the security guards are still digging."

"What...?" His fist comes down softly on the table and he slumps back into his chair. He straightens up and turns to Laura who has just left the shower and disappears behind the curtain. "Laura? You better come and join us."

"I'll be right there," is her response.

Miguel asked me quietly, "How many?"

84

"Thirty dead, possibly more."

He pulls a face and curses under his breath, "Shit!"

He reaches for the pot on the stove and pours some more coffee in our cups. Nothing more is said until Laura joins us.

She has put on a blue and green dress with native embroidery typical for the Michoacán region. Her hair is held together in the neck by a golden brooch. Looking ready to go out or to travel somewhere, she is setting a signal whose significance escapes me for the moment. The way she smiles and sits down with a suave, elegant move reflects her composure and good spirits.

She puts her hands together near the edge of the table, loosely intertwining her fingers, and gives Miguel a pensive look before she turns to me.

"What do you have to tell us, Rigo?" she asks.

Without embellishments I relate the facts of the mine accident, Arbuckle's death, and my encounter with the mob. My observations of the miners having become a lot of selfish individuals, the directors covering up Arbuckle's death as an accident and the priest claiming that there have been no deaths in the mine in over a year takes a little while to convey. Beyond the observations, I relate my suspicion about the white and black smoke from the smelter chimney and the beeping brown box near the church.

I am on the verge of summarising facts and observations and supply Miguel with the ammunition needed to call a strike, when Gabriel, Pilar, and Benito stroll in looking bored. Laura cuts me off patting my hand. She looks after the children's needs giving them each a rolled-up tortilla sprinkled with a bit a salt and asks them to be patient for a little while. After lifting Benito onto her lap, she puts her arms around Pilar and Gabriel standing to the left and right of her. She looks a picture of serenity when she addresses me.

"Rigo," she begins in a measured tone, "I can see where this leads. But before you proceed, let me tell you that Miguel and I have decided to leave this town. What you told us only confirms it was the right decision. Besides the underlying reason, of which you may be the only person aware except those people directly involved, Miguel and I want to leave for other reasons, too.

"There is no proper medical care, no school, no library, no community centre, not even a football pitch in Tepetapa. There is no future for our children. There is nothing in this valley to keep us here. This town isn't even a real town. It is a company compound without a mayor, an administration or representation of its inhabitants. It was taken over and is run by foreign bosses who oppress, humble, deprive, manipulate, and exploit.

"For the sake of just feeding your children, you have to turn into a human robot, subject yourself to the will and whim of those in power, and never raise your voice in protest. The directors have put a machination in place, as you just told us, with the aim of controlling each individual and family, every activity, almost every thought and turning each man against the other.

"The total loss of identity and identification with one's past, heritage and culture is the result. I don't want my children to grow up without a past, present or future. The system has grown so large, and it is so overpowering with its controls and security that we can't fight it and bring about change from within, from the position of a pawn. That's why we decided to leave. I hope you can and will respect that and you will still respect us."

Laura's monologue has pierced my balloon. It has put Miguel's response, anxiety, and lack of determination in perspective as well.

While he has deflated my high-flying ideas about an uprising, Laura has brought me down to earth with her concern for her children and her assessment of the situation in Tepetapa. The more I get to know her, the more I recognise the complexity of her personality that would not allow me to get to know her fully. She represents two incongruous opposites packed into one.

Laura is everything a woman has to be to succeed: - smart, intelligent, strong willed, determined and not shy to be manipulative. At the same time, she is what all people fear to be: - locked in, cut off and living in abject poverty.

Taking Miguel's considerable skills and talents into consideration, I wonder why this couple had come to Tepetapa in the first place and how they had got stuck in this dump.

I must befriend myself with the idea that Miguel and Laura would soon be gone. I will have to think of leaving as well. It is only a question of when. Perhaps I should leave with them, I think, drop everything, pack my bundle, and hike across the plateau. If my car ran, I would give them a ride wherever they wanted to go, provided we could make it past the gate down the road.

86

I study the grain of the wooden tabletop, sigh, wipe away an invisible crumb and say, "You have put Mexico's never-ending history and the guiding principles of the information age, the second industrial revolution, if you will, in a nutshell. When are you going to leave?"

"Soon," says Laura.

"And how?" I ask. "I mean, you can't just walk down the road. You'll never get past the gate or over the fence that blocks the valley. Besides, don't you think the company would want to hold you back? You still owe for the smashed-up store, don't you?"

Laura smiles mysteriously. Ignoring my questions referring to the guards and the debt, she says, "We'll travel very light. A path behind the church leads out of the valley and onto the plateau beyond. The highway to Zacatecas and San Luis Potosí is not too far. We'll find a way."

Zacatecas? San Luis Potosí? South! They want to go south. Michoacán is south of Tepetapa, too. Suddenly Laura's dress makes sense.

"All the way to Michoacán?" I ask with a grin.

Laura smiles happily and draws her children closer. "Yes," she says dreamily, "all the way to Michoacán."

"I have never been there," I say. "Is it nice?"

"Nice?" Laura asks and laughs. "No, it's beautiful. Often, I dream of its green meadows and the cloud forests on the mountaintops with the myriad of Monarch butterflies. That's where I long to plant a garden, take long walks where the air is filled with the fragrance of wildflowers and herbs, or take a refreshing dip in the sparkling clean water of one of the creeks. It is a little paradise."

Her gleaming eyes reflect happy memories and expectations of a near future. She lets the children run back outside and clasps Miguel's hands as if to give him the final persuasive nudge that was necessary for him to get moving.

He responds with a vague smile, evidently not quite convinced of Michoacán's paradisical qualities. He clears his throat.

"Sorry to disappoint you, Rigo," he says. "But as you just heard, we have other plans."

I nod and look into my empty cup. The dark-brown, mud-like residue reminds me of the dark-brown box I had passed on my way down from the plateau and something begins to dawn on me.

When the two guards blocked my way, they never asked me for my number. The first question upon every contact with any of the guards is always for your number, especially in a situation they consider to be a potential infraction of security. So why hadn't the guards asked me? Did they already know my number? If so, how? Could the beeping brown box have anything to do with it? Was it possibly a scanner that could identify my number? But then again, I didn't carry anything on me that could be scanned. Or did I? I came to the conclusion that it had to be put to a test.

"You intend to leave on foot?" I ask Miguel.

"Yes, of course," he replies matter-of-factly. "Growing wings and learning to fly would take too long."

"Indeed," I say. "Leaving on foot may pose a problem."

"What do you mean, 'a problem'?" Miguel asks.

"Have you ever been up that path you want to take to the plateau?" I ask Laura.

"Yes," she confirms, "I have gone up there a few times."

"And on the way down? Did a couple of guards block your way asking what you were doing or who you are?"

"Yes, of course, but they are everywhere asking stupid questions and snooping around, aren't they?"

"Sure, but not on the way up. Right?"

"Well… yes. What are you getting at?"

"What I am getting at is simply that some kind of control mechanism identifies anybody going up that path. It sends a signal to the guards telling them exactly who went up to the plateau. Then they come after you to see what you are doing."

"Forget it," protests Miguel. "That's science fiction. How could they possibly identify you?"

"That I don't know," I admit.

A disparaging wave of his hand seems to conclude this matter for Miguel. "Even if you are identified, what's the difference? All the guards know is that you have left. Before that troop of layabouts gets moving to do anything about it, we'll be in Zacatecas and on a bus to Michoacán."

Vehemently I shake my head in disagreement. "I don't think so! Listen, Miguel, I was up there this morning. I saw the plateau. How far is it from the valley to the highway? Ten, twelve kilometres? That will take you three to four hours on foot under the best of circumstances, that is, if you don't encounter an

88

insurmountable obstacle like a wide crevasse. And you'll have the children with you. That'll slow you down. Let's say, you get to the highway within five hours. On the way south to Zacatecas it intersects with the road from the valley. The guards don't need to run after you. They'll get on a truck, drive up the highway and you'll walk right into their arms. So there."

A glum silence follows. Miguel and Laura look at me, he with an air of defiance, she with doubt in her eyes.

"You have to put my assumption to the test," I say.

"How?" Laura asks.

Drumming my fingers on the table, I am trying to think of a simple answer to her simple question.

Miguel interrupts my train of thought. "Look, Rigo, I don't think we have anything to worry about. We'll leave early in the morning, before sunrise. The guards won't even see us. Your assumption that they can identify anybody walking up that path sounds too farfetched. I mean, we aren't exactly walking around with dog tags around our necks."

"Dog tags!" I shout. "That's how they identify us!"

"What?" Miguel asks. "Have you gone nuts? I don't wear a dog tag."

"You just might, Miguel, you and I and everybody in Tepetapa just might," I say.

Ignoring their derisive laughter, I continue, "About a year ago I read an article about domestic animal identification in North America. You know how they do it? They implant a microchip under the skin, a microchip that contains the information about the owner, the pet's name, its medical history, and so on. It can easily be read with a scanning device. Why wouldn't the mining company do the same to us? You wouldn't even know about it and never feel the difference."

That assumption really hit the funny bone with Miguel and Laura. They laugh at me to their hearts' content and only calm down because I retain my stoic expression.

"I don't recall having undergone an operation to have a dog tag implanted in my chest," says Miguel.

"Of course not," I agree. "And you didn't need to. But you and Laura and your children, you are subject to annual medical check-ups by Doctor Gomez. Right? And you never find out why or against what you receive the three injections you get every year.

Correct? How the hell do you think the microchips are implanted? With a syringe, an injection under your skin!"

"Oh, come on now, Rigo," protests Miguel. "That's ridiculous! You think I wouldn't notice it if one of those, uh, what do you call it, was implanted in my chest?"

"No, Miguel, you wouldn't notice it, and I didn't say it's implanted in your chest. It could be in your neck, in the tip of your nose, even in your eyelid and you wouldn't notice it because it's so tiny."

Inevitably Miguel and Laura rub their eyelids, tweak the tips of their noses, and scratch their necks. They look highly uncomfortable all of a sudden.

"How small are these things?" Laura asks with a shaky voice.

"I don't know," I reply. "But I know there are microchips not bigger than your fingernail that can hold the information of all the books of an entire library. And some time ago I read that tiny robots are being developed. They can be inserted into a blood vessel, crawl up to your heart and perform surgery. That gives you an idea of scale. Imagine how small a microchip has to be to hold only your name and number and medical and work records."

"A tiny robot crawling around inside of me performing operations?" Laura asks. "That's creepy."

"No," I disagree with her. "It's not creepy if you are informed about it and the little robot saves your life. What is creepy is the possibility that the mining company is using microchips without our knowledge or consent for a total and perfect control system."

Miguel turns pale. "How the hell can we find out if there's any truth to what you say?"

"You have to put it to the test," I say emphatically. "And here's how. Laura, listen to me. You'll take Benito for a walk up the mountain path. About a hundred meters beyond the church there is a brown box standing in a crevice. I think that the box is the control device, the scanner. I suggest you hide behind one of the boulders and tell Benito to run in a circle in front of the box. That should trigger the alarm and at least two of the guards should come trotting up the mountain within about fifteen to twenty minutes. It would prove that the box identifies you. Finally, give the guards a fake four-digit number for yourself."

"But I don't have a number," says Laura. "Only Miguel has one."

90

"That's what we're supposed to think," I say. "But I am certain every miner's family has numbers and microchips implanted. Otherwise, they could walk about willy-nilly without any control. You'll find out if there's anything to my assumption as soon as they hear the fake number. They'll react accordingly and may arrest you."

"Arrest her?" mutters Miguel. "Forget it. I am not going to let that happen. No way."

"But Miguel," I object. "You and I will wait behind the church and come out as soon as the guards walk past."

"What? And get into a fight with them? No, I don't like it. It'll put our entire plan in jeopardy."

"Let's put it to the test, Miguel," urges Laura. "It's the only way to ascertain that we can ever get away from here."

Miguel gives Laura a very dark look. "We won't get out of here, if he's right about these controls."

They both look at me when I get up to leave, open the door, and say with a wry grin, "In that case, I guess, you'd have to organise a strike, an uprising against the directors' machinations. I'll go home and change. See you in fifteen minutes."

18

THE HEAT is almost unbearable. The midday sun stands right above the small garden behind the church and burns down through the naked branches of some trees.

Miguel grabs the thin trunk of one of them, shakes it, and pulls a face. He must think the tree is dead, which it isn't. In the hot, dry regions of the country, deciduous trees drop their leaves during the summer to conserve energy. Come October, November with the autumn rain, they sprout a rich foliage and stand once more in full bloom almost overnight.

It presents a fitting analogy to the miners, whose sense of community appears to be as dead as the trees seem to be but needs only the right stimulus to blossom again. At least, that is what I hope will happen if Miguel turns out to be the rainmaker this town needs so desperately.

We lean against the relatively cool whitewashed wall of the sepulchre with two sealed and ten open tombs. Hidden by a large bougainvillaea, it is an observation point to oversee the terrain without being spotted by somebody walking up the winding path past the church and into the rocky flank to the plateau.

Not a breeze brings relief from the heat. Despite our broad-brimmed straw hats and white cotton peasant shirts, loose slacks, and open sandals, we feel uncomfortable. The slightest movement of waving a hand to chase away the irritating flies causes us to break into a sweat. Fortunately, Miguel has brought along some small bottles of water. They should last us a while, if we take only small sips to prevent our tongues from swelling up and sticking to the roof of the mouth.

Laura and her children are walking up the path. Concerned about the outcome of an encounter with the guards, she decided to take Gabriel, Pilar, and Benito along. It isn't safe to leave one of them behind at home, she told me.

They pass the recess where the brown box is installed. They settle down behind a jagged boulder and disappear from view.

Miguel and I are on high alert listening for anyone coming up the path. The scanner would have sent a signal and raised the alarm to set the guards in motion, if a control system actually exists as opposed to my sense of paranoia.

Time flows by as slow as ice-cold molasses. Five minutes feel like half an hour. I am checking my wristwatch almost every twenty seconds.

Against the muffled background noise of the mine's hum, drone, crunch and hiss and the incessant buzzing of the flies, everything else remains quiet. No footsteps, no voices, nothing. After fifteen minutes Miguel raises one eyebrow in a critical look, after twenty, he raises both with mockery in his eyes. After twenty-five minutes he tilts his head with a smirk and casts a glance up the path indicating that he wants to join Laura and the kids. I signal him to stay five more minutes and remain quiet. Miguel opens his mouth to say something when the sound of crunching gravel and muffled voices of two men are heard. We can't see who it is, but we can hear what they say.

"Man, why are we doing this?" complains one of them. "It's so stupid! Running up a mountain in this heat! Why can't we wait until dusk when the sun won't fry my brain?"

"Shut up, Cardozo, just shut up!" barks the other one. "Don't fuck with me! Shut up and keep going!"

"Phhhht! Don't fuck with me!" mocks him the first one. "Man, I haven't even started yet! Why won't you tell me why we are sent up her to check on the woman and her kids? Because we're the idiots of the company?"

Two personified beefcakes in sweat-stained uniforms come into sight and stop at the corner of the church. They continue their verbal exchange while looking up the path. The argumentative younger one is the taller of the two but the other one is bulkier. If either one of them looks into the garden, Miguel and I will be spotted right away. That isn't part of our plan.

I turn to look at Miguel for some advice of what to do. He is gone! Silently I creep sideways towards the narrow opening between the church and the sepulchre when a big hand reaches out of one of the open tombs and tugs at my slacks. I am ready to jump out of my skin. It takes all of my constraint not to scream and run away. The hand points to the next tomb. Quickly I slip into it feet first and use my sombrero to cover me from view.

In the excitement of the moment, I don't listen to the guards' continuation of their argument. But what I do hear next is enough to make me want to scream. The older guard has lifted his cap and wipes forehead and balding pate with the sleeve of his shirt.

"Listen, Cardozo," he addresses his colleague while squeezing his cap back onto his bowling ball. "It's our job to assure that nobody walks out of here and escapes! Anyone trying to run away has a bounty of five thousand pesos on his head! We can make some quick cash bringing them back dead or alive!"

He points a hand up the path. "That woman and her three brats intend to escape. Believe me. They are easy money. Ten thousand each for you and me. Let's go."

They walk up the mountain path. The younger guard asks, "What happens to them once we hand them over?"

His colleague shrugs and says, "Who cares? They are never seen again and as long as we get our money…"

His voice tails off and blends into the background din of the mine.

Miguel scrambles out of his tomb and curses under his breath. He looks into my tomb and urges me to come out. In my devastation about what I overheard, I am incapable of moving. He grabs me by the collar and drags me out.

"You can cry and commiserate all you want after we have finished off the guards," he says with a pressed voice and shakes me by the shoulder.

He walks off through the garden and picks up fist-sized rocks along the way. At the church's corner he turns and looks back angrily, eyes full of rage and chin jutting out. In contrast, I am a pathetic sight. My knees are shaking. I am on the verge of bursting into tears and clutch my sombrero. I feel so guilty. The mess Laura and the children are facing is my fault. The guards are armed with pistols and riot-truncheons. We can't possibly overpower them.

"Are you coming or what?" Miguel asks very quietly.

His deep voice seems to reverberate off the church wall and the sepulchre. He looks utterly disgusted at the state I am in, turns, and silently rushes after the guards taking long, cautious strides. I can't leave him in the lurch, I think, raise a hand, and open my mouth to shout to wait for me. But I manage only a garbled whimper. I fall into a knock-kneed trot and follow him at a distance.

About halfway between the church and the spot where Laura and the children are hiding, Miguel is less than ten meters behind the guards. Still arguing, they didn't hear him coming up from behind.

Miguel takes a few more steps to shorten the distance. He holds a rock in his right hand, levels his arm back at shoulder height, stops and shouts, "Heh! Cardozo!"

The younger guard turns his head with a surprised look on his face and the projectile, catapulted by Miguel's powerful arm to high velocity, hits him square in the forehead. The peak of his cap softens the blow somewhat but still he topples like a felled tree. His body hits the edge of the path where gravity takes over and pulls his limp figure down the rocky precipice.

Miguel jumps out of sight behind a boulder while the other guard watches his colleague disappear. The guard turns and draws his gun, but all he sees is a babbling, crying figure trotting up the path about fifty meters away. That is I, holding my hat in my left hand and waving my right, in a limp gesture.

The guard is dumbfounded, lowers his gun, and pushes back his cap. He looks up the rocky flank and back at me again. His shiny forehead offers the perfect target. Miguel gives him something to think about with his second rock leaving an indelible mark above the guy's bridge of the nose. The guard falls to his side and rolls down the path a couple of turns.

Both guards taken out of commission gives me back my strength and I rush up to Miguel.

"Well done," says Miguel. "You make one hell of a decoy."

He flings the guard's firearm down the precipice and fetters the guard with the handcuffs taken from his belt. He turns and rushes up the path. Hot on his heels, I stop him just short of the brown box.

"Don't go past the scanner," I pant.

"The what?" he asks and wants to take another step.

I haul him back and say, "The brown box. The scanner. If you walk past it, they know that your entire family is on the run, and they will send out the guards in force."

"Who is 'they'?" he asks angrily.

"I don't know!" I yell. "It doesn't matter who will send the guards! But they are sent up here when somebody crosses the line. That should be quite obvious to you."

"Yes, sure," he shouts back. "But who the hell do you think I just flattened with a couple of rocks? The guards, right?"

"Just two of them!" I shout and point a finger at the mine. "There are more than fifty if not over a hundred vultures waiting for the computer to signal an easy twenty-five thousand pesos to be made when you cross the line."

"Computer? What the hell is that?" he asks and points at the brown box. "I thought you said this was a scanner."

"Yes! It is a scanner that is hooked up to a computer," I say heatedly. "Look, Miguel, this isn't the time or place to explain everything to you! I'm not an electronics expert! I have only a rough idea of how this stuff works! But believe me, it is not idle chit-chat when I tell you that Laura and the children have to come down here and go past the scanner to deactivate the signal and take them out of danger."

"Alright, alright," says Miguel, "I'll call Laura and the children to come down here, Rigo, though it doesn't make any sense why they have to go twice past the brown box before we go up to the plateau and take off."

"Take off? You mean, try to escape? Are you crazy?" I struggle to retain what little is left of my composure. "You can't do that, Miguel! You must go back to your house!"

"Out of the question!" protests Miguel. "We're not going back! We can't! If they find out…" He stops in midsentence and gives me a nervous stare. He looks up at the path and speaks in a quaking voice, "Laura and I decided we should get away from here and go for it if the path is clear. We will take that chance now and nothing can change my mind."

His sudden change in demeanour is very peculiar. Miguel is hiding something. He is afraid to be found out about something he doesn't want me to know. That means, whatever he is so secretive about has nothing to do with Laura's whorehouse caper. It must be something far worse, something that carries consequences so severe that he fears going back to the house and seeks safety in flight across the plateau with three small children. Not knowing what his big secret could possibly be, I decide to play along.

"All right," I say, "go ahead."

I give him a slap on the shoulder, the kind of combined slap and push that says, 'Go for it and damn the consequences.'

Instantly, I feel some resistance as Miguel stiffens and pushes his shoulder back just that tiny fraction that says, 'Don't push me! I'm thinking!'

"Miguel," I assure him, "you have my blessings. Go ahead and have yourself and your family killed."

I watch him look at Laura and the children who got up and are ready to go up to the plateau. Impatiently, Laura waves an arm telling Miguel to get moving and join them. Miguel turns to look at me. His expression is one of complete indecision. It is like an invitation to strike him and strike him hard.

I continue, "When the guards drag your limp and bloodied bodies back into town, I will tell everybody that you were a man of your word to the last. And when one of the guards flings Benito's body by one of his little legs into the smelter to remove any trace of him ever having existed, I will say a prayer for his soul. Should I ever find your grave, Miguel, I'll put a tin-wreath on it so you can hear when it rains. Now go already! Go! Your mind is made up, isn't it?"

Miguel's eyes fill with horror when I mention Benito. He is incapable of moving. I turn to walk away.

Miguel's big hand drops on my shoulder. He tears me around. His face distorted in a grimace of pain, he grabs me by the front of my shirt, lifts me up, and shakes me like a rag doll. I am dangling over the precipice, some twelve meters of sheer rock, and the ground Miguel stands on doesn't look too secure, either.

Through clenched teeth Miguel cries, "What do you mean?"

Waving arms and legs about, I stammer, "C-C-Careful now! My sh-shirt might rip!"

Miguel hauls me in and plants my feet on the edge of the abyss. I grab him by the sleeves and hold on for dear life. Looking down, I almost faint and try to get onto terra firma. But Miguel still shakes me and wants an answer to his repeated question, "What do you mean?"

"Call Laura and the kids down here and I'll tell you," I say hastily and hold on to his shirt when he lets go of me to wave to Laura.

Unwilling to come down, Laura slaps her thighs, looks skyward and quietly curses. She is furious but makes a move. With Benito on her arm and Gabriel and Pilar trailing her, she stomps towards us, walks past the beeping brown box, and addresses Miguel angrily while giving me a furtive glance.

"What's going on? Why aren't you coming, Miguel? There are no guards! The path is clear! Let's go already!"

I clear my throat to draw her attention, but she avoids looking at me and keeps on staring down Miguel with unabashed anger in her eyes. It is time for a shot in the dark.

"Laura," I say with a stern voice, "it doesn't matter how you enriched yourself. Nobody cares or will come after you because you filched Arbuckle's money."

Bullseye! Laura puts Benito down and stares at me. She puts a hand over her mouth with horror in her eyes. Miguel put his arms around her and turns to me.

"How do you know?" he whispers.

I shrug and wave my hand telling them to follow me. I turn and walk down the path towards the sanctuary of the little church building.

19

THE CHURCH proves to be a good sanctuary. Dressed like country folk in their traditional Sunday best, we blend seamlessly into the congregation, a small gathering of about twenty-five men, women, and children facing the ornamental altar for noon prayer. Miguel, Laura, and I have split up. We take separate seats in between other people. The children seem to have sensed the tension that grip their parents and me and stay quiet. Laura has moved to the left front, Gabriel and Pilar to the centre on the right, Miguel to a pew farther back on the left, and Benito and I have slipped into the nearest pew on the right.

Several guards enter the church barely fifteen minutes after we are on our knees and bow our heads. Unable to find a woman with three children in the company of an armed and dangerous malefactor who had given lumpy foreheads and concussions to two of their colleagues, they withdraw from the place of worship and gather outside.

I leave the congregation with Benito on my arm. We pass the scrutiny of the Brownshirts without hindrance and go to the cantina. Within a few minutes Gabriel and Pilar join Benito and me for refreshments and a short while after their arrival Laura and Miguel sit down with us. I order a hearty meal of *sopa de carne*, a clear beef-soup, and *champandongo*, a layered dish of ground beef, ground pork, cheese, grated walnuts and almonds, *móle* hot sauce, and tortillas. I know nothing about cooking, but I sure know how to eat well, and I am glad that Miguel and his family enjoy my selection and pay for it, too, as I am practically broke.

Little is said during the meal. But during the two-hour afternoon lull, Miguel, Laura, and I engage in a whispered conversation. Several times we order soda pop or beer, a bottle at a time, to get rid of the waiters lounging around in our vicinity trying to catch snippets of our subdued chat.

It proves extraordinarily difficult for me to explain the function of the control system that prevents anyone from leaving the valley unnoticed. Miguel and Laura have no knowledge of even the basics of electronic signal transmission.

They wonder if they could get rid of the microchips, which I presume have been implanted in all of us. Although I don't know if it is possible, I assure them that the chips can be extracted. They believe me. It makes sense to them that the microchips in our bodies are the reason anybody wanting to leave is caught by the guards. Should it ever be found out, I argue, how the gringos have obtained total control of the miners' every move in contravention of the most basic of human rights - the right to privacy and freedom of movement - an international hue and cry would bring their scheme of things down with a crash.

I observe with some glee how my reasoning brings Miguel to a boiling point. He appears to develop a firm resolve to rebel against the system the more he learns about its intricacies and despicable implications.

Possibly in return for enlightening them, Miguel and Laura begin to trust me enough to let me in on their secret that scared them into their escape attempt.

Laura provides a fragmented narrative of observations and events. It includes her belief of having heard beeps in the company store and every room of the whorehouse. She claims they were identical to the sound emitted by the scanner on the mountain path. She digresses to Lucy's relationship with Juanita, the male prostitute. She conveys in detail Arbuckle's visit to the whorehouse the previous night and a fight that ensued between Arbuckle and Juanita. She explains how she had got a hold of quite a bit more money than was owed to her by Lucy. But the scenario she lays out begins to make sense only once I hear the last bit of her information, because she conveys the fragments as jumbled as pieces of a jigsaw puzzle. Putting the pieces together and filling in the gaps with my knowledge of events and a bit of imagination, it begins to dawn on me why Laura, even more so than Miguel, has reason to be afraid.

It began with Miguel's visit to the whorehouse. When he entered "Lola's" room blindfolded as was required of her clients, Laura recognised him of course immediately. Quietly she pleaded with Lucy to take him away. But Lucy had simply shut the door and left Laura to her own devices.

Torn between outrage about Miguel spending what little money he had in the whorehouse and a deep sense of guilt about her own caper, Laura decided to throw caution to the wind and

100

allow herself to be carried away by her passion for Miguel. She wanted to give him the full and honest treatment.

That meant no fudged, lubricated hand-job all other clients were given with her sitting on top pretending to ride a wild mustang while jerking off his wiener. No, this deal was for real.

She gave herself completely, passionately, responding to his every move with limbs locked in a firm embrace and urging Miguel on to a rousing climax that left them both exhausted and content. She was filled with heavenly happiness and began to cry, which in turn gave Miguel good reason to rip off his blindfold to see what was wrong with "Lola". Seeing his wife, her arms around his neck, a smile as wide as a barn door and tears of happiness streaming down her face, he went into a state of shock.

Not being versed in the world of make-believe of a professional whorehouse where clients are rarely, if ever given real penetrative sex for their money, Miguel believed that the treatment he had received was what every other client was given as a matter of course. Recalling the stories other miners had told about "Lola", he thought that he had one recourse only to restore his honour and to right the wrong inflicted upon him, and that was by killing "Lola".

In the absence of any useful weapon, he put his hand to her throat to strangle her but was overcome by an inner conflict that drained all power from his limbs. As much as he wanted to kill "Lola", he could never raise a hand in anger against Laura for whom he was ready to give his own life.

Stroking her neck gently, he belted out his emotional pain in a primeval scream that shook the house and brought Lucy and two muscular *maricas*, Juanita and Armandita, onto the scene. Fearing the worst, they dragged Miguel out of the room.

Confronted by two guys wearing curly wigs and lots of make-up, he regained his powers and let out his rage on them thrashing about like a madman. It took the help of several girls to subdue Miguel, get him back into his pants, and throw him out.

After the screaming and fighting, Laura was in as much of a state of shock as Miguel. It took Lucy over an hour of reproof as well as encouragement and several snifters of fine French cognac to uplift Laura's spirits enough to stop her talking about suicide.

It was during this crucial hour when Lucy brought Laura back from the brink and I had gone down the road in search of Miguel that Arbuckle showed up at the whorehouse. He had had a bad day. Someone had scratched the lacquer of his shiny luxury limousine. The battery of his cell-phone was dead leaving him without a lifeline. Mine inspector Mendez had questioned his expertise and, contrary to his view, considered a stope unsafe just because one lousy miner had been killed by falling rock. Miguel had actually threatened him with perverse retribution for declaring the drift safe and he fired him. Callaghan had bawled him out in turn for firing foreman 1-8-0-3, the miner with the highest productivity rate, and forced him to reinstate Miguel. Small wonder Arbuckle was in a foul mood and in dire need of a release of his frustration.

A blowjob and a glass of champagne on the house, the usual perk for the director collecting the cut of Lucy's income, simply wouldn't do this time. He needed rough sex, wanted to domineer, and inflict pain. Juanita obliged.

Lucy and Laura sat in the monitor room next to Lucy's private quarters. On one of twelve closed circuit TV-screens they observed and listened to the ugly proceedings in the "dungeon", a padded room outfitted with torture instruments and a rack with chains and spiked belts for shackling the submissive party. Arbuckle whipped and slashed Juanita until he drew blood and then proceeded to sodomise him. Still unable to get his jollies, he tried to get more than a submissive response out of Juanita and screamed that Hernan Godoy was dead, that he, Arbuckle, had killed him.

Juanita bucked, screamed, strained, and somehow freed himself of the shackles and his tormentor. Arbuckle was suddenly on the receiving end of punishment, but he laughed at the blows he received and seemed to enjoy bleeding from mouth and nose. Lucy had had a brief fainting spell and Laura helped her to her bed. As soon as she recovered, Laura learned from her that the killed miner in question was Lucy's son, her only child, and that Juanita was his father.

Hernan had been the result of one night of mad love many years ago when Lucy had saved Juanita from a gang of police officers who had maltreated and heaped scorn on him for being a *marica* and then proceeded to gang rape him. With the death of Hernan, the tie was gone that had bonded Lucy and Juanita and had given their lives a semblance of meaning.

Lucy switched off the constantly jangling background music and rushed downstairs together with Laura to be by Juanita's side. In the silence that followed, Laura noticed a faint beeping sound every time she passed through a doorway. She wanted to ask what that sound was but forgot because by the time she and Laura had got to the dungeon, they had to attend to more pressing matters.

Arbuckle was knocked out as a result of the severe beating. Juanita had gone stark raving mad and needed to be constrained by several people forcing him to the floor. Lucy had Arbuckle cleaned up and dressed and told two of her girls, Maria and Martha, to walk him over to the mine and pass him into the care of the guards.

Lucy declared the whorehouse closed for the night and threw the remaining clients out. Laura wanted to leave as well and asked for the pay that was due to her. In the unceasing confusion of getting Arbuckle out of the house and keeping Juanita in, Lucy told her that it was in a brown envelope on the dresser in her private quarters. There were two unmarked and sealed envelopes on the dresser and a receipt with Arbuckle's signature for the directors' cut. Laura took both envelopes and went back to ask Lucy which one was hers but the whorehouse had turned into a madhouse.

Juanita had escaped. Ignoring her questions, Armandita pushed Laura out of the house through the back door in the basement and told her on order from Lucy to leave and never to return. Clutching the two envelopes she took a roundabout way home past the mechanic's workshop and along the mine gate. In the dim moonlight and from a distance she saw a naked man with a blond wig in front of the pawnshop wielding a huge rock and slamming it a couple of times down on a man lying stretched out on the ground. She knew who the naked man was but would never have sworn to it because she hadn't seen his face.

She didn't stop and rushed home where she found me lying on the table, knocked out, bruised, and bleeding. Thinking I was dead, she suffered a severe panic attack, wanted to dress her children, and run away with them. But then Miguel turned up with a box of adhesive bandages and a bottle of hydrogen peroxide he had stolen after breaking into the company store.

In bitter silence they cleaned and patched up my wounds. It was Pilar who brought Miguel and Laura together again. She had woken up, left her bed and began to cry at the sight of me. Miguel and Laura brought Pilar back to bed and made sure their three children were fast asleep. Then they had a long talk, a real exchange of minds they had never had before, until they succumbed to emotional and physical exhaustion.

Taking catnaps, waking, dozing, watching over each other, they spent a restless night that led to accepting each other's failings and capers. Ultimately, they forgave each other and made up. It was only later in the morning, after I had left their house that Laura thought of checking the envelopes and counting the money. They had never seen so much money in one pile. Together with the savings she had accumulated during her four weeks as "Lola", it was enough to buy a small plot of land and the material necessary for building a modest home somewhere far away from Tepetapa. That's when they decided to leave for Michoacán.

Unfortunately, I had turned up and told them about the electronic control system and they wanted to leave immediately.

They have reason to be afraid of the control system, if Laura was correct with her suspicion that scanners are installed in the whorehouse and selected spots all over town and the mine. Her and Miguel's every move could be traced and analysed with the help of a computer. It could create a data shadow pointing out unequivocally their involvement in Arbuckle's death. A thorough search of their premises would yield a pile of money, that is to say the evidence if not the proof of robbery as a motive for killing Arbuckle. It was an amount of money they couldn't possibly have obtained through frugality. It was more than twice Miguel's annual income. It was more than the amount of the directors' cut of Lucy's monthly gross income, which Arbuckle had collected but which had not been passed on to them.

Taking into account that Miguel had threatened Arbuckle with severe retribution, the directors' "legal expertise" would be sufficiently satisfied to take immediate action. They wouldn't bother with yet another kangaroo court but mete out punishment based on the "evidence" they had. At best they would push Miguel and his family back into abject poverty and to the abyss of disintegration. At worst they would let this couple of malcontents and their brood disappear without a trace.

I mull over my theory of the directors' anticipated path of action for a moment. It is a worst-case scenario based on the assumption that the directors knew of or for that matter cared about the disappearance of their cut of Lucy's earnings. In our reality it is of course a vast amount of money, enough to purchase a small plot of land and build a modest home. But to them, the directors, what is it to them? Almost nothing, a mere trifle of cash anyone of them would spend without thinking on some friends for lunch in some exclusive greasy spoon or club in any of the metropolitan areas of North America.

It isn't the money they want, I concluded, it is control they are after, the control inherent for example in collecting cash from Lucy and matching it to the amount their computer had calculated. And Laura said that she had seen a receipt for the money signed by Arbuckle. That means the control function had been carried out. Lucy is off the hook. Neither is there an obvious reason to link Laura to the disappeared money.

That link could only be established if the entire collection of data signals was examined in detail and conclusions were drawn as to the multitude of possible scenarios. But that would require patience, diligence, perseverance, and the ability to draw logical conclusions, facilities I denied anyone of the directors to have.

The directors are a bunch of greedy control freaks driven by the bottom line and their craving for power. In short, they pose no real, imminent danger to the livelihood and well-being of Miguel and his family.

It is certain that the directors rely on their electronic gadgets for the control of their venture and the mineworkers. And whatever the computer system doesn't tell them they don't act upon.

Like the majority of their peers in the industrialised world, they substitute common sense, sound judgement, and business acumen for a computer and accept the machine's answers as the equivalent to the wise utterances of a super brain.

However, a computer is a machine that responds only to commands permissible within the limits of the logical functions that are inherent in its structure and for which it is programmed. Therefore, the answers the machine supplies are nothing more than the reflections of the directors' limited vision, imagination, creativity, and instincts which focuses entirely on the requirement dictated by the bottom line and the status quo of their power structure.

I conclude that Miguel, Laura, and their children are not in any danger of being persecuted.

A hand is waved in front of my eyes and snaps me out of my thoughts.

"Are you still there?" Miguel asks.

"Uh… yes," I say. Looking at Laura, I continue, "You can go home. As a matter of fact, you should go home."

"Why?" Laura asks. "What makes you so sure?"

"To avoid suspicion among your neighbours," I explain. "If anyone of them blabs about your absence, it could provide the pointer the directors need to investigate your movements. Only then could you end up in trouble."

"What do you mean?" Laura asks anxiously.

I sigh and explain, "The directors rely on the computer system for any information they need. But the computers will only provide answers to the questions they ask - nothing more, nothing less. If they don't suspect you, they won't ask the computer any questions concerning you or Miguel, you understand? Go home and tell the neighbours what a lovely time you and the children had in church. That should forestall any chin-wagging."

Laura lowers her head in tacit agreement. Over the noise of the squealing brakes of two gleaming charter coaches coming to a stop in front of the mine gate, she says, "Let's go, Miguel. You have to change for work."

I put a hand on her forearm. "No, Laura. Miguel and I must take care of some business that just cropped up. Don't we, Miguel?"

Miguel watches the buses and the disembarkation of men, women, and children. A group of ten security guards form a cordon and encircle the new arrivals to Tepetapa. Miguel looks at me, nods, and goes to the bar to settle our bill.

"You're not going to do something stupid, are you, Rigo?" Laura asks.

My indignant look turns into a grin. "Miguel and I? Do something stupid? Whatever gives you that idea?"

Laura is not amused. She gets up, picks up Benito who fell asleep in his chair, takes Pilar by the hand, and indicates to Gabriel with a tilt of her head that it is time to leave. She gives me one last dark and doubtful look and slowly walks up to Miguel. He says something that seems to reassure Laura and waves after his kids

106

as they leave the cantina. Although brief, it is a long farewell for a man with a mission.

When he looks at me and tilts his head briefly towards the plaza, I can see it in his eyes and his whole demeanour that he is ready to take on the directors in a fight against schemes, intrigues, and machinations. I know he is not going to quit until he has reached his goal - at whatever cost.

20

In constant fear of death or failure,
life can neither be enjoyed
nor lived to its fullest.

THE CHARTER COACHES stand idle. Their engines are turned off. Under the watchful eyes of the guards, suitcases of all sizes, cardboard boxes held together with rope and huge bundles of goods knotted into blankets are hauled off the roof racks and out of the luggage compartments. Once empty, the drivers search the interior of their vehicles for items left behind by the weary travellers. When nothing is found, the drivers salute and start the engines. The buses draw a large circle on the plaza and depart with a mighty, thundering roar of their exhaust pipes.

Thirty-two men and their families, a crowd of about one hundred and forty people is left behind in twirling clouds of slowly settling yellowish-brown dust. The coughing and cursing newcomers take a cautious first look at the "attractions" of Tepetapa.

Swiftly the guards separate the men and the women and children. The crowd falls silent in expectation of further orders shouted by the guards. But none come forth. The officer in charge is still searching on the mountain path.

Miguel and I stroll out of the cantina into the gleaming sunshine of the plaza. All eyes turn towards us. Dressed in white peasant shirts and slacks, sandals, and wide-brimmed straw-hats, we lack only colourful ponchos slung over our shoulders to create the impression of having stepped straight out of a movie set.

The awe-inspiring figure of Miguel gives the women cause to pick up or hold back their children and step aside. Miguel walks towards the guards who huddle between the separated groups of newcomers. He tips the brim of his sombrero and addresses the grinning Brownshirts in an authoritative tone of voice.

"Well done, boys," Miguel compliments the guards. "I am the foreman of level eight, and these men are my new recruits."

He points at the group of thirty-two men, a rough-and-ready bunch of tough guys and addresses them. "Welcome to Tepetapa! You have arrived just in time."

Turning to the guards again, he says in a sharp tone, "On orders from President Callaghan, these men are to be outfitted immediately! They must be ready for tonight's shift with overalls, helmets, and boots! I will take care of them! You will take care of the women and children! Who has the list of assigned accommodations for the families?"

Flabbergasted the guards look at each other. The initial smirks upon seeing Miguel disappeared when Callaghan's name was mentioned. One of the guards raises a hand asking for permission to speak and gets the nod.

"It's in the guardhouse, uh, I think, Sir," he says.

"Get it!" orders Miguel in response and turns to address the women and children. Pointing to the rows of bundles, boxes and suitcases, he says, "You will proceed in orderly fashion to pick up your luggage. Items too heavy to carry you may leave behind to collect later. The guards will accompany you to your assigned accommodation. You will have plenty of time to settle in. Your medical appointments have been moved to tomorrow morning eight o'clock. Now pick up your luggage."

The guard returns with a list. Miguel looks at it briefly and tears it into ten strips with three to four names per strip of paper. He hands one strip to each of the guards and says, "These are your respective charges, boys! Take them to their hovels! And be courteous! I don't want to hear any complaints!"

The guards, happy to receive clear orders, give their affirmative response shouting in unison, "Yes, Sir!"

While the guards scramble to gather their respective charges and lead them away, I cast a wary look around. Had nobody yet become suspicious of Miguel's activity, I ask myself. Evidently not! The mine gate is slightly ajar without a Brownshirt in sight. In the distance, near the church and spread out along the path leading up to the plateau, I can vaguely make out some fifty or sixty guards searching and poking around in the cracks of the rock-face. The entire mine complex has been left unguarded! I wonder if Miguel is aware of that. I want to point it out to him, but he orders the men to follow him and leads them to the company store as soon as the last of the guards has marched off with women and children in tow.

I stay behind and sit down on the one remaining piece of luggage, a big pink suitcase. After only twenty minutes, Miguel and his recruits come out of the store outfitted with brand-new black overalls, helmets, and safety boots. They march towards me in a broad front and carry their personal belongings in white plastic bags.

I get up and look around. Three gringos stand at a window of one of the offices. I recognise Callaghan, the only director with a semblance of character. He and his two cohorts observe the scene below with expressions of satisfaction. Townspeople walking by either pay no heed to the newcomers or give them scant attention at best. Miguel approaches me with a request.

"Rigo," he says in a low, conspiratorial tone of voice, "get four cases of cold beer at the cantina on Callaghan's account. If the barman balks, tell him to step outside and wave to the three gringos. Go!"

He turns to the men to address them. On the way to the cantina, I hear what he tells them while I cast suspicious glances back.

"Aren't you glad you're finally in Tepetapa, all outfitted with new gear and ready to make some money?" he hollers.

Some of the men mutter their affirmation, others just nod.

"What I want you to do now," continues Miguel, "is to look up at the big window on the second floor of the office building behind you. Three gringos are gawking at you like a herd of monkeys. Show them how happy you are to be here. Turn around and wave your helmets!"

Tripping into the cantina, I look back. The men are swooning as they rip off their helmets, laugh, and shout, "*¡Viva Tepetapa!*"

For good measure Miguel has joined the joyous outburst and waves with both hands.

Standing at the bar and placing the order, I can hardly believe what I see next. The three men at the office window look surprised at first, then laugh and wave back. When the barman refuses to accept my "order on account", I ask him to step outside and wave to Callaghan, as per Miguel's instruction.

The barman and I stand shoulder to shoulder and wave with varying degrees of enthusiasm, he with a certain reluctance and I as if my life depended on it. It works better than a charm. The three gringos respond with more laughter to our message of cheer and wave back. When the barman holds up a hand with four fingers spread apart, Callaghan shrugs. He waves both his hands with fingers and thumbs spread apart.

"Oh well," I say, "I guess I must have misunderstood him. Make it ten cases then."

The barman accepts the order. I sign a note with "Callaghan", and promptly ten cases are loaded onto a dolly and delivered to the loud cheers of the men. The first bottles are drained in seconds flat and lustily the men help themselves to more of the free brew.

The gringos had grown tired of gawking and stepped away from the window before the beer delivery. As a result, they don't see Miguel get a grip on his recruits. He gets the men's attention when he bellows, "Drink and be merry! This is the last drink you're going to get for a long time! Welcome to hell!"

His diabolical laughter that follows the gloomy outburst has a distinctly infernal ring to it. The men gulp, and it isn't just the beer. It is the sudden change of tone. They swallow hard upon hearing what Miguel tells them next with an inscrutable smile.

"In case you were wondering, there is no way out of here!" His arm draws a large circle. "You are enclosed by a three-meter high, industrial strength chain link fence topped by coiled razor wire!"

His hand points up to the path along the rock-face. "The heavily armed guards are under orders to shoot to kill you on sight should you want to escape! You are trapped! Imprisoned! And as of tomorrow, once you are dog-tagged with microchips, every one of your steps will be monitored and registered."

The men's expressions change from the moronic grin of good-time Charlies to the curiosity and suspicion of worried men afraid to have realised too late that they sold their souls to the devil for a mere handful of silver. The first reaction of shocked silence gives way to grumbling. One of the men steps forward and addresses Miguel.

"Why are you telling us all this?" he asks. "What's your name? And who the hell are you?"

"Good question!" says Miguel. "My name is Miguel Patín. I am your foreman. What is your name?"

"Diego," says the man. "Diego Zacala."

"Pleased to make your acquaintance, Diego," says Miguel. "You want to know why I am telling you that there is no escape? Because in two to three days you will think of nothing else but escape."

"Nonsense!" shouts Diego. "We didn't come here to run away! We came here to work and make some money!"

"Of course, you did," confirms Miguel. "So did the thirty-two miners you're here to replace. Guess why they don't work here any more? Because they quit their jobs and moved to another town? Or because they ran away? No! They were killed underground last night when a drift collapsed!"

He pauses and looks at the glum faces. Only Diego's stony expression shows solid defiance.

"Bullshit!" he scoffs. "Thirty-two miners killed! That's a disaster that wouldn't go unnoticed. There's not a word in the press, on TV or the radio about it!"

"Would you have come here had you heard or read about the disaster?" Miguel asks.

"Of course not!" says Diego.

"That explains it, doesn't it?" is Miguel's enigmatic reply. He looks from face to face and focuses on Diego who wants to say something but holds back when his eyes meet Miguel's steady gaze.

Miguel speaks to him when he continues, "Tepetapa is a company town. It is a compound with restricted access. A fence has been put up right across the valley to prevent anybody, especially newsmen from entering and snooping around. That's why you didn't hear or read anything about the disaster of last night. We are under the total control of the gringo directors!"

He pauses and rips open the lid of another case of beer, takes out two bottles and offers one to Diego. They unscrew the crown corks, clink the bottles, and take a swig. Pointing at the remaining six cases of beer, Miguel encourages the other men to help themselves.

The consumption of beer in the blazing sunshine expedites the alcohol's effect on the brain. Some of the men look ready to start a brawl right on the spot. Miguel should hurry up and finish his speech, if he doesn't want their attention to slip and a fight to break out. But he takes his time as if he knows exactly what he is doing. He looks again from man to man with that inscrutable smile.

"Now for the bad news," he says with a barely suppressed chuckle in his voice. "It concerns your pay. I don't know what divine wages you were promised. But your hourly rates were cut by fifteen percent and the daily drilling and blasting quota was raised to two meters per shift."

The ensuing uproar drowns out Miguel's voice. The men rush forward, a howling mass of beer fumes and desperation. Each one of them clamours for his attention. Miguel has his hands full trying to contain the sudden onslaught. He barely stands his ground raising his hands and ordering them to be quiet with little success.

It takes Diego waving his arms to silence the men. He shouts at Miguel, "If that is true what you say, why are you still here?"

Miguel reaches for Diego and pulls him around to stand by his side. Facing the other men, he puts an arm around his shoulders and says, "Did you hear Diego's question? He wants to know why I'm still here. Here's my answer. I'm still here because I'm still alive."

He pauses to allow the dramatic message to sink in. He pulls me to his other side and says, "This man, Rigoberto, saved me and my family from certain death today. He investigated the control system in the mine and the entire valley. He told me how it works, how it controls your every move, and why the guards come after you to kill you when you try to escape. Rigo stopped me from running away. Had he not done so, my family and I would be dead and cremated in the smelter right now. Look up at the path in the rock-face. The guards are still searching for my family and me. They want to kill us because our microchips gave them the signal that we wanted to escape. Tomorrow morning, during your medical check-up, you will be dog-tagged with microchips. And then every one of your steps will be monitored and registered as well. You will be at the mercy of the men you saw at the window and their cohorts. Right now, you don't carry dog tags! Right now, you are renegades! You are still beyond the control of the gringo directors of this mine! You can try to run away with a slim chance of succeeding if you leave your families behind! Your alternative is to stay and fight for fair wages and the liberty to come and go as you please! Do you want to break the control system? Do you want to be recognised as men of dignity and honour? Are you willing to stand up for your rights? Are you ready to help me? Are you ready to help yourself?"

The response Miguel gets is not the overwhelming vote of confidence he might have expected. That is due to some disturbances on the fringes of the small crowd. During Miguel's quest for the newcomers' hearts and minds and muscle, some early arrivals of the late shift drift up to the crowd wondering out loud what is going on. The beer-soaked replies they get in answer to their questions centre on dog tags, the only term the minds of the miners, unadulterated with electronics terminology, seem capable of comprehending.

An argument has broken out between a newcomer and an old hand when the newcomer asks to show him his dog tag, and the old hand mistakes the request as an insult of being taken for some street mutt. The raised fists promote the tension. The argumentative mood spreads in circles. Miguel must do something to stem the tide of anger that threatens to wash away his call to disobedience and kill the seed he has planted before it had a chance to germinate. He figures pouring on a little more liquid might do the trick.

"Anybody here who hasn't had a drink?" he hollers. "Step forward and help yourself!"

It works! Eager to grab a free beer, the firebrands drop their quarrelsome attitudes. Cooling the hot tempers with barley-juice also improves the crowd's willingness to listen to what the big guy has to say. Expectant looks are cast in our direction when Miguel confers with me briefly in a whispered exchange. I suggest he drop any reference to the microchips, scanners, computers, or control system. It is too complex to explain in simple terms. He balks at my suggestion and insists that the miners must be made aware of the sinister control system and that it must be destroyed. I agree with him on that point and mutter that I would take care of the computers. Somehow! When he frets how I was going to do that, I tell him to let it be my concern. He should concentrate on the need for a safe workplace and draw the miners' attention to what really riles them - their reduced pay. At last Miguel put his big hand on my shoulder. He looks full of doubt but nods and lets go of me.

The gate moves silently, when I push it open just enough to slip through. I pull it by the spring-loaded release handle until the

114

lock snaps shut. A sharp cracking sound tells me that some part of the lock broke. The lock is set between two large metal plates welded to the frame that makes it impossible to inspect it. The heavy handle, normally standing in an upright position, dangles down with a rusty squeak and falls off as soon as I let go of it. I have busted the damned lock! I am trapped inside the mining compound! I pick up the handle, turn it over a couple of times, and finally fling it onto the flat roof of the guardhouse.

Walking along the narrow space between fence and guardhouse, I avoid the scanner that, if at all, is installed facing the gate and driveway. At the back of the barrack, I rush along close to the wall and watch the windows of the office building. Quickly I cross the patch of lawn and hurry around the corner to the entrance of the medical station. Looking back, I see Miguel on the plaza facing the growing crowd. Cases of empty beer bottles serve as his platform. He stands head and shoulders above the men. His elevated position assures him of their rapt attention. They respond to him with angry shouts of support and raised fists. When he looks in my direction, I wave to him in a reassuring gesture, although I have no idea what I am going to do next.

My hand resting on the handle of the door to the medical station, I hesitate. This isn't the path to get to the computers. Those machines are installed in the offices. I contemplate entering the building through the main entrance when I see three men, a director, a guard in a neon orange overall and a grey-clad smelter worker come into view between machine shop and ventilation house. I have to act and get out of sight before they spot me. I push the door open and enter the waiting room of the medical station.

21

IN THE WAITING ROOM four security guards in neon-orange overalls wait for their turn to be looked after. At first sight of the goons, I want to turn on my heel and leave again. But I force myself to stay calm and sit down looking at them without uttering a word. Their attire tells me that they are part of the crew that "cleans up" level eight. They glance at me and continue an exchange of expletives while gingerly touching their scrapes and bruises. I don't detect any major injuries, just the usual scuffmarks resulting from a day's work underground. Had a miner shown up in that condition, he would have been thrown out on his ear.

I doff my hat. The plaster on the side of my head gets almost torn off. The serous fluid of the laceration had soaked the plaster that got stuck on the hat's sweatband. It is a good enough reason to be there, I think, should anyone bother to question my presence.

I look around the room and commit all details to memory while desperately trying to think of what to do next. I am facing the door to the patients' lavatory. The consulting room and the surgery is to my left, the door to Doctor Gomez' office and the door to the yard to my right. A sad looking, neglected yucca-palm stands in a plastic pot next to the lavatory door. A couple of framed photos of the mine hang on the wall. Out of the ceiling and next to the neon lights extend the gold and silver-coloured valves of the sprinkler system with their built-in heat and smoke sensors. Otherwise, this mono-coloured room is bare of decorations.

There is only one access route from here to the rest of the building. If I want to get into the administrative section upstairs or the basement rooms without stepping outside and entering the building by the main entrance, it is through the consulting room and another small waiting room at its other end for the office workers. That would lead me to the central staircase. But how could I sneak through the consulting room unseen? And in the event of making it to the staircase - then what? If I should get as far as the offices, I wouldn't know what to do. I don't even know what type of computer system the company uses to store the scanner signals or where the machines are located. In all likelihood they are those inconspicuous looking, grey or khaki-coloured boxes with monitor screen and keyboard. In other words, they would look very much the same as all other terminals and computers of a network. How would I know what was what? And even if I found the control computer and disabled it, wouldn't there be a back-up system that takes over and carries on as if nothing happened?

The flood of questions crossing my mind and the lack of answers give me a severe bout of anxiety.

What am I doing and what am I after? Am I just chasing ghosts? What do I really know about this allegedly sinister control system? Nothing! Except for the brown box on the mountain path and Laura's claim to have heard beeping sounds in the whorehouse and the company store after I made her aware of the possible existence of scanners, I have nothing, not a shred of evidence of the system's existence.

Have I not worked myself into a frenzy and start to believe in a phantasm of my own creation? What if the brown box isn't a scanner but simply a sensor that causes a bell to ring somewhere in the guardhouse alarming the guards of a potential security infraction? Am I not going down the same road I accuse the directors of taking, that is to say, passing judgement on flimsy if not non-existent evidence? And why do I think of the directors as such evil characters? Isn't that simply a result of not knowing anyone of them on a personal level? Maybe they won't turn out to be all that bad a crate of apples once I got to know them.

Doubts gnaw away at me. Doubts about my assumptions, presumptions, and suppositions come to the fore, and the observations, events, and incidents that raised my suspicions in the first place are pushed aside. Perhaps it is all a matter of my wary mind having led me astray, having prevented me from inviting Doctor Gomez for a beer and a friendly chat at the cantina. Why couldn't we be friends? Why shouldn't we?

A repeated subdued shout tears me out of my thoughts while I stare at one of the sprinklers in the ceiling. I lower my sight at the four guards grinning at me.

"Are you deaf?" one of the boneheads asks sharply.

"What? Uh…no," I reply quietly.

"So why don't you answer?" the bonehead inquires with yet more venom in his voice.

Facing the sadistic grin of four guards, I yearn for Miguel's authoritative voice to make these clowns stand to attention. But I don't have his voice and there is no time to lose with wishful thinking.

The guards expect an answer and show signs of unrest. I take on a stiff posture and lock eyes with the loudmouth for a measured period before I speak.

"Who gave you authority to address a private friend of Doctor Gomez in this tone?" I ask quietly.

The guards look stunned for a moment. But their quandary doesn't last. They stare at my bruised face and grin again. I must up the ante before they come back with a retort.

"I will bring your insolence to the attention of President Callaghan," I say with an angry undertone.

The guards, thick as they are, may not have understood a word I said, but the names Gomez and Callaghan cause alarm bells to go off in their heads. Their shifty eyes and expressions changing from cocky to dense give that much away.

"What do you want, boy?" I address the young guard closest to me. He doesn't respond.

"Señor?" says the guard at the far end in an apologetic tone. "He only asked if you have a cigarette for us."

Cigarette? What do they take me for? A tobacconist? I want to give a response to that effect when the door to the consulting room is opened. Mireilla wants to call the next patient. I see Gomez at the other end of the room ushering another neon orange clad guard into the small waiting room. Quickly I get up, give Mireilla a cordial smile, and walk right past the four guards.

"Mireilla! My dear, is Doctor Gomez in?" I say in a low voice, step into the consulting room, and shut the door. I point to the wet plaster on the side of my head.

Mireilla looks irritated from me to Doctor Gomez who is still at the door talking to the guard. Resolutely she pulls me to a stool by the operating table and motions me to sit down. I flinch when she tears off the plaster and turns my head to have the light of the overhead lamp on the laceration. Swiftly she applies ointment, gets a fresh plaster ready, and whispers, "What are you doing here? You are up to no good, aren't you?"

Before I can answer, the door to the small waiting room snaps shut and Gomez asks, "And who have we got here?"

118

I wait until Mireilla has stuck the plaster onto the wound, before I turn my head and give Gomez a broad smile. I get up, reach for his hand, and pump his arm. "Doctor Gomez! Nice to see you, Sir! How are you today?"

He is taken aback by my friendly demeanour and tucks in his chin. "Oh, it's you again. What happened to your face?"

"My face? Oh, that's nothing," I say with a laugh. "Just a stupid little accident. I was gardening for the priest? Behind the church? I stepped onto a rake that was lying on the ground and - bang! - the handle hit me right in the face! Imagine! Isn't that stupid?"

"Sure is," agrees Gomez and looks uncomfortable when I take a hold of his elbow.

"But I want to talk to you about something completely different," I say and guide him through the waiting room past the four security guards to his office, shut the office door behind us and lead him to his chair. "Lately I fraternised with some of the guards and had very interesting discussions. We talked about the mine and, of course, the type of people who make good workers."

My roaming eyes notice a sprinkler sticking out of the ceiling directly above the laptop computer on his desk.

"And I must say," I prattle on, "I gleaned some very interesting information about myself. It is sometimes so difficult to recognise how other people see you. So, I am truly indebted to my friends, the guards, who were completely frank with me. Uh, which reminds me… Some of my friends are in the waiting room. Totally stressed out they are after their rescue work on level eight. They would love to have a smoke. Calms their nerves, you know? Could you spare a few cigarettes?"

Gomez eyes me with increasing suspicion. I can't tell if he is amused or bemused when he opens the top drawer of his desk and pushes a pack of American cigarettes and his gold lighter across. I thank him, take cigarettes and lighter, and step out of his office with the words, "I won't be a minute."

There are only three guards left in the waiting room. They are surprised to see me come out of Gomez' office and are absolutely delighted when I offer them cigarettes and a light. Eagerly they take the first drag and voice their thanks.

I go into the lavatory and lock the door behind me. Standing on the seat of the toilet, I can barely reach the sprinkler in the ceiling. I light a cigarette and take a couple of puffs. Carefully I blow the smoke away from the sensor in the valve. I jam the cigarette with its filter horizontally into the fingers of the water diverter and hope that it will hold. With any luck the glowing end will indicate a major fire to the heat sensor and kick-start the sprinkler system at high pressure. I get down in a hurry, flush the toilet, and leave the lavatory.

When I enter Gomez' office, he is typing on his computer. It is hooked up to the thin black cable of the power supply and a thick beige cable attached to a wall-outlet with a round socket. Gomez looks up, folds his hands behind his head, and leans back.

"So, you've been fraternising with the guards," he says with a haughty smile around the corners of his mouth. "Funny, but I have no record of any guards fraternising with you. Strange, isn't it?"

"No, not at all," I reply, sit down, and continue in a confidential tone. "You know how the miners look down on the guards, don't you? Scum and criminals they call them. I kept my meetings rather low-key to avoid running afoul of the nameless and unwashed riff-raff, you know? A chat at the gate, sharing a beer with a couple of them passing by my abode on patrol is the best way to keep my contacts under cover."

"Can I have my cigarettes back?" he asks unmoved.

"Of course," I reply, pass the pack and lighter across the desk, and watch him light a cigarette. "Anyway, I was going to tell you how these little chats with the guards helped me to understand you much better."

"What?" he asks and flips forward in his rocking chair.

"Yes, yes," I insist. "Don't you remember what you told me after my accident? People like me are not held in high regard around here, you said. And I can only agree with you. That's why I have come to a decision."

"Is that so?" he asks.

"Yes, indeed," I confirm. "I reckon it would be best if I left Tepetapa, went back to the capital city and tried to make a living there. So, I have decided to quit my job."

Gomez laughs. "Hang on, you can't just walk in here one day, demand a job and walk out again as and when you please. Creating a workplace for you has cost us lots of money. You have collected sick benefit for ten weeks. You owe us a lot and must deliver in terms of productivity. No, my friend, you're committed to your

120

job. Nobody walks out of here and away from the company. That's against our policy."

"Yes, of course," I agree and look straight at him. "Is that because of the microchip you implanted in my neck? Or do you fear I'll tell the press what you do to the bodies of the miners who are killed underground and are never seen again or buried?"

Gomez gives me the strangest look of fury, surprise, and calculation mixed into one. He types something into his computer and mutters under his breath, "You son of a bitch! Guess who else will never be seen again?"

I say nothing and watch him type. Into that moment of silence bursts the wailing siren indicating the change of shifts. It almost drowns out the distant ringing of an alarm bell and the simultaneous clanging and banging of water pipes. A second later a brief hiss of air advances the sprinklers' discharge of water. Gomez looks up in surprise, as he gets drenched. He forgets to close his laptop computer. After emitting some warping noises, it exhausts itself with a couple of sparks flying out of the keyboard that are followed by a puff of smoke.

He blinks through the veil of water, takes the dripping wet cigarette butt from his mouth, and shouts, "You idiot! Did the guards smoke in the waiting room?"

"Yes, of course!" I answer and can barely contain myself seeing him tap the keyboard of his dead computer.

Gomez slumps in his chair, takes off his glasses, and clasps a hand over his eyes.

Through the downpour I look out of the window. The entire late shift of miners, mill, and smelter workers surround Miguel. All of them turn and stare at the office building. In the distance, the guards are trotting down the mountain path. The administrative employees, soaked to the bone, vacate the building in haste.

Mireilla storms into the office and shouts, "Fire! There's a fire! Get out!"

I grab her by the hand, pull her into the waiting room, and out into the yard. Gomez stays behind as if glued to his chair.

Outside we mingle with the other wet figures. Everybody looks dumbfounded. One of the office workers says to another, "I wonder why the sprinklers don't shut off again. There must be one hell of a fire in the building. But I don't see any smoke."

"Perhaps it's a malfunction," says the other man and adds, "Do you know what the water will do to the computers? Irreparable damage, for sure. The computers are shot because the electricity won't shut off until there is a short in a circuit. We can go right back to manual record keeping."

"Yes, you are right," confirms the other. "The directors are such a bunch of idiots. I don't know how many times I told them to have the sprinkler system updated to a compartmentalised one that only functions in the area of an actual fire. But no, would they listen to a lowly office employee? Now we have the disaster of the entire building getting drenched."

22

THE ALARM BELLS stop ringing, but the water keeps on gushing out of the building. The crowds on both sides of the mine gate are getting restless. The labourers of the day shift inside the compound want to get out. The men of the night shift outside voice their refusal to go to work by chanting demands for fair wages and a safe workplace. The guards, down from the mountain path, are caught in the middle. They stand at the gate and gruffly cast nervous looks in every direction. The white-collar workers stand on the patch of lawn and give the grimy black, green, and grey clad blue-collar workers disparaging looks from a safe distance. Everybody waits for the directors to provide some directives. But none are voiced, and it doesn't look as if that is going to happen soon.

The guards have no way to open the gate. The key they stick into the keyhole might as well be a swizzle stick. As much as they twist it around, it won't release the lock. Neither can the guards see that the release handle has gone missing. When the officer orders a miner inside the gate in a sharp tone to pull the handle, the grimy face responds by blowing a raspberry. He doesn't understand what the officer is talking about, laughs, and demands a fifty-thousand-peso bribe to touch the non-existent handle. The commissioned Brownshirt becomes highly offended and threatens the most severe repercussions. But the miner doesn't seem to care or feel threatened. The officer's further cries for help are greeted with catcalls, raucous laughter, and insulting remarks. Nobody steps forward to come to his aid. His efforts frustrated, he gives up. Sensing the growing unrest and prevalent rebellious mood, he orders his men to ready their riot-truncheons and firearms.

The few neon orange clad guards inside the mining compound are assigned to guard the entrance of the administration building. They stand in a semi-circle, three meters in front of the door and are armed with riot-truncheons but no firearms. Not one of them makes a move to go to the gate and help their officer. They are under orders of a higher authority - two directors standing behind them. Dumas, the pig-eyed nonentity, and Henderson, the Spanish speaking empty suit, are engaged in a heated argument in English. They fight over the responsibility of shutting off the deluge that is seeping out of every crack and orifice of the building. Both claim vociferously that the janitorial duty of finding and shutting off the sprinkler system's main valve is not within the scope of their defined activities. In the meantime, the building is getting washed away. Evidently, neither one of them gives a damn about the damage as long as the other doesn't piss on his respective pea-patch of authority.

Ironically, or typically, the solution to their problem is located right next to the entrance. A thick red water pipe with a polished valve protrudes from the ground and leads into the building. An affixed brass plaque states in English, "Sprinkler Valve".

Other drenched directors escape the in-house downpour to the dry outdoors, listen to their fighting colleagues, and take sides. The exchange of denials becomes one of insults of anal fixations, sexual preferences with animals, their adversaries' wives' promiscuity with football teams, and orders to perform fellatio. The spectators, with no or very little knowledge of English, look on dumbfounded. If they understood one word of the dispute, they would understand it even less.

Callaghan steps outside under the protection of a giant, rainbow-coloured umbrella. He brings the dispute to an end and restores a semblance of order and calm. He points to the sprinkler valve and orders Henderson to order a guard to shut it off. A few moments later the water flow stops and the run-off from the building is slowly reduced to a trickle. Callaghan confers with his cohorts to decide what to do next. He sends them into the building to assess the damage and check the electrical system. The fuses are blown and none of the electronic gadgets work. Then he orders the gate to be opened. He waves his folded umbrella about and shouts. When his order appears to be ignored by guards lounging around at the gate, he makes a couple of crucial mistakes.

Callaghan disregards the chanting crowd of miners and mill and smelter workers and steps out from behind his safety cordon of guards, thus making himself vulnerable to direct confrontations with the nameless, unwashed masses. Had he ever bothered to learn a word of Spanish during his years in Mexico, he might have understood the miners' chant and possibly grasped that it was a thinly veiled threat. But he hadn't and he didn't, and he walks like a babe in the woods through the crowd of miners inside the mining compound. They begin to converge on him as soon as he walks past the guardhouse. Amid laughter they shout: *"¡Señor Calajana, guarda tu banana!"*

Simple words, which, taken literally, give Mr. Callaghan the innocuous advice of keeping an eye on his banana. What it implies, of course, is for Callaghan to be on his guard, for the miners are after his family jewels.

The miners inside the compound have realised that the gate can't be opened by conventional methods. That message has gone back by word of mouth through the restless crowd. A couple of two-meter-long crowbars, the variety strong enough to shift a weight of several tonnes, are retrieved from the machine shop and passed from man to man. Thrust into their hands, the guards at the gate apply the crowbars with force to break the lock.

Callaghan sees the men straining and wants to stop what he considers wanton destruction. Arms flailing and shouting at the top of his lungs, he pushes his way through the crowd only to be held back by one man. It is Raúl. He grabs Callaghan by the white silk shirt with his grimy talons, slams him into the wall of the guardhouse, and demands his five-thousand-peso reward for having found and delivered the murderer of Arbuckle. Other miners come to Raúl's aid and lay hands on the soft, clean cloth of Callaghan's shirt.

Callaghan doesn't understand a word. He sees only filthy fingers clawing his chest. He stares into grimy faces smeared with the dirt of a hard day's work. He smells the bad breath and rancid body odour of undernourished men who had slaved away in the foul air and unsanitary conditions of the mine. He looks into the sunken, yellowish, pus-filled eyes telling the irrefutable tale of unhealthy food, dust penetration, and lack of medical care. He recognises the despair of his making. He lives his worst nightmare - the physical confrontation with "the scum" that always wants more of his money! He screams in panic the very moment the lock gives way with a sharp report that sounds like a gunshot.

The gate slides aside silently on its well-greased overhead castors. The officer hears the shot-like sound, turns, and sees his master besieged by scum and riff-raff. Like the good, homicidal maniac and soldier he is, he raises his large calibre pistol, aims, and fires. After the first shots have rung out, Raúl and several other miners lie dead or are gravely injured. Callaghan disappears under the collapsing miners' bodies, and nobody cares what happens to him as the gunfire continues. While the officer is pumping bullets into the crowd, the other guards raise and fire their guns, blindly and insanely, not aiming at anyone or anything in particular, overcome by their pent-up hatred for the miners and a thirst for blood and action. Out of bullets, they follow the officer's example and lash out with their riot truncheons at anybody standing within reach and not getting out of the way fast enough. Limbs are shattered, eyeballs beaten out of their sockets, ears torn off, heads split open - the bloody mayhem has no limits.

A small, wiry miner, one of the nameless, unwashed numbers, who helped to break the gate open, stands in the doorway to the guards' office holding one of the crowbars. He watches the guards in horror as they lash out at the slowly retreating crowd. When the officer labours away right in front of him whipping miners writhing on the ground, he steps out of the doorway, raises the massive crowbar, and brings its sharp point down on the back of the officer's head with all his might. Brain matter and blood squirts in all directions as the skull cracks wide open. Stunned by the effect of his action, the small, wiry man stares at the dead officer. He drops the crowbar and stands quite still and defenceless. He becomes the target of three of the raging guards who transform him into a bloody pulp of torn skin and broken bones in less than a minute. The flesh of his cheeks ripped to his ears, he gives his tormentors a final, ultimate grin of death.

The savage manslaughter triggers the miners on the plaza into action. They watch the outbreak of violence in silence and shrink back in fear at the sound of the gunfire. Once they realise that the thrust of the attack hasn't been aimed at them, their courage is rekindled, and they mob together at the gate. Although their postures and faces reflect anger, outrage, and resolve, they hesitate. Diego and Miguel break through the front row of teeth gnashing, howling onlookers, and lunge at the nearest Brownshirts. The other men join the attack in a two-pronged formation and split the horde of over sixty guards into three manageable groups. Without weapons, they rely on fists, boots, and body tackles to bring the guards down. All their contempt for the Brownshirts is packed into every blow levelled at them. Noses are bloodied, eyes are bruised, and teeth are knocked out. When

126

the guards are lying face down in the dirt, every one of them, for good measure, is shackled with his own handcuffs.

In the ensuing calm, the men who fought so bravely to bring the guards' murderous rage to an end become fully aware of the extent of the slaughter. Overwhelmed by the sight of the dead and the gravely injured miners, mill and smelter workers, some can't help but cry like little children.

23

CRIES, GROANS AND WHISPERS pierce the silence. Including the guards, well over a hundred men lie where they have fallen on the dusty ground of the battlefield. The stench of blood and cordite hangs in the air. In the blazing sunshine and heat of the late afternoon, the spilled blood dries rapidly. The men, who brought an end to the bloodshed, stand or kneel by their slain or beaten comrades and are quite helpless beyond trying to give some comfort muttering words of sorrow in the face of horrendous injury and death.

In a state of shock at the terrible sight, I lean against the far corner of the guardhouse. Mireilla frees herself of my grip and, walking from man to man, inspects the injuries and assesses the extent of medical aid required. She talks to Miguel and Diego and points to the back of the administration building. Both men nod. Miguel shouts that he needs volunteers. The men at the gate respond without hesitation. About forty of them step cautiously over the bodies near the guardhouse and gather on the patch of lawn where I join them. Mireilla leads us and we rush past the remaining early shift miners standing in front of the headframe.

Next to the garage gates at the back of the building is a steel door. Mireilla unlocks and opens it, and we step into a large, fireproof safety room. It is a supply store with rows of shelves and gleaming, stainless steel cold-storage cabinets. The lights don't work because electricity has not yet been restored. Mireilla takes flashlights from a shelf next to the door and hands them out to the men with instructions what to pick and pack from the boxes and cartons. In a short time, we are loaded up with stretchers, body bags, medical instruments, cartons of bandages and medication, and sealed styrofoam boxes filled with bags of plasma.

Plastic-wrapped cardboard boxes emblazoned with the words "The Peacemaker" are stacked in a corner next to the stretchers that stand upright against the wall. At the front-end of one of the cartons hangs a content description with a picture of the riot-truncheons that had been used by the guards for their pernicious attacks a moment earlier. I tear off the sticker and stuff it in my pocket, grab a stack of five stretchers and leave with the others. We rush back to the battleground.

The medical supplies are brought into the surgery. Mireilla has to check the water damage and asks some of the volunteers to help with the clean-up. The rest of us, loaded down with stretchers and body bags, go ahead to attend to the wounded and take care of the dead. Many more miners and most of the office workers step forward to assist in whatever way they can. The disparity between the two groups of employees is forgotten or at least put aside in the shared effort of alleviating the suffering. A short while later Mireilla and some volunteers rush outside with boxes of medical supplies and instruments. She wears a fresh uniform and under her direction the men give first aid, stem the bleeding, and carry the most severely wounded into the medical station. Everything goes well until electricity is restored.

A gurgling, gushing sound interrupts the hectic proceedings in the driveway. Three large pipes sticking out of the basement of the office building spew dirty water forth in streams as thick as a leg. A veritable flood of oily sewage is discharged into the driveway. The miners, who stand in front of the ventilation house and headframe, scramble aside to avoid a mud bath. The brown maelstrom advances rapidly towards the men lying on the dusty ground.

Mireilla lets out a piercing scream and shouts to pick up the wounded and take them to the plaza out of harm's way. Without a second to spare, her orders are being followed, and a long line of volunteers carries men on stretchers away from the rushing flood to safe ground in front of the whorehouse.

Miguel and I contemplate asking Lucy to open her house as a shelter for the injured when a high-pitched squeal causes all heads to turn to the mine gate. The beaten and handcuffed guards get up and stand alongside the pay-office. They stare at the guardhouse where corpses are moved by the onslaught of the flood and piled up near the door to the guard office. An arm reaches up clawing the wall. It is Callaghan.

He wails in English, "I've been hit! I've been hit!" as far as I can discern. It isn't clear if he refers to an injury. He sees himself confronted by the grinning death mask of the small, wiry man's corpse. Callaghan scrambles to his feet and goes into a mad frenzy. Leaning against the wall, he bellows out his horror at the sight surrounding him. His pudgy, overfed, wrinkle-free baby face distorts in a grimace, he bawls in anguish, and kicks at the corpse to push it away from him.

Watching Callaghan, Miguel mumbles, "Have a good look at the disaster of your own making, Mister President."

The outflow of sewage from the office building's basement stops suddenly. The brown flood runs off and the mud settles rapidly. Several men, Miguel and I amongst them, return to the gate to have a look at the screaming, trampling, and mud-caked president.

Confronting him, Miguel reaches out with his right hand and gives Callaghan a resounding slap in the face that makes the guy's head spin.

Callaghan stops his tantrum instantly and screams with unrestrained fury, "You hit me! You attacked me!"

"What did he say?" Miguel asks me to translate.

"He said that you hit him," I say.

"Oh, he noticed," says Miguel. "That's what I wanted to do since the first day I laid eyes on his pouty mug. So, what's he going to do about it?"

I turn to Callaghan and ask him. He looks from face to face of the men confronting him and shouts, "You will suffer the most severe repercussions! I'll remember you… you scumbags! Human garbage! Yes, that's what you are! Human garbage! How dare you lay a hand on me? I'm your president!"

Unmoved I translate his tirade into Spanish. Miguel reaches back with his left and gives him another resounding slap in the face. Callaghan loses his balance and slides into the mud. He holds his cheek and stares at us in utter disbelief.

Turning to the miners standing by the ventilation house, Miguel waves to them to leave the mining compound. He opens a door to the guardhouse and orders the guards to enter the room. They follow his order slowly, reluctantly, and the passing miners subject them to well-aimed kicks, blows, and insults. Miguel locks the door with two sliding bolts mounted on the outside when Callaghan can be heard again making whiny noises. Miguel loses his cool.

He pulls Callaghan up by his shirt, clamps a hand around the back of his neck, drags him along and forces him to look at each one of the dead men.

"These men you shall remember, you fat son of a bitch!" he shouts angrily. "Every face of these innocent men shall be burnt into your godforsaken soul, you murderous bastard!"

I hobble along through the ankle-deep mud in my open sandals and translate as best I can. The men, who had been on the way out of the mining compound, stop and watch the rare spectacle. Fighting words are heard and some clenched fists indicate readiness to beat Callaghan to a pulp. Miguel hears the shouts for the president's hide, pulls him into the upright, and forces him to look at the miners.

"Did you say you are our president," Miguel asks him quietly, "the president of these men?"

Callaghan gives him a frightened stare in response to hearing the questions in English. Miguel points at the crowd of angry men with a sweeping gesture.

"That's really good to know that you are the president," he says in a loud voice. "Most of these men don't know you and were wondering with whom we have to negotiate! In case you didn't know, Mister President, we're on strike! You hear? I said, we are on strike!"

A roar of approval from the miners and mill and smelter workers turns into the chant, "We're on strike! We're on strike!"

But some of the men look full of doubt at that dirty, shapeless man with rapidly drying mud flaking off his trousers. He is supposed to be Callaghan, the president? Dishevelled, as he is, he looks so much like one of us. He would fit right in with any of the underground crews, if it weren't for his gringo face. Any doubt about his identity vanishes, though, when he opens his mouth.

"You can't go on strike," Callaghan shouts in response to my translation of the chant. "Strikes are forbidden!"

The Spanish version of his statement causes uproarious laughter among the men. They crowd around and jeer the frightened looking president.

"Strikes are forbidden?" Miguel asks. "You mean to say that every activity in Tepetapa requires your permission?"

"Yes, of course!" confirms Callaghan hearing my translation.

Miguel points his thumb over the shoulder at the corpses and snaps, "Which implies, that everything that does happen in Tepetapa is done with your knowledge, approval and permission! Correct?"

Callaghan listens to my translation and casts a furtive glance at the corpses. He realises that his claim to supreme authority has put a noose around his neck. He admits having approved the slaughter of these men. There are no guards to protect him, no subservient toadies to take the blame for his blunder. Surrounded by grim looking miners, there is nowhere to run and no place to hide. He straightens up and scratches mud out of his hair, trying to give himself a semblance of dignity.

"Yes, absolutely!" he says in a firm voice while avoiding eye contact with anyone in particular. "Those lamentable victims of an uncontrolled act of outrageous violence by some of the guards is proof of what happens if anything is done in Tepetapa without my knowledge, approval and permission! Now we have a real mess on our hands! It will take all my effort to straighten it out and get the mine operational again!"

When I convey his statement in Spanish there is a moment of silence. Callaghan wants to jump into the breach and continue his speech. But Miguel cuts him off.

"Nice try, you windbag!" says Miguel and clamps his paw on Callaghan's shoulder. "But you are not talking to the press! You won't get away with feeding us clever lines, blame the results of your murderous schemes on your bloodhounds, and continue with business as usual! Your game is up! You will have to meet our demands before it's back to business for you and your cronies! Do you understand me?"

Callaghan is obviously not used to being addressed in this manner and has difficulty to constrain his flaring rage when he hears the translation of Miguel's response and the initial demands.

"First you will requisition the whorehouse to serve as a hospital! Then you will get coffins for each of the dead of last night and today and give them burials at the surviving families' place of choice anywhere in Mexico! You will pay the survivors compensation of an amount to be negotiated by us! All other demands concerning fair wages, safe work conditions, and health services will be presented to you shortly by the representatives of the mineworkers! But first we must take care of the injured! All right?"

Miguel doesn't wait for Callaghan to provide his approval. He drags him along in a quick march as we rush through the crowd and up the steps to the door of the whorehouse.

132

Lucy's initial resistance to running a hospital is quickly overcome when Miguel mentions that Callaghan is going to pay compensation for the loss of her son Hernan Godoy and arrange a proper burial for his remains. Bursting into tears, she opens the door wide and bids us to enter. She rushes around and informs her "girls and boys" of the new situation while the volunteers pick up the injured men and carry them on stretchers together with the medical equipment and supplies into the large vestibule. Mireilla rushes in and begins immediately to instruct the volunteers in the cleaning of wounds and applying antiseptic ointments and bandages. She gets down to the more demanding tasks of giving injections, drip-feeds and clamping or stitching some of the wounds. She reminds Miguel and me of the seriously injured men in the surgery and urges us to assist Doctor Gomez until she has looked after the injured in her care and is free to join him.

We rush back across the plaza and drag Callaghan along. After we enter the medical station, I lock the entrance door and the door to the stairwell. We don't want any interruption from the other directors roaming in the office building.

24

THE SCENE we encounter in the medical station is reminiscent of a field hospital without medical staff behind the front lines of a war. A row of eight stretchers with wounded men is laid out in assembly line fashion from the entrance to the very end of the consulting room. The volunteers kneel or squat next to the injured. They have limited knowledge of first aid and try to the best of their ability to keep the battle victims alive. The gauze patches and bandages have soaked through and mopping the seeping fluids is done with paper towels. The volunteers don't have any pain-killing medication, nor would they have known how to administer it. The injured men are left to suffer in pain. Hearing their cries and moans is as heart-rending as seeing some of the terrible lesions and lacerations.

I ask if anyone had seen Gomez. Several hands point to his closed office door. A good kick at the repaired doorknob breaks the lock and the door flies open.

Gomez sits at his desk unmolested by the human suffering he had sworn the Hippocratic oath to relieve, if indeed he is a bona fide medical practitioner. Stacks of white linen towels and sheets, in sterilised condition intended for his patients, are strewn over the floor. He uses them to mop his desk and the floor of his office. On his desk lies an array of small tools. His laptop computer is taken apart into its major components.

I grab the first larger piece of the computer within my reach, the lid with the screen, and smash it on the edge of his desk. Mad with rage he gets up, lunges for my throat, and clamps a hand around it. In the ensuing struggle, the rest of the computer parts are pushed to the floor and trampled beyond repair.

Miguel brings the fight to a quick end. He snatches Gomez's glasses and plants his fist on the doctor's right eye. Gomez howls and falls to the floor.

"What kind of a doctor are you?" shouts Miguel. "People are dying in your surgery! They need your help!"

He picks up Gomez and throws him into his chair. Gomez gets up and points a shaking finger at Miguel.

"Your days are numbered!" he screams. "You are dead, man! Dead! Get out of my office!"

Miguel reaches for the doctor's shaking hand, wrapped his huge, calloused paw around it and squeezes. Gomez screams and sinks into his chair. Miguel leans on the armrest and moves nose to nose with the doctor.

"I'll give you a choice, doctor," he says. "You can go out there and save some lives or I'll give you the thrashing of your life. And then I will operate on you with a blunt knife! You understand?"

Raising his fist ready to strike the first blow, I am certain that Miguel would have followed up on his promise within a second if Callaghan hadn't intervened.

"Alex, I need first aid," Callaghan says sharply. "I've been hit by a stray bullet. You will look at that first and then at the men in the surgery."

Gomez looks surprised. He stares at Callaghan and screams, "You, Callaghan? You are on their side? I don't believe it!"

"Oh, fuck off! I'm not on their side," barks Callaghan. "We have a situation on our hands here! I am seriously injured, and the men outside look like they could do with an adhesive and a couple of aspirin. Everything else we can discuss later. Come on! Get going! That's an order!"

Gomez grumbles and defiantly remains seated. Covering the swelling side of his face with a hand, he stares angrily at the president with one eye. Callaghan looks at him and scoffs in a threatening manner. Whatever the unspoken exchange entailed I don't know, but it was very effective. Gomez turns pale and cowers for a moment. Then he puts on his glasses, goes to his wardrobe, and takes out blue scrubs. Putting it on, he looks briefly into the consulting room and decides to attend to Callaghan in the office. He opens the door to the waiting room and asks Miguel and me to leave. But Miguel shuts the door brusquely.

"Just look at that injury Callaghan claims to have suffered," he says to Gomez, "and be quick about it. I won't leave until I see you treat the men in the surgery."

Gomez looks at Callaghan in the hope of some support, but Callaghan shrugs and pokes a finger through a hole in the sleeve of his shirt. Gomez cuts the sleeve open with surgical scissors all the way up to the shoulder. It reveals the red stripe of a scrape or burn-mark on the upper arm. There is no bullet-hole and not a trace of blood. Gomez touches the bruise gingerly and mutters something about the seriousness of grazing shots. He reaches for ointment, gauze patches, and bandages.

Miguel looks on in utter disbelief. He cuts the fussing short when Gomez wants to dress Callaghan's scrape as if the arm had been amputated. Shoving Callaghan aside, he takes Gomez by the scruff of the neck and shunts him into the surgery.

"I want to see you do your job on some real injuries!" he shouts. "I'll stay right here and watch what you're doing! One slip-up and you're under the knife!"

He points at one of the wounded men with severe head injuries and motions the volunteers to put him on the operating table.

Callaghan comes into the surgery and barks, "Now you listen to me! I've had quite enough of your bully tactics! I admit there has been an unfortunate infraction that led to a few men being injured. I understand that you two are upset over this incident. But that doesn't give you any special rights! You can't tell us how to run this company and certainly you can't interfere with the doctor doing his job! I won't allow it! And I won't let you stand around here either! Get out! Leave the company premises immediately! You are off limits here!"

Callaghan points to the door. Evidently, he doesn't understand the gravity of the situation at all.

His callousness of mentioning a "few injured men" as an aside while many of them are dead and some of them lay near death right under his eyes is astounding. Only ten minutes earlier the grinning face of death scared him out of his wits! Has he wiped the incident from his memory? I have difficulty recognising let alone comprehending his frame of mind.

He knows that he has no protection or support, no guards, and no control system! Yet he acts as if nothing has changed from a couple of hours earlier. Is he as dumb and ignorant as I suspect him and his cronies to be? Or is this a cold and calculated move, a tactic he employs in the hope of intimidating us and making us toe the line like the subhuman species, the unwashed, nameless numbers he considers us to be?

Ignoring Miguel, I launch into a counter-offensive. Unflinching, I say, "Callaghan, if anybody is off limits here it is you! We are in charge now and give the orders! If you don't like swallowing your medicine we are dispensing, then you're shit out

136

of luck! Gomez and you start treating the injured men this very minute while we watch, or we will leave you to the mercy of the men outside! The choice is yours!"

Callaghan gawks at me in surprise and then breaks into shrill laughter. Voice tilting, he shrieks, "Leave us to the mercy of the men outside? Is that supposed to be an ultimatum or a threat? That's a joke! What will you and those little brown men in black pyjamas out there do if I ignore you? Huh? What will you do?"

"Beat you to death," I say calmly and add, "you and all your directors with your own riot-truncheons. And your corpses will disappear without a trace in the smelter like the thirty-two miners that were killed last night."

Callaghan is taken aback by the matter-of-fact announcement of his imminent death should he refuse to cooperate. He looks from me to Miguel to Gomez. Valuable seconds tick away while nothing is being done. It is too much for Miguel to bear. He grabs Callaghan by the arm, drags him into the bathroom of the medical station, and turns on the cold water. Against howls of protest, Miguel tears off the president's shirt, trousers, and underwear and hoses him down.

It is a humiliating experience for Callaghan to be manhandled like that. Within minutes Miguel has him half decently cleaned, dressed in grey scrubs, and standing by the operating table.

Gomez watches the struggle unmoved. He pre-empts such a strike against his dignity, washes his hands, and puts on latex gloves. He turns to Miguel and points a thumb at Callaghan. "How can I perform surgery with that guy as my assistant? He knows nothing! I need Mireilla."

"Mireilla is unavailable," says Miguel dismissing the demand. "You can tell Callaghan what's to be done, can't you? Now get going. I'm really losing my patience with your stalling tactics."

Without another word, Gomez begins to administer sedatives and analgesics to the injured men to relieve them of their pain. Miguel and I stand back and watch Callaghan, who until now has only known how to have suffering and pain inflicted through his henchmen. He actually helps Gomez repair some of the damage applying himself as a reluctant Samaritan.

Despite their shortcomings, he and Gomez proceed quite rapidly. After two hours of intense work, they are down to the last case. Miguel observes them constantly while I look out into the yard from the doctor's office. The guards, under the direction of Diego and his men, are rinsing the corpses, identify them, put them into body bags, and lay them out in a row. The men of the late shift still crowd around their foremen and discussions are going on.

Miguel brings Callaghan to the doctor's office as soon as he sees him peel off his latex gloves. The three of us stand by the window and look at the crowd in the square that slips into the shadows of dusk.

"Look at those men, Callaghan," says Miguel. "That is your labour force refusing to go back to work under the present conditions. We demand fair wages, a safe workplace, and destruction of the control system. We will accept nothing less than the removal of the dog tags."

Callaghan looks puzzled after hearing my translation and asks, "Dog tags?"

"Yes, dog tags," I say. "That's what we call the microchips you have implanted without anyone's consent in the men, women and children to control their every move."

Callaghan's protest is immediate. He shakes his head and repeatedly points a finger at me while mouthing his response. "That is utter nonsense," he says haughtily. "Your claim is tantamount to defamation. It is downright slanderous. Microchips! Ridiculous! I demand that you provide absolute proof of the existence of such microchips and the control system this instant. Or else!"

I tell Miguel what has been said. Cunningly or by instinct, Callaghan has hit on the weakest spot of our argument, the terrain of electronic control systems, which is completely foreign to Miguel. But I have an idea and pursue a line of argument that puts Callaghan back on his heels.

"Absolute proof?" I say with an accommodating smile. "That's no problem. But in view of your computer system being down, we'll have to take a little detour in your limousine to provide the proof you want. We will have to take a scanner and a woman and a child along to San Luis Potosí. I know a veterinarian there who uses the microchip pet identification system. He has the equipment to provide absolute proof that microchips are implanted in all of us. I know an electronics expert who will enthusiastically dismantle the scanner and determine its function.

138

He doesn't get too many opportunities to inspect state-of-the-art, cutting-edge technology. I'll ask him as well to come here and ferret out all scanners installed in Tepetapa. He will trace their hook-ups to your computers and provide the absolute proof of your control system's existence."

Callaghan's face is getting longer with each sentence. He is on the defensive. Before he can come up with a reply, I continue, "What do you say, Callaghan? Shall we go and get the absolute proof you want? Come on then! Let's go for a ride in your car!"

That jovial invitation to take a jaunt in his jalopy is a bad mistake. Callaghan recovers instantly. I realise too late that I should have ordered him to drive us to San Luis Potosí. Weasel that he is, he turns the table on me.

"Aha!" shouts Callaghan. "You don't have any proof, do you? You want to go for a joyride to visit friends who'll manufacture evidence to back up a figment of your imagination. Don't be ridiculous!"

He points to the crowd outside. "Let me say this! This entire discussion is over! You understand me? You've wasted enough of my time! I have to get this mine up and running again. And you… you will go out there and tell those men to report for work immediately! Or else!"

"Or else what?" I bark back and poke him in the chest with my index finger. "Your Americanisms of 'or else', 'now you listen to me' and 'let me say this' don't have any weight around here. We are on strike! You are an economic terrorist whose bluff has been called! You have no 'or else'! You have no guards! You have no control! You have only one option to get this mine up and running again! That option is to meet our demands!"

Callaghan has his back against the wall, literally and figuratively. He stares over my shoulder at Miguel who stands behind me, flashing a perverted grin and cracking his knuckles. He looks ready to put Callaghan through a meat-grinder.

"I'm not being talked to in this tone," says Callaghan with chattering teeth.

"You better get used to it!" I shout back poking his chest.

He ducks and raises his hands. "Stop it already," he begs. "What exactly are your demands?"

"If you had listened to Miguel, you would have heard the demands three times so far," I answer. "But you don't listen to riff-raff, do you? Consequently, you will have to sit down with the negotiators, the group of eighteen foremen speaking on behalf of their crews and listen to their demands."

"A group of eighteen?" he says. "I don't negotiate with groups. I will talk to them only on an individual basis."

I belt out a laugh and tell Miguel what has been said. He doesn't laugh. He doesn't see anything funny in Callaghan's attempt to divide and conquer. He is quite angry when he insists that all negotiations must take place between the workers' representatives as a group and the board of directors as a group. No side deals, no special interest considerations, no fudging of the issues is his clear demand. Work will be halted until negotiations have resulted in an agreement and a legally binding contract has been signed.

I convey the demands to Callaghan with Miguel standing behind me staring him down. Callaghan doesn't like what he hears but figures that he has no choice. He says as much and asks for a couple of hours to prepare himself and the other directors for the first meeting. In a sudden change of attitude, he agrees with Miguel quite amiably on the venue and an approximate time for the initial meeting. We part ways on the understanding that one of the directors would call on the group of foremen in the cantina within two to three hours and bring them to the boardroom.

Once outside, I am overcome by a feeling of gloom. It isn't just the sight of the body bags that pulls me into an abyss of fear and loathing. It is my deep-seated mistrust of the directors in general and Callaghan in particular. Some nagging doubt in the back of my mind persists in telling me that the bloodshed isn't over yet.

25

THE NEXT TWO HOURS pass quickly in hectic activity. Miguel and the seventeen other foremen representing the crews of miners and mill and smelter workers sit in the back of the cantina and hammer out a list of demands. I have been asked to be their interpreter and join them when they are going to sit down opposite the board of directors.

The men on the plaza have been told to grab a bite to eat and be back for an all-night vigil. The crowd thins out a little but quite a few men return with their families. Soon more than a thousand men, women, and children mill about and chat with just about anybody in an atmosphere of excitement and expectation of better times to come. There hasn't been such animated and spirited conversation in Tepetapa in a long time. Even joyous laughter can be heard on occasion.

The interim hospital serves its purpose well. Several men were released and sent home to recuperate. They make room for the patients from the mine's medical station who are transferred. Fortunately, there is no shortage of volunteers. Even some of the miners' wives, despite their initial reservations about entering the whorehouse, step in to lend a hand and assist in changing bandages and administering medicine. I go to see how Mireilla is getting on with her patients. I arrive just in time to be asked to fetch more medical supplies. She gives me a long list of needed materials, and I rush with five volunteers to the storage room. We decide to take double the requested material and clear some of the shelves of all supplies. Faced with a mountain of boxes and cartons, we take three stretchers, put a box of riot-truncheons on each as a base, and stack the goods on top. That way a total of sixty truncheons ends up in the whorehouse. This goes against Miguel's strict directive not to touch or utilise the arms employed by the guards. But I feel better knowing that these weapons are out of reach of the guards. The feeling of gloom in anticipation of more bloodshed to come just won't let go of me.

I take time out for a meal. Waiting to be served, I read the sticker I ripped off a box of truncheons. It is a revelation to see in print how the so-called defenders of law and order see us, and what ghastly weapons they employ to achieve their end of maintaining oppression and dominance.

The truncheon has the wonderful name "The Peacemaker". It is declared to be the weapon of choice of police and security forces around the world to maintain law and order. It is a proven tool in facing riot situations of mobs of terrorists and anarchists. The tapered steel whips with star shaped serrations at their points cut through the toughest materials including rubber, leather, vinyl, and skin to keep rebellious hordes under control. The truncheons are "Made with Pride in Singapore". That tells me more about that city-state than I ever wanted to know.

I fold up the sticker and shudder. Terrorists and anarchists refusing to abide by the law! Yes, indeed, I could see how the directors viewed us as rebellious hordes.

Don't the tormentors see anyone who stands up and fights dehumanising oppression and ruthless exploitation as a terrorist? Aren't the people who dare to question the status quo of any type of power structure considered to be anarchists? You bet, they are! And they are investigated, spied upon, harassed, incarcerated, and, when deemed expedient, killed by the respective bum-sniffing agencies in the name of security, stability, progress, and law and order.

How do you like your peace and freedom so far?

Singapore! That name holds such promise of the cultural magic of a far-off land. Just saying "Singapore" conjures up images of a gentle, industrious people living in peace and harmony.

That image and promise has been destroyed for good after reading the sticker of the box of riot truncheons. If that was the type of "peace-keeping" equipment they invent, manufacture, and use in Singapore and sell to anyone who wants to maintain a graveyard peace and the harmony of oppression, then that country must be one hellhole of hypocrisy.

The waiter serves the *salchichas*, the *guacamole*, and the beer I ordered. I look up at the big clock on the far wall. Nine fifteen! The two hours are almost up! I must dig in and eat fast to finish my meal before Miguel calls on my services as a translator. The plaza has sunk into darkness. The lights of the mine, the whorehouse, the company store, the alleys, and the cantina don't cast enough light on the crowd to recognise individual faces or to

142

read the banners some of the men have crudely fashioned out of bed sheets and broomsticks.

The mine is silent. Only the soft whir of the two big wheels spinning atop the headframe give an indication that it is still in operation. In the distance the sound of engines of approaching vehicles can be heard. I don't give it any thought. It is probably the change of shift for the guards and a bus to pick up the office employees, who are still waiting outside the administration building for their ride home. I am munching on the last chunk of ham sausage when the lights go out with a discernible "clack" coming from the transformer station.

In total darkness, shouts of surprise and curses are heard from the people on the plaza and the buildings along its perimeter. An eerie silence takes over, interspersed only by timid cries for light and some yokel's remark about the president not having paid the electricity bill. Nobody laughs. In the pitch-black darkness, the fear of the unknown holds us in its clutches.

The soft sound of quick footsteps coming towards the cantina adds another dimension to the spooky scene. Unable to see anything, my other senses have been put on high alert. I can sense somebody rushing into the cantina, then a second person, a third and more until I lose count. In the air turbulence created by the people rushing past, I catch a whiff of stale body odour mixed with the sweet scent of make-up. What is going on? Is this an invasion of transvestites? Before I can say Teotihuacan, which is easy when you speak Aztec, I am knocked sideways and fall with my chair into the corner near the entrance of the bar. The table topples over next to me. The crash of furniture, crockery, and cutlery drowns out my brief curse of protest. Just as well. Because the next thing I hear is somebody barking an order. Blinding light floods in the direction of the foremen's table.

A platoon of the Special Forces of the Motorised Cavalry in combat gear with night vision goggles and spotlights mounted on their helmets point snub-nosed automatic rifles at the foremen. The commandos' faces are covered with camouflage paint. They shout and scream incoherently and slowly advance trampling their feet nervously, thus giving away their American training.

The foremen and everybody else dives for cover. Tables are tipped over to serve as shields. Chairs, beer bottles, plates, and heavy mugs are flung in a broad barrage at the commandos, some of whom, including the officer in charge, suffer direct hits and are knocked out. One commando crashes to the floor next to me and smashes my table and the chairs. His flailing arm drops a rifle into my lap.

Miguel's voice booms, the miners rush the commandos and take them by surprise. Using the sturdy tables as shields, they push the soldiers back onto the plaza. The helmet-mounted spotlights mark the commandos as easy targets. Each one of them is jumped by two or three miners at the same time and beaten up.

Two muffled shots are heard, and a couple of flares rise into the night sky. They descend slowly dipping the entire plaza into intensely orange, blinding light. The full extent of the military invasion becomes visible. The crowd of men, women, and children is encircled by a riot squad of over three hundred baton-wielding soldiers and security guards in riot-gear with helmets and man-high shields. The guards are as mad as hell and lash out with their riot truncheons.

Back on the road next to the company store, a huge diesel generator on the flatbed trailer of a truck roars into action. More than a dozen trolley mounted massive mercury vapour floodlights that will turn the night into day are pushed into strategic locations.

The riot squad advances beating the shields with batons to intimidate men, women, and children. A detail of commandos pushes its way through the crowd towards the cantina to aid their troubled comrades.

It is time for me to get out of there, and I do just seconds before the floodlights are switched on.

26

THE GAUDIESQUE BALCONY of Lucy's private quarters is the ideal lookout point. The small embrasures of its curved sandstone balustrade allow us to observe the plaza without being seen when lying down. Lucy had dragged me up there the minute I arrived in the whorehouse by way of the basement back door.

I had escaped from the cantina through the small window of the urinal. I was loaded down with a snub-nosed automatic rifle fitted with a telescopic night-vision sight, a spare magazine, a can of pepper-spray, two stun grenades, and four tear-gas canisters. It would have been a crying shame to leave all that stuff behind, I figured, since the special commando, unconscious as he was, had no use for it. I took care of his wallet, too, lest it fell into the wrong hands. You can't trust anyone these days, least of all corrupt soldiers, policemen, and security guards.

Lucy crawls onto the balcony wearing a dark tracksuit, a black baseball cap, and thin leather gloves. She squats next to me and watches me going through the contents of the wallet.

Credit cards, birth certificate, social insurance and health insurance, driver's licence, military identification - this is testimony to a man leading a stink normal life.

The commando's data shadow identifies him as an exemplary citizen with a steady job and regular income, and probably a bank account with a small balance, a mortgage, a wife, and three and a half children.

How many people has this exemplary citizen killed in the course of his steady job? What is the balance of his bank account in a tax haven where he deposits without a doubt the kickbacks and graft money he receives for the officially sanctioned killings he commits in the name of law and order?

The bill compartments of the wallet contain five crisp one-hundred-dollar bills and a batch of over two thousand pesos. That is an awful lot of cash to carry around for a soldier of the rank of sergeant with an official annual income of less than thirty-six thousand pesos. I take good care of the money by depositing it in my pocket.

The wallet I pitch over the balustrade where it disappears in the melee of people in front of the whorehouse.

"Now that you have some blood-money in your pocket," whispers Lucy with a scowl, "you better get some blood on your hands to show you've earned it."

She snaps the release of the gun and thrusts the weapon into my hands. I break into a cold sweat holding the rifle and shake my head vehemently.

"I can't do that," I whisper.

"Why not?" she asks angrily.

"I'm a terrible shot for a start," I say. "And then… if I shoot, the soldiers will shoot back, and we'll have a bloody massacre."

She rips the rifle out of my hands. "That depends on whom you shoot first," she says and points the gun at my crotch. "What are you going to do while everybody else is fighting? Sit there with your thumb up your arse? What are you? A man or a cockroach?"

I swallow hard after her outburst. She is right. I have left friends and colleagues behind, sought refuge in the makeshift hospital, and enriched myself on ill-gotten gains. I must do something, support the struggle, and help turn the tide. I look at my small arsenal.

"Have you got black socks and some strong elastic band?" I ask holding up the silver-grey can of pepper-spray.

Lucy looks at me for a moment, puts down the gun, and crawls into her room. She returns with black stockings and a box of elastic bands.

The stockings cover the bright metallic sheen of the grenades and the canisters perfectly. The dull, black material will make the missiles' trajectory almost invisible in the bright light when I toss them onto the plaza. Six elastic bands would be sufficient to keep the handle of the pepper-spray depressed. The two grenades, the teargas, and pepper-spray would cause confusion among the soldiers and create the diversion we need. Hopefully it will lead to their limited use of firearms and allow us to use our gun without being detected.

I ask Lucy if she is a good shot. She smirks, turns to lie flat on her belly, and aims the rifle through an embrasure.

I pull the locking pin from the handle of the pepper-spray, point the nozzle away, squeeze the handle, and snap the elastic into place. The pepper-spray is blowing out with force, and I lob the

146

can over the balustrade. It lands in front of the cantina amidst a group of guards lashing out with their batons. The pressure of the spray keeps the can spinning and tumbling. It distributes its load evenly on friend and foe alike and breaks up the melee in a few seconds as everybody gasps for air and screams for water.

I withdraw to Lucy's quarters with the grenades and tear-gas. I need room to hurl my projectiles as far as possible. In quick succession I pull the pins and pitch the two grenades. For five seconds nothing happens.

Nervously I rip the seal off a canister of tear-gas. It starts to fume right away. I panic and want to pitch it the very moment the grenades go off! The intensity of the explosions, one under the truck with the generator, the other between two floodlights near the company gate, startles me and the canister flips only over the balustrade. Mad at myself, I hurl the remaining three cans as far as I can.

Enormous confusion breaks out among the soldiers near the store and the pawnshop, and blindly they fire their guns at some perceived but invisible enemy. That is the diversion we need.

Lucy aims the rifle at an officer who gets out of an all-terrain vehicle parked next to the generator truck. He stands on the running board and barks orders into a radio transmitter.

She fires and her shoulder is thrown back by the rifle's recoil. In the same instant the commanding officer's head explodes. Bone and tissue splatter car and truck. His torso drops away. The radio transmitter keeps on squawking.

Lucy looks at the rifle with a mixture of disgust and surprise. She curses quietly that it is loaded with dumdum bullets. She turns back to take aim through the embrasure and picks off the floodlights at random. One light after another explodes as it is hit with deadly accuracy. The response of soldiers and guards becomes more erratic. Innocent bystanders are shot and rushed to the makeshift hospital. With only one floodlight left, Lucy shifts around and carefully takes aim at the office building through the night-vision telescopic sight. She fires twice. The boardroom window shatters and the radio transmitter in the officer's car stops squawking. Almost instantly the soldiers cease fighting.

Lucy shifts back and blasts the remaining light to smithereens with a single shot. Where in hell did she learn to shoot like that, I wonder.

Darkness engulfs us once more. The steel door below the balcony slams shut. The small lights of a control panel on the generator glow brightly until somebody shuts down the diesel engine. An intense silence sets in. It stretches my nerves to the limit.

The clicking sound of metal hitting metal makes me jump. Lucy is changing the rifle's magazine. I suspect that it can be heard right across the plaza.

A barrage of shots fired at the whorehouse confirms my suspicion. The bullets hit the balustrade and walls near Lucy. Her sniper's hideout has been discovered.

I can hear the ricochets zing, shatter and spray fragments of metal and sandstone. Lucy cries out in pain. I crawl onto the balcony at all speed, throw the rifle over the balustrade, put my arms around her chest, and drag her inside.

Our battle is over.

27

WARM BLOOD oozes from innumerable small wounds on Lucy's shoulder and her back. Lying on the floor next to her in the total darkness, I gingerly try to assess the extent of the injuries. Her tracksuit makes that impossible. I unfasten the zipper of her jacket and peel off the blood-soaked garment.

Lucy whimpers every time I touch another one of the painful cuts, but she seems to understand what I am trying to do. She holds my wrist to guide my hand when I take off all her clothes. Cautiously I probe her lower back and the inside of her left leg. Most of the wounds aren't large, but I fear that she will bleed to death due to the sheer number of cuts and the fact that shrapnel is stuck in a lot of them. She needs first aid urgently but without light I can't do anything to help her.

I remember the candles that stand on every table, shelf, and ledge of her room. Crawling around on hands and knees, I bump from one piece of furniture to the next until I have found two candles and a book of matches.

I pull the day cover off her bed, make my way out into the hallway, and lay out a narrow resting-place for her. I crawl back and carry Lucy into the hallway. I shut the door and light a candle revealing a horrible sight.

Lucy's face and shoulder are covered in blood. The skin on the right side of her forehead and cheekbone looks shredded. Large wounds are located above her hip, on her buttocks and the worst one on the back of her left thigh. She flinches and curses quietly when I remove a large shard from her rump. I take off my shirt and rip it into strips that I fold into several compresses and press onto the wounds.

It is a futile attempt to stem the bleeding. I must get proper medical supplies and equipment and, if at all possible, some professional guidance and advice. I light the second candle and go downstairs in search of Mireilla.

The vestibule is a ghostly tomb sparsely lit by candles and some flashlights. Some of the people being treated look in far worse shape than Lucy.

Mireilla is extracting a bullet from a man's smashed shoulder, and volunteers tend to men, women, and children with lesser injuries.

Miguel sits in a corner next to the medical supplies. He is stripped to the waist. His chest is bandaged. He is engaged in a lively conversation with Juanita and Ismelda. It surprises me to see him talk to a *marica* and a bloated old prostitute. He had never minced words when it came to dismissing them as the scum of society. Yet here he is involved in a lively and by all accounts friendly discussion with two of the most stalwart representatives of their profession. While I pick the material I need from the pile of supplies, I overhear briefly what is being said.

"How would you know what went wrong?" Miguel asks Juanita.

"Because I'm an old fag, hombre," says Juanita. "I say it with all respect, but you can't even start to imagine what my thirty years of feeding off the underbelly of society have taught me. I know human greed and fickleness. Alarm bells go off in my head when somebody vile and ruthless suddenly gives the appearance of being friendly and cooperative. You didn't recognise that. You trusted Callaghan and let him out of your sight. That was your mistake."

"Oh yes, oh yes!" agrees Ismelda. "You can't ever let any of the gringos out of your sight. I wouldn't do a doggy-style turnover for anyone of them, even if I were offered a hundred dollars for the trick. You can't trust them. No, no. Oh no!"

Miguel pats Ismelda's hand and asks, "So what do you suggest we do now that we've been had doggy-style by the gringos?"

"You have only one option left to get at the gringos," says Juanita. "You have to grab them where it hurts."

"What are you saying?" protests Miguel. "I wouldn't touch them there if I was paid a thousand dollars!"

"No, hombre," says Juanita. "Grabbing them by the balls wouldn't hurt them at all. Most of them would love it! But from experience I know there's one thing they really fear, and I have an idea how to hit them and get them where they'll really hurt."

"Let's hear it," says Miguel and the three conspirators stick their heads together.

I have picked the supplies I need including a small flashlight and rush back upstairs without anybody paying particular

150

attention to me. When I get to the landing, I can see that Lucy is in bad shape. She must have tried to get up and collapsed.

The candle by her side has been knocked over and is extinguished. The door to her quarters is open. I drop the supplies, switch off the flashlight, and rush into the room to quietly shut the French windows and draw the heavy velvet curtains. Then I grope my way to her bedside table, light a candle, duck, and wait for gunfire to shatter a window. When nothing happens, I light every one of the thirty candles in the room, place them on the bedside table and a ledge above the headrest, spread extra sheets on the bed, go to pick up Lucy and carry her inside. Her arms draped around my neck, she holds me when I put her on the bed. She pulls me towards her until my ear was close to her mouth.

"Do you think I look beautiful?" she whispers.

Taken aback by such a question under the prevailing circumstances, I straighten up. My eyes skim over her trim and bloodied body lying naked before me. I take her hand in both of mine, lean towards her and say, "Yes, you look beautiful. But now I must take care of your injuries, Lucy. You could die."

"Oh, I will die, Rigo, I will die," she whispers, clutches my hands, and rambles on at fever pitch. "But I want to die happy, Rigo. I liked you since I first saw you. Tell me you like me, too… just a little bit. I'm an old woman, much older than you, but I want you to like me. I want to die happy, Rigo. Don't I have a right to be happy? You can make me happy. Look at me. Kiss me…"

I look at her wondering what she has in mind but all I can see are her wounds oozing blood onto the linen. I am getting desperate and hoping to let me get on with tending to her injuries, I kiss her.

She almost sucks the tongue out of my throat but gives some peace at last and allows me to free my hands from her grip. Gently I turn her onto her left side and prop her up on pillows. Dazed from the loss of blood, she watches me with tired eyes.

I lay out the supplies next to her. In the bathroom I wash my hands and find a small bowl. I fill it with a bottle of vodka and dump the instruments into the alcohol hoping to sterilise them.

Kneeling by the bedside, I work feverishly taking care of the larger wounds first. Holding the flashlight between my teeth, I extract a clump of metal, a deformed bullet, from deep in the back of her thigh and close the wound. All the other cuts I check for shards, remove debris, dab and clean the surrounding areas with gauze soaked in hydrogen peroxide, apply antiseptic ointment, and clamp the wounds with narrow strips of elastic adhesive strips. I make good progress, but Lucy still passes out. At first, I think she has died when she goes limp, but then I notice her breathing and I carry on with double the effort. After about an hour all but her face is patched up. I take great care to put the puzzle of shredded skin back together on her forehead and cheek and hope it won't leave too many scars once it heals.

After midnight I am finished. I replace the bloodied sheets with clean ones, put Lucy to bed and tuck her in. She is fast asleep. Her breathing is a bit shallow but regular. Her face seems to have aged dramatically. Her cheeks appear hollow and the lines on her forehead and around her eyes are more pronounced.

I feel a close bond with her since our caper on the balcony. I laid the groundwork and single-handedly she had brought a battalion of special commandos of the Motorised Cavalry to a standstill. We had been a real team. Gently I rub her cheek and hold her hand. A faint smile seems to play around her pale lips.

I fill a tumbler with Dutch egg liqueur I find in the liquor cabinet. In the absence of food this would be the next best thing to reawaken her spirits once she recovers.

When Juanita looks in, he is shocked at the sight of Lucy's face and wants to know what happened. He can't believe that I patched her up all by myself. I mention that Lucy should undergo a thorough medical examination in a proper hospital. He agrees but can only shrug at the impossibility of getting her to a hospital.

Juanita blows out all the candles but one and says that Miguel wants to see me. He adds ominously that our counter-offensive has started and leads the way downstairs.

28

A CONSPIRATORIAL MEETING of sorts takes place in the almost empty vestibule. A sofa and six chairs have been moved in a circle and provide seating for nine people. Miguel and five foremen sit in the chairs. They lean forward and talk to each other in low voices.

One of Lucy's girls, Vanessa, sits on the sofa and shows no interest in the discussion. Bored she picks her nose, pulls up a leg, and shows off her skimpy underwear.

The injured men and women have been moved to adjacent rooms normally reserved for whorehouse clients. Two volunteers mop the floor. They douse candles as they go along until only two in the centre of the vestibule are left burning.

Mireilla is slumped into an armchair at the far end of the room, legs stretched out, head propped up on a fist. She looks exhausted. Her blood-spattered uniform and shoes would suit a butcher better than a nurse. Her eyes open wide when she sees me coming down the stairs. She gets up and stands in my way fists akimbo.

"Twenty-three dead and fifty-six seriously wounded! Is that what you wanted to achieve with your schoolboy prank?" she asks with rage in her voice.

"Schoolboy prank?" I inquire a bit baffled.

"Yes, you pulled the stunt that triggered the sprinkler system and brought everything to a standstill so you could have a day off at full pay. Isn't that so?"

"A day off at full pay? Is that what you think the strike is about? And you think we get paid, too? How often have you been down in the mine?"

"Never! And that's beside the point!"

"Beside the point? That is the point! That's what this strike is about! Unsafe work conditions! Miners getting killed on the job every week! The rock fall last night killed over thirty men! That's what we have to stop! The killings! You must know about that!"

"No, I don't know about that," says Mireilla and continues quite agitated. "And I don't believe a word you say! I would know if thirty miners had been killed last night. I work hand in glove with Doctor Gomez and there's no record of thirty miners killed by a rock fall!"

The five men of the conspiratorial meeting sit up and take notice of our argument.

"Of course, there is no record," I say. "Doctor Gomez is the worst perpetrator of the dastardly system that covers up the fatal accidents. He lets the corpses disappear and has them burned in the smelter. He implants every man, woman, and child with microchips to control their every move. Surely you know that! You are present when the microchips are implanted, aren't you?"

"What are you talking about now? Microchips implanted? Corpses burned in the smelter? Covering up fatal accidents? You are all over the place! You are making this up to justify your prank, don't you?"

I look at Mireilla in utter disbelief. Does she know nothing of the work conditions, the fatal accidents, or the control system? How could it have been kept hidden from her who is working right in the eye of the storm?

It feels so futile to continue the argument, I want to turn away and join the five men and Juanita who are waiting for me. But I have one last thought.

"When did you get your last raise?" I ask her.

"I don't see why that is any of your business," she answers sharply. "But if you have to know, I got one three months ago."

"Was it a good one?"

"Yes, thank you, it was all I asked for."

"Good, I'm happy for you. Then you should be aware out of whose pocket your pay rise comes. The minimum drilling and blasting quota was raised to two meters per shift! The pay of each miner was reduced by fifteen percent! For seventy hours of work per week we don't get paid enough to put decent food on the table. That's why we are on strike! A day off at full pay doesn't even come into the picture! None of us gets paid right now and we won't get paid until we succeed!"

Abruptly I turn away from her, walk to the sofa and plunk myself down between Vanessa and Juanita.

I am incensed and it must have shown on my face. Miguel and the other foremen grin.

Miguel leans forward and whispers, "Good show, Rigo, but don't get mad at her. She's only trying to get your attention."

"What do you mean?"

"Well, she was full of praise for you until she went upstairs and saw you treat Lucy. She came down here and was furious. She muttered, 'Kissing the naked shaved slut!' and stomped her heels like a mare in heat. I think she's in love with you."

I am shocked. "In love with me? I think she's nuts. Lucy is badly injured. She was hit by shrapnel. I gave her first aid and cleaned and patched up her wounds. I didn't screw her."

"You didn't?" Juanita asks with a chuckle. "You'll be in deep trouble when she wakes up."

"If she wakes up," I say. "She has lost a lot of blood."

"Ah, she'll pull through," says a foreman. "Sluts heal fast."

I give that guy an angry look. I have to restrain myself from getting up and punching his lights out.

"She may be a slut to you," I growl. "But she's still a human being deserving of as much care and compassion as anybody else. And remember, if it weren't for Lucy's marksmanship, you wouldn't be sitting there all smug and superior. You'd be rolling in your blood on the plaza under the jackboots of the special commando of the Motorised Cavalry. It was Lucy who blew away their officer and their lanterns. She's gutsy and courageous, more than you'll ever be!"

Stunned silence and long faces follow my outburst. Juanita puts an arm around my shoulder and gives me a hug. Vanessa reaches for my hand, gives it a gentle squeeze, presses it to her thigh, and cuddles up to me. Their gestures of appreciation give me a lump in the throat.

"So, what's the big plan?" I ask Miguel with a thick voice.

He gives Vanessa and me a probing look and says, "You look very tired. Are you still fit?"

"Depends on what you want me to do," I say.

"Drive a car."

"No problem," I say. "I can do that in my sleep." I pause and sit up with a jolt. "A car? What car?"

Juanita jingles a set of keys. "Arbuckle's Mercedes."

"Sure…but… but…" I stammer.

"Yes or no?" Miguel asks.

"Yes, of course," I reply.

"Let's go then," says Juanita and gets up. "Come on, we have to hurry. I'll explain everything as we go along."

He pulls me up from the sofa. I go over to Mireilla. She curled up in the armchair and seems to sleep. When I reach for her chin, she snaps back her head and breathes fire and fury. For a second, I think that she would jump me like a cat with all four paws and tear the flesh off my face. I get right into the thick of it sitting down on the armrest and putting a hand around her shoulders. Swiftly I pull her towards me and talk to her.

"How would you feel, if I acted the way you do right now every time you jingle some guy's nuts or rub ointment on his frazzled love gherkin?" I ask her.

She looks up, chuckles, and covers her face with her hands. Suddenly she hits me in the chest and says, "Treating a patient isn't the same as cavorting around with whores."

"That's true," I say, "but giving first aid to a whore is not exactly cavorting around with her. Right? Lucy needs your help. When I get back, I'll cavort around with you. Do we have a deal?"

Mireilla becomes very quiet. Her head bowed, she gives Vanessa a furtive glance and then stares at the floor. She gets up without looking at me, takes a small flashlight out of her pocket and rushes up the stairs past Juanita. He waves to me, bidding me to hurry up and follow him.

At the end of the third-floor hallway is a room I had never entered during my time of dusting and sweeping. It is the stockroom with racks of dresses, costumes, suits, shoes, shirts, accessories, and rubber and leather paraphernalia.

Juanita gets right down to business and picks a chauffeur's outfit of white shirt, blue tie, charcoal suit and peaked cap as well as socks, underwear, and shoes for me.

"Here you go, Rigo, try this on," he says and starts a long monologue while he picks clothes for himself and gets dressed. "I'll play the part of Arbuckle and you are going to be my chauffeur. You'll drive us out of the mining compound and past the military to Zacatecas. I have a few hundred dollars to bribe our way out should the soldiers demand money to let us pass. You'll drop me off at the express bus station in Zacatecas and park the car in a garage across the street. I should make it to Mexico in about five hours. You will take a bus back to Torreón. Ask the driver to let you out three kilometres beyond the turn-off to Tepetapa. You will have to make your way back on foot across the plateau. These guys here need you as a translator once the

156

directors are cornered and forced to negotiate. How does the suit fit you? Looks good. Put on the cap. It'll do. The shoes fit? No? Try another pair. We must hurry. I don't know how much time we have. We sent out Armandita to check the commandos. He has great night vision, can find a safe passage from here to the garage, and clear the path to Arbuckle's Mercedes. We will have to call the whole thing off if Armandita doesn't come back. He may get arrested or killed by the special commandos. If he does come back, he should be here any minute. How do I look?"

"Incredible," I mutter.

Juanita has undergone a transformation. A navy-blue silk suit, white shirt, red tie, and wide-brimmed fedora have made a gringo businessman look-alike out of him. Holding a cell-phone to his ear, his face is obscured, and he could be anybody. He pats me on the shoulder and points to the door. I turn and jump back.

Armandita stands in the doorway dressed in a black body stocking and Balaclava. He carries a long-handled pair of wire cutters. I didn't recognise him and thought for a second that he is a special commando who is going to attack us.

"Put on black sneakers and take your shoes with you. Don't forget your papers," he tells us.

Grinning broadly, he hands me my wallet. The son of a bitch must have searched my abode and found the secret place in the cistern of the toilet where I hid my papers in a sealed plastic bag!

After we put on the sneakers as we are told, Armandita and I wait in silence while Juanita collects a heavy travel bag from his room.

Quietly the three of us go down the servant staircase and leave the house through the basement door at the back.

29

THE COOL AIR of night makes me shiver. In a crouch we slip past the back of the pawnshop. Armandita leads the way, I follow, and Juanita brings up the rear. A cord is our lifeline in the darkness. We have it slung around our left wrists so we wouldn't lose touch with each other. Pulling and easing the cord in a slow, steady motion is the signal that the way is clear. One strong, short pull signals caution and stop. Two pulls mean, hit the ground, and find cover, if at all possible.

Proceeding in the pitch-black of a moonless night with a thin cloud cover preventing even the stars to shed sparse light on our way proves to be a tremendous mental strain. I can't see a thing. With every step, I seem to dip my foot into a bottomless pit. The uneven terrain makes things worse. A couple of times Armandita signals a stop to allow Juanita and me to regain our senses. I can only wonder about Armandita's fantastic ability to see in the dark. His mother must have fed him nothing but carrots as a baby. How could that guy sleep at night? I mean, he must stare clear through his closed eyelids. Perhaps he sleeps like a rabbit with his eyes wide open.

I am certain that it will take hours to get to the garage at our slow pace if we ever make it there. But step-by-step we advance along the rusty fence at the back of the mechanic's workshop.

The cord is pulled twice. We hit the ground. I am ready to scream, when Armandita approaches me silent as a shadow and whispers in my ear, "Three commandos having a smoke, rifles by their hips. Night vision goggles. Let's wait."

With my head resting on my hand and staring into the black of night, I start to feel drowsy. I fall asleep and dream of Lucy floating in mid-air her eyes firmly shut. I hear her say, "You'll be in deep trouble when I wake up, up, up, up."

But it is Armandita who urges me, "Up, up, up!"

I look around. I see nothing. I get up, grope for my leather shoes and curse under my breath when I am pulled around a corner. A few metres on, we pass through some wire mesh fence held open by Armandita. I have no idea where we are. Quite rapidly we advance for a distance, turn another corner, and walk down a ramp. We are in the garage.

Juanita presses the car-keys into my hand. We have arrived at the Mercedes. It takes a bit of poking around to find the keyhole. A hand clamps down on mine before I can unlock the driver's door and pull it open. Armandita whispers, "Wait a second. Let me get out first. Good luck."

I expect to hear his footsteps. I hear nothing and wait.

Juanita becomes impatient and growls, "Are you waiting for better weather or what? Open the car! Let's go! Let's go!"

When I open the door, the interior ceiling light of the car reflects off the chrome parts despite the tinted windows. It stings my eyes. I swing inside, press the button on the centre console to unlock the doors and Juanita gets in.

I insert the ignition key and look at myself in the rear-view mirror. The swellings and bruises on the right side of my face look very bad and make me an unlikely candidate for chauffeur of some gringo businessman. I put on the cap and pull it down on my forehead. It looks a little better. I dust my jacket off, adjust the tie, and check the car's interior to familiarise myself with all the buttons and switches.

In the glove compartment I find several thousand pesos crumpled like play money. I shut the compartment and we are ready to go.

I turn to look at Juanita. He clutches his travel bag on his lap. His suit and shirt are covered in dust and bits of dried grass. I press the button that pops the lid of the trunk open, get out of the car, and open his door.

"What are you doing now?" Juanita asks nervously.

"Give me your bag."

He quivers. "No! I won't! I got all my stuff in there."

"I know! Let me put it in the trunk."

"No, you won't. It stays right here with me."

"Give me your bag! A businessman doesn't travel in his car with luggage on his lap."

"This isn't my car."

"But it's damn well supposed to be, isn't it?"

He gives me a haunted look and shakes his head. Oh great, I am thinking, that's what we need - a conspirator suffering a bout of the jitters and frozen in fear. I grab the handles of the bag and pull. I might as well have tried to dislodge a rock. All I need now is Juanita starting to cry and talking in a fake falsetto voice.

I point to his shoulder. "Look there! A spider!"

Juanita shrieks. "Where?"

"On your shoulder. And another one is crawling up your tie."

Juanita shrieks again and hits his shoulder and chest raising clouds of dust. I snatch the travel bag, swiftly deposit it in the trunk, and pick up an executive briefcase that is stowed there.

Juanita jumps out of the car and performs a strange, convulsive dance. He groans and rolls his eyes evidently suffering a severe bout of arachnophobia. I shut the trunk and try to calm Juanita.

"It's okay, it's okay," I say. "They are all dead."

Juanita doesn't react to my efforts of calming him. He has gone mental and keeps on jerking. I place the briefcase on the backseat and open it. It contains business papers relating to the mine and several bundles of one-hundred-dollar bills. I fold and pocket the papers, take two wads of money and shut the briefcase. One bundle I keep for myself, the other one I give to Juanita. He stares at the bundle and his convulsions subside a bit.

I retrieve the cell-phone from his jacket, flip it open, and check that it is switched off. Gently but firmly, I guide him into his seat, adjust his tie and jacket, and squeeze the fedora onto his head. I put the cell-phone into his hand and make sure he holds it to his ear.

"It's your mother on the phone," I say. "Her voice is very weak. You have to listen carefully, or you won't understand what she wants you to do with your money."

Juanita stares straight ahead and earnestly listens to the silent phone. I shut his door, slip into the driver's seat, start the car, put on the parking lights, lock the doors, and pull out of the garage. It is up to me now to get us out of the mining compound and onto the road to Zacatecas.

Driving towards the gate, we pass the silent buildings, the body bags, and the watchtower. Past the gate I turn left towards the road and switch the headlights to high beam. Fearful miners and their families huddle on the plaza and get out of the way squinting into the light.

At the back near the company store stand several guards and special commandos in small groups. They smoke and guzzle beer. Cautiously I drive towards a soldier waving a red light. He stands

160

between the flatbed truck and the officer's car. I break into a cold sweat as I pull up next to him and open the window.

"Where do you think you are going?" the commando asks in a harsh tone.

"I'm driving one of the directors to a meeting at the Ministry of Mining and Natural Resources in the Federal District," I say and switch on the interior light.

The commando stares at Juanita listening intently to the phone. "What's his name?" he asks.

"Arbuckle."

"Tell him to take off his hat."

"I'm sorry, I'm his chauffeur and in no position to tell him anything. Neither does he speak Spanish."

I switch off the interior light. The commando straightens up and the muzzle of his automatic rifle points at my head. He doesn't notice when I push the muzzle away. He puffs up his cheeks and does some thinking moving his lips. I imagine him flipping through a miniature card deck of ready-made excuses between his ears. "We have strict orders not to let anyone pass," he says.

I have to suppress my urge to grin. I wonder why this corrupt bastard doesn't muster the courage to demand a bribe in a straight-forward manner and instead relies on the roundabout approach of using the age-old excuse of "strict orders".

I turn in my seat and pretend to speak with Juanita while trying to get the wad of money out of his hand. But Juanita won't let go. I reach for the briefcase and manage to extract two bundles of dollar bills. I turn to the commando and hold out one bundle.

"Here are the papers that say that your strict orders don't apply in this case," I say.

The soldier grabs the money and flicks through the bundle. He grins and barks, "Yes, Sir!"

"Are there any other checkpoints along the road?" I ask. "You better get that information to them, or your arse is on the line."

"Yes, Sir! I will, Sir!"

I hold up the second bundle. "Here are some more papers," I say and pull it back when he reaches for it. "These are your strict orders to blow up the gate down the road, station all vehicles and men in the mining compound, restore electricity, open the company store and the cantina to the public and cease fire. Is that understood?"

I hand him the money. He flicks through a total of twenty thousand dollars and can barely contain himself.

"Yes, Sir! Gate to be blown up! Vehicles and men to be stationed in the mining compound! Restore electricity! Open store and cantina! Cease fire!"

He salutes with a broad grin, switches his flashlight to green, and waves it about in a straight up and down motion.

Life with corrupt soldiers and policemen can be very uncomplicated - if you have the money!

I shut the window and pull away. As we drive past the long line of military cars and trucks, ambulances, a field kitchen, and even a couple of armoured personnel carriers, I wonder what lies the regional Brigadier General of the Motorised Cavalry was told and how much of a bribe had to be paid in cash under the table to activate a force of this magnitude.

The car accelerates smoothly as it shifts through the gears. Soon Tepetapa is left behind and we hit the highway to Zacatecas.

30

IT IS STILL DARK by the time we approach Zacatecas. The traffic is light, and the one-and-a-half-hour journey was relatively uneventful. Except the occasional rabid dog breaking out of the bushes and a dead horse lying in the middle of the road, we don't encounter any obstacles.

Juanita holds onto the cell-phone during the entire trip and stares straight ahead, eyes vacant and showing no emotion. I feel sorry for the poor sod. It hadn't been my intention to put him into a state of shock. Had I known of his arachnophobia, his fear of spiders, I would never have played that trick on him. Against our plan of dropping him off at the express bus station in Zacatecas, I stay on the four-lane highway that passes the town. It would be inhumane to let him loose among people in his condition.

The fuel gauge indicates that the car's tank is empty. I keep my eyes open for a gas station. South of Guadalupe, where the road forks to Aguascalientes and San Luis Potosí, I spot a modern, spacious service centre with a restaurant and pull up to a gas-pump.

The attendant, an old man with a deeply wrinkled face, is awake. He will give the car a fill-up, an oil check and a wash and wax while Juanita and I go for a bite to eat in the restaurant.

It is a job in itself to get Juanita out of the car and persuade him to let go of the wad of money and the cell-phone. He is disoriented. I have to guide him up the steps and through the glass door to a seat by the window. We are the only customers in the cavernous establishment. The clock on the wall shows a quarter to four. Juanita sits down slowly and turns his back on the darkness outside. He fixes his gaze on the bright lights above the service counter. It seems to give him some balance though he doesn't respond when I ask him what he wants to eat and drink. Assuming that he will be satisfied with coffee and some pastry, I go to the counter to place our order.

A young girl, she can't be older than fourteen, in a green, white, and red uniform is the only person in attendance. She tells me with an embarrassed smile that the pastries on display are plastic imitations and that the coffee is cold. Fresh pastry is being baked but will be ready only in half an hour. I ask her to make some fresh coffee. She gets right down to it with the awkward and at the same time endearing movements of a child trying to please an adult. Several times she looks back at me with a vague smile while she handles filter, ground coffee, and a water jug to see if I approve. I nod to encourage her, and she seems very happy. We exchange names and chat for the time it takes to brew the coffee.

Her name is Rosa, a name that matches her blushing cheeks perfectly. I learn that the old man outside is her grandfather and only remaining relative. Her family of father, mother and four younger brothers and sisters had disappeared one day just like that, she says and snaps her fingers. They have probably forgotten her, Rosa surmises, because she had to stay behind to go to school in Guadalupe and they had to leave. A bit restless she fidgets about, props herself up with her skinny arms on the edge of the counter while she assures me that she is living with her grandfather and that she is all right. Intrigued, I inquire why her family had to leave. Her father had found work, she explains. A big bus had come more than two years ago and taken him and her family away. Whereto, I want to know. A small place of which I have probably never heard, says Rosa, a place so small it was not on any map. Her father had joked that it was so small that he had to duck to do his work. And what work did he do, I ask. Carpenter, she says with some pride. So, what is this place called where he has to duck to do his work, I want to know. Tepetapa, she says quietly, and her eyes become overcast.

The coffee is ready, and Rosa occupies herself with filling the cups. She puts the coffee and spoons, napkins, cream, and sugar on a tray and insists on serving us. I pay, give her a generous tip, and sit down with Juanita who still stares at the lights.

Rosa serves the coffee and says that she will bring the pastry as soon as it comes out of the oven. She gives Juanita a frightened look. Before she turns away, I ask her for her father's name. Juan Antonio Gonzalo, she replies. I try to lift her spirits telling her that she should not give up hope to see her family again. It may happen sooner than she thinks. She gives me a doubtful look.

After she leaves to go back behind the counter, I pull the folded papers out of my pocket. I remember having seen a list of names among them. It is a twenty-page computer printout with columns

164

of numbers, names, and dates. I put sugar in my coffee, stir it, and take small sips while I go over the list.

The numbers and names are in no particular order and at first the list doesn't make any sense. I notice that several names have been marked with a pink highlighter. When I find Miguel's and my name among them, I realise that the names are grouped by crew and list the workers and their families by number within those groups. This could be proof that all inhabitants of Tepetapa have microchips implanted and are identified by their numbers. Quite a few names, including Hernan Godoy's, are marked with a thick black dot. Presumably they are the men who had been killed on the job.

It seems hopeless to search for Juan Antonio Gonzalo. I fold the paper and stash it in my pocket when I notice Juanita staring at me. It is an expectant stare as if he is waiting for me to say something.

"Drink your coffee," I say in an amiable tone.

"Did you find it?" he asks in response.

"No," I say somewhat surprised and take the list out again, "the list is too long with thousands of names that are not in alphabetical order."

"Damn," he mutters. "Look again! How can I invest my money if I don't know the name? You must find it!"

"Invest your money in what? What name?" I inquire with my curiosity suddenly aroused.

"The company my mother mentioned. I forgot it," he whines.

That response tells me almost everything there is to know about his mental state.

All of a sudden, the strain of the past thirty-six hours catches up with me. My shoulders sag and I slouch forward. I recognise the profound implications of the problem I have on my hands. The purpose of our trip and Juanita's destination in the metropolis of Mexico, a huge city with millions and millions of inhabitants, is a mystery to me. I don't know where to go or what to do unless Juanita will tell me. He is supposed to give me the details of our plan of action, the counter-offensive. But Juanita has become totally disengaged from the moorings of reality. He is rearranging deckchairs on a rudderless boat tossed about on the stormy seas of his mind and I can't even get a sensible answer out of him. I am getting desperate.

My head feels stuffed with cotton wool, too numb to formulate a thought. It crosses my mind to cancel our trip and turn back.

"Do you know where we are?" I ask Juanita.

"Of course," he assures me and nods emphatically.

A faint feeling of hope arising is quickly dashed when he says, "Santa Fé!"

He points to a colourful sign above the counter that advertises the brand of the coffee I drink and he ignores.

Rosa comes to the table and serves two plates of pastries that smell delicious and look scrumptious. They are shaped like stars with eight crusty, slender extensions and a glazed apricot half and a cherry on a bed of vanilla pudding in the centre. Rosa gives me a warm smile and I respond in kind. She is like a little ray of light in the darkness that still surrounds us.

"Thank you," I say to her. "The pastries look marvellous. What are they called?"

"Just pastries," says Rosa with a giggle. "Most customers just point a finger and say, 'That one'. But because they have eight legs, I call them apricot spiders."

Juanita hears the word, stares at the pastries, and goes berserk! He shrieks! His fist comes down hard on his "spider" and squashes it to a pulp! Pudding squirts and the plate is shattered. A fork goes ballistic and gets stuck in the ceiling. The coffee cups dance and spill their contents.

Juanita jumps up and grabs his chair to smash my pastry as well. Luckily his steel and plastic stackable seating contraption becomes entangled in other chairs behind him. He rips it free and overturns a table and chairs in the process.

I push Rosa out of the way and tackle Juanita. Ramming my head into his midriff and grabbing him around the waist, we crash to the floor. He hits the back of his head hard on the shiny tiles. After a short slide, we come to a stop, and I get up.

Juanita is out cold. Rosa is crying. It won't relieve her anxiety and shock trying to explain to her that Juanita is suffering from arachnophobia. I give her a hug, guide her back to the counter, and tuck some money into her apron.

Juanita's floorshow cuts our stay at the hospitable place unceremoniously short. I grab my folded, wet, and coffee-stained papers, lift Juanita, put him over my shoulder, and carry him out to the car.

The old man is taken aback by the sight of us, but he helps me getting Juanita onto the backseat and lay him down. I explain briefly what happened in the restaurant, ask him to help Rosa with the clean-up and give him enough dollars to put a big smile on his wrinkled face.

Ten seconds later Juanita and I are back on the road. Forced by the highway median to travel south, I continue in that direction in the vain hope of Juanita coming around with a clear head before we reach the city of Mexico.

31

IT IS HALF PAST FIVE in the morning, and we are in the fast lane on the highway to Querétaro. The first light of the rising sun creeps over the horizon. Some serious groaning comes from the back seat of the Mercedes. It blends into the rap music of a radio program. Juanita regains consciousness. I can see him in the rear-view mirror holding his head while we pass an endless convoy of trucks that crawls up a lengthy gradient.

"Stop the car! I'm going to be sick!" he moans.

Quickly I push the button on the centre console, lower the rear window on the passenger side, and shout, "Stick your head out the window! I can't stop right now!"

He hangs out of the window and heaves and retches to his heart's content. The huge vane of bile he releases is caught in an updraft of air turbulence as I pull past the convoy. It splatters onto the windshield of the leading truck. The incensed driver shakes his fist and blasts his horn. The truck doesn't have wipers. The trucker splashes soda pop on the windshield to wash the slime away. But his efforts result in getting splattered by the diluted vomit spraying into his cabin. Mad as a hatter, he flashes the one working headlight and honks the horn furiously. Stopping the car is out of the question. I boot the accelerator and speed away.

Once Juanita has finished tossing his stomach's contents to the wind, he sits back and closes the window. On the rear windowsill is a box of tissue paper. He uses it freely to clean up his face and suit. It doesn't make much difference to the fine silk. The large spots emit a choking stench. I open the windows and turn the ventilation to full blast.

When the volume of traffic slows us down, Juanita casts suspicious looks around.

"Can we stop somewhere?" he asks. "I need a drink. Where are we anyway? Shouldn't we be in Zacatecas by now?"

A look in the mirror tells me that the old self of Juanita is back. Relieved, I belt out, "Welcome back and good morning!"

He doesn't understand my greeting. He asks what time it is and then apologises for having slept through the entire trip since he got into the car. He doesn't remember a thing of the incidents in the garage in Tepetapa or the restaurant outside Guadalupe, and I am certainly not going to jog his memory.

At a convenience store along the highway, I stop to get us bottles of soda, beakers of coffee and sandwiches. Juanita moves to the front seat, and we eat and drink as we speed towards Querétaro. During the hour and twenty minutes it takes to reach the outskirts of that city, he fills me in on the plan of action and a lot of background information.

The counter-offensive he outlines is simple. It involves blackmailing some of the most upstanding and respected members of the media into coming to Tepetapa and covering our dispute. I have my doubts that the plan is going work but don't want to put the brakes on his enthusiasm. Consequently, I shut up and listen to his life's story that explains the background of his plan.

After Lucy had picked up Juanita off the streets of Tlalnepantla, a northern suburb of Mexico City, it took her about a year to turn the young man who survived on giving sexual favours to male clients into a high priced, high-class male prostitute in the city of Mexico.

His clientele included politicians of every stripe and members of the press and television. He gained a reputation for discreetness and was favoured for his services by those "pillars of society" that publicly defend Christian family values, clean living, and law and order. He rode the crest of a wave of success for eight years, but a nasty series of murder, assassinations, and the disappearance of journalists and politicians brought his lucky streak to an abrupt end.

A new breed of incorruptible investigators probed deeply into the private affairs of most of Juanita's clients. He and Lucy were paid off in return for their silence and were asked to leave the country for a while.

After five years in Nicaragua, where Lucy had befriended an American "security advisor", who taught her to shoot to kill, they returned to Mexico to pick up where they had left off. But things had changed drastically. The fear of contracting AIDS had reached epidemic proportions and practically all of Juanita's old clients had become "consumers" of young, clean boys. Lucy found an alternative by offering her stable of "girls and boys" to North American convention visitors.

Her regular customers included a group of businessmen with whom she built an excellent rapport. They were mine operators and managers from the USA and Canada who weren't very popular any longer up north. Their management methods had led to the death of hundreds of miners and their strike breaking and dubious business practices had caused the bankruptcy and closure of mines back home.

Therefore, they were on the lookout for greener pastures in Mexico and took full advantage of the North American Free Trade Agreement.

Led by Callaghan, they regarded Mexico as an industrial, economical, and cultural backwater in dire need of "American Business Savvy" and "Canadian Corporate Culture". The object of their desire turned out to be the ghost town of Tepetapa and its abandoned mining operation.

Callaghan, a capable geologist, had investigated the valley and found rich ore deposits to the north of two abandoned shafts. A new shaft was sunk, and the town needed to be revitalised to accommodate miners and mill and smelter workers. That's where Lucy and Juanita came into the picture. They were contracted to organise the social element of the town and provide "rest and recreation" by setting up and running the whorehouse and cantina. Close ties with the management as well as the board of directors' careless handling of confidential information during the construction and initial operational phase of the mine and town gave Juanita access to discarded documents.

On Lucy's orders he compiled a file of telephone messages, letters, the directors' family addresses in the USA and Canada, bills of lading, and minutes of meetings retrieved from waste bins, taken from cars, or forgotten in the whorehouse. It provided profound insights into the gringos' fraudulent schemes.

A huge bribe had been paid to the state governor to eliminate the quarrelsome property owners and secure a ten-year lease of the valley. Cooked books persuaded various authorities that the mine's operation was of an exploratory and non-profit nature. Extracted precious metals were smuggled out of the country. All the plotting and scheming required heightened security measures and gradually the entire valley became a corralled prison camp and a death trap for any of the mineworkers entertaining the idea of leaving.

170

The fence across the valley, the implanted microchips, the control system, and the trigger-happy guards made it impossible to get out of Tepetapa. These "security measures" were as illegal as the mining operation itself. Hence, the directors couldn't afford any publicity and were loath to let even their presence in Mexico become public knowledge. But that is exactly where Juanita wants to grab them because he knows that a media circus will hurt them most. To achieve his end, he intends to blackmail his former media clients into visiting Tepetapa, sending a crew, and bring cameras, lights, and action into town.

So far, so good, but there is a final catch to the plan. Juanita also wants the media to report what is going on, and that is most unlikely. In scandal-plagued Mexico some nine hundred miners and some hundred mill and smelter workers getting shafted and staging a strike for fair wages is hardly considered news.

When I ask Juanita how the impossible could be achieved, his mocking smile turns into a hearty belly laugh, and he says, "We'll put on a show, Rigo! When you return to Tepetapa today, you'll find out what I mean!"

32

THE WALK across the plateau from the Zacatecas highway back to Tepetapa turns out to be far more arduous than I had anticipated. The sun has turned the flat terrain into a hotplate. I have to place my folded jacket on a rock to avoid burning my bum when sitting down to change my shoes. The black rubber sneakers, presumably made by some ten-year old kid in Vietnam, are torture instruments that turned my feet into wet, smelly clumps of goat cheese within an hour of trekking. My toes feel much better once I dry and rub them in the sunshine. I open the travel bag I purchased in Querétaro, take out a clean pair of cotton socks and my leather shoes, and put them on. In the bag is also my driver's cap, a file of Juanita's papers, my wallet, money, and car keys, two bottles of water and fruit and bread. I have a bite to eat and a sip of water and continue my hike in good spirits and much welcome foot comfort. Along the way I contemplate Juanita's mysterious plan of action.

The key to the success of our counter-offensive is timing. If Miguel and the mineworkers start too early, that is before the media circus arrives, our strike could lead to a bigger bloodbath than we had seen so far. Should he miss the correct point in time and start the action after press and TV had arrived, the journalists, commentators, and photographers would become bored, pack up their stuff, leave, and write the whole thing off as a non-event. The only part of our strike action of interest to them, according to Juanita, will be the "show" that has to coincide with the media's arrival. Miguel will have to keep the mineworkers in a constant state of alert without overdramatising their need for readiness until the media rolls into town. He has a formidable task on his hands.

I don't have a clue what the "show" entails. I know only that it is supposed to start today at approximately six o'clock in the evening or about ten-thirty tomorrow morning depending on the outcome of Juanita's attempt of blackmailing his old clients into coming to Tepetapa. He told me that he would send notice by taxi two hours in advance of the media circus' arrival. The delivery of a huge bunch of flowers for Lucy will be the signal for Miguel to call the mineworkers to come to the plaza and get past the preliminaries of presenting our demands to the directors and receiving a response. Depending on the directors' answer, which we presume will be negative, Miguel has to fire up the strikers with a short speech, just long enough for the cameras to be set up and the commentators to comb their hair, before he gets on with the "show". It is my sincere hope that the "show" does not involve a violent charge and clash with the security guards or the military. That would be a disaster.

I check my watch. It is synchronised with one Juanita purchased for himself in Querétaro. It is just past two o'clock.

Seeing what time it is, suddenly an unreasonable sense of urgency, a panic attack has me by the throat. I want to run, but my legs won't cooperate. Standing still, I am panting and sweating like a long-distance runner. The desolate ochre landscape loses what little lustre it has. In my visual perception, sky and ground blend into each other and engulf me. I want to scream but my parched throat won't let me. I get a bottle of water out of my bag, snap it open, take a sip, and pour some over my head and neck. Exhausted I lean forward, prop myself up on my knees and close my eyes.

I had a similar panic attack earlier in the day. It was a most unpleasant sensation of having reason and structured thought suddenly swept away by a flood of doubts and questions. After stationing the Mercedes in a guarded parking garage in Querétaro and while I was still shopping for a travel bag near the city's centre, the Plaza Obregon, my thoughts began to race, and I started panting and sweating in the grip of uncontrollable mental spasms. Inside a store, I grabbed the next best bag off a rack, dropped money on the counter, didn't wait for the change, and dragged Juanita outside. Jabbering madly, I urged him to let us take taxis for our respective trips and jumped into the first available jalopy at a nearby stand.

Fortunately, Juanita had kept a cool head in this critical situation and dragged me back out of the dilapidated vehicle that had an almost flat front tire. Suave businessman that he appeared to be, decked out in a new suit, shirt, and tie, he picked a sound looking car and did the haggling with the veteran taxi-driver until they agreed on a fixed price for my trip of over five hundred kilometres. Juanita gave me a copy of a thick file that he had made first thing in Querétaro and told me to pass it on to Miguel. We parted ways at a quarter to nine in the morning.

It took two hours for that first panic-attack to subside, which was the catalyst for the taxi ride to take under four hours. The driver stepped on the gas every time he caught a glimpse of my bruised face and wild-eyed stare in his rear-view mirror. He was scared of me and that was good. It kept him from getting funny ideas about his fare. I was scared, too. I don't trust taxi-drivers and as a result I didn't sleep a wink. After I had been dropped off and the taxi was gone, I wanted to crawl into the ditch by the side of the road and take a nap. But exhausted as I was, I soldiered on and began the last stage of my return to Tepetapa by clambering up the steep embankment to the plateau.

I stay in my bent forward position until the feeling of panic abates, and I am breathing calmly again. I look up and recognise the desolation around me once more in its pallid colours. I drag my feet for another hour through the dust, sand, and pebbles of the plateau. The surrounding landscape bears not a single sign that would tell me where I am. I arrive at the bottom of a shallow and check my watch once more trying to figure out where the sun should be at this time of day in relation to the valley. It takes several attempts to determine that I have been walking in a general northerly direction parallel to the valley but slightly away from it. A sharp right turn corrects that mistake.

With the sun burning down on my back, I walk up an incline and suddenly through the glimmering heat I see the flickering image of the headframe's spinning wheels on the horizon to my left. It is like seeing an old, long lost friend. Strange emotions get the better of me. I fall into a trot and promptly trip over a rock. Hitting the ground brings me back to my senses. I get up and march on at a steady pace. Still, having a target in my blurry vision seems to give my feet wings. A short while later I reach the top of the narrow mountain path. I begin my descent down the rocky flank.

Once the width of the path permits it, I take a look down at the town. The plaza is teeming with people. It seems that everybody is up and about. The deep grumbling sound of diesel engines wafts up. The vehicles of the Motorised Cavalry are still parked in the mining compound in compliance with my "order". A couple of helmeted soldiers in combat gear are talking to three men in white

174

shirts at the entrance to the office building. Suddenly one of the soldiers waves his arms in a gesture of rejection and walks away. The other soldier follows him to an all-terrain vehicle with a red pennon attached to the aerial, steps on the running board, and shouts to the crowd while waving an arm in a broad sweeping gesture. The people clear a path, and the vehicles pull out.

Regardless of one's attitude towards the military and other uniformed forces, it is impressive to see the precision of a well-disciplined motorised company in motion, especially when it withdraws.

The vehicle with the red pennon leads the way and one with a blue pennon brings up the rear of the convoy while it moves like a giant centipede along the road leaving behind nothing but a huge cloud of exhaust fumes and dust and welcome peace and silence.

As quickly as my feet carry me, I rush down the path, past the church, along an alley to the plaza and up the stairs of the whorehouse. It is a quarter to four. Puffing and panting, I demand entry banging on the door. The taxi delivering flowers could have come and gone by now or could be arriving any minute. Time is of the essence more than before. Why doesn't anybody answer?

People gather around and watch me banging my fist on the steel door. Some of them mutter, some shake their heads in disapproval. What is the matter with those people? Don't they know what is at stake? The door opens and two miners carry a stretcher with a shroud-covered body out of the house. Mireilla stands in the vestibule. She looks devastated and bewildered. I reach out for her hand and greet her, but she doesn't respond. Her empty eyes are fixed on the stretcher that is carried away through the crowd.

"Cyanide," she mutters suddenly. "They used cyanide. You were right, Rigo. They didn't want to uphold law and order. They came here to maim and kill."

Tired as I am I don't grasp what she is talking about. I look to the plaza and see that quite a few men are sobbing.

Near the back of the office building, I see a convoy of directors' cars taking shape. A bus is being loaded with boxes of papers and computer terminals. The directors are trying to leave! And by the looks of it they aren't just going to leave for the day to be back the next morning. They are packing it in, giving up, and leaving us! That is a new ball game! They must be stopped!

I hand Mireilla my travel bag and jacket and say, "When a taxi delivers flowers for Lucy, you must tell Miguel that the action has to start immediately!"

She didn't grasp a word. Her looks tell me that she thinks I lost my mind. A taxi delivering flowers in Tepetapa? Get serious.

I storm down the stairs and across the plaza while yelling, "Shut the gate! Damn it, shut the gate, and keep it shut!"

Some men pull the gate shut. I shout they should follow me and jog to the mechanic's workshop. I break the rusty gate to the yard to get chains and steel pipes to lock and block the mine gate.

Watching the men carry away lengths of chain and pieces of pipe, I doubt that it would be enough to stop a three-tonne sport utility vehicle from crashing through the gate and creating a breach.

My eyes fall on my dusty and forlorn looking minivan beside the workshop. I open a door. The key sticks in the ignition. I move the gearshift to neutral and shout to the remaining men to give the van a push. Together we get the vehicle moving and roll it to the mine gate. Blocking it with the van's full length, there wouldn't be enough room for a bus or a car to squeeze through.

We wrap the chains around the posts of fence and frame of the gate, when a black truck on all terrain tires and a wide, rectangular snout speeds up to the gate. The powerful engine roars and its shrill horn demands room to pass. I almost flip my lid when one of the grey-clad smelter workers actually tries to remove the chains.

He turns to some men standing nearby and yells, "Heh! Move that rust bucket! The boss wants to leave!"

I knock the guy's hands off the chain. "Are you crazy? Why do you think we lock and barricade the gate? We have to prevent these guys from leaving!"

"But he is a boss, hombre," answers the man innocently. "He wants to leave. We can't stop him."

"And why can't we? Do we have to do whatever the boss asks us to do?" I shout.

"Yes, of course," is his prompt reply.

"And if that fat son of a bitch in the truck asks you to work for nothing and starve your children to death, you would do that, too, wouldn't you?" I bellow.

"Of course not!" is his angry reply.

Raising my open hands, I force my tone of voice down and ask him calmly, "So what do you think this strike is about?"

"Strike?" he asks surprised and gives me a close look. "You are the friend of that guy Miguel, aren't you? Now I recognise you. There's no strike. No more."

"No strike? What do you mean?" I demand to know.

He hesitates and clears his throat. "We've reached an agreement with the directors. Since they learned that Miguel is dying, they promised us a raise if we return to work peacefully. We'll get paid tomorrow. So, there's no more strike."

"Get paid tomorrow?" I am furious with the smelter worker's naïve faith. "Have you got eyes in your head? Can't you see the directors are leaving never to return? Have you got an agreement in writing? Of course not! And what do you mean Miguel is dying?"

Before he can answer, the driver of the black vehicle steps up to the gate. It is Blaskiewicz, a short man with a squat figure. He holds his right hand behind his back and shouts in English, "What the fuck's going on here, you dumb shit eaters, eh?"

Hearing him use the expletive referring to Mexicans, I am sorely tempted to sink to his level of gutter language.

Restraining myself, I reply, "A strike is going on, if you don't know by now! We are sick of your trickery, and we won't take it any more!"

"A strike?" he shouts. "You call this a strike, wetback? I've faced real men and broke their back! I won't be beat by a bunch of shit eaters! I know how to deal with a strike, you shit bag!"

"Of course, you do!" I yell back. "The dead miners and bankrupt mines you left behind in Canada and the United States bear ample testimony to your skills!"

He gapes at me for a brief moment before his narrow set eyes turn to slits of fury. His right hand comes up and points a large calibre automatic pistol at my head. Spittle sprays from the corners of his mouth as he screams, "Open the fuckin' gate and move that van, motherfucker! On the count of three or I'll fuckin' well blow your fuckin' head off!"

Seeing the gun, the men around me step back. I have to face Blaskiewicz alone and remember an old question and answer joke we used to tell in school so many years ago. Question: What do you call a psychopath with a loaded gun? Answer: Sir!

In line with that old joke, I look at him and say, "That's a very persuasive argument you hold in your hand, Sir! But I can't remove the chain alone, Sir! If you pull it through on your side, we should have it removed in no time, Sir!"

Impressed by being addressed respectfully, Blaskiewicz tucks the gun into the waistband in the small of his back and grabs the loop of the rusty chain on his side of the fence.

I reach for the long end of the heavy chain dangling to the ground and give it some slack. The instant both his hands clutch the chain I yank the loose ends with all my might and squash his fingers. I prop a foot up against the post. My pent-up rage and hatred give me the strength to hold the chain ends with one hand and still muster the dexterity to reach for a piece of rusty pipe jammed against the post. I poke it through the wire mesh and ram it into his gut. Already in pain from his squashed fingers, he begins to squeal like a pig being slaughtered. I ram the pipe again and again into his abdomen.

Blaskiewicz crawls on hands and knees leaving a trail of blood. I scream after him, "Die, you bastard!"

I wanted to kill and would have killed him if a heavy hand on my shoulder hadn't pulled me back. Diego yanks me around. "You better come with me," he says. "It concerns Miguel. My people will guard the gate. Come along, Rigo."

I tear myself out of Diego's grip, pick up another pipe lying on the ground, and ram it through the front grill of the black vehicle. The engine is still running. On the fourth or fifth jab, the pipe penetrates the radiator. A jet of boiling coolant shoots through the pipe and is followed by a stinking plume of steam. Some of the men standing nearby get it up their trouser legs and curse while Diego and I rush towards the whorehouse.

"A taxi delivered flowers for Lucy a minute ago," says Diego. "I can't make sense out of what Mireilla told me, except that you want to see Miguel."

"Yes! Where is he and how is he?" I ask.

Diego mutters, "He's not in good shape, I'm afraid. He's dying, I think. He may be dead by now."

As I run up the stairs, he stands back and asks, "Where are you going? Miguel is at home."

"I have to pick up my bag and jacket," I call out and disappear in the vestibule.

On an armchair next to the entrance lies a huge bouquet of flowers. I pick it up and rush upstairs.

Lucy looks terrible. Dark circles under her eyes give her face the appearance of a death mask. She manages a smile when she sees me approach with the colourful bunch of flowers. She is very weak and fails to prop herself up on her elbows. Tears stream down her face. I lay the fragrant flowers down next to her and fill a small bucket with water in the bathroom. When I return, she is asleep with a faint smile on her face. I place the bouquet in the bucket on her bedside table.

Lucy, the old fighter, who never accepted things the way they were unless they were right, looks at peace with the world. I leave her room also feeling peaceful and strangely confident.

Diego and I hurry along the alley towards Miguel's hovel. I express my hope that he will be alive and well, at least well enough to give me instructions how to pull off the strike.

"Strike?" Diego asks a bit out of breath. "More than one hundred people died in the past twenty-four hours, Rigo, including the Brigadier General and a lieutenant of the military. Are you sure, a strike is still on the books?"

"Oh yes, Diego," I reply. "All the bloodshed and death are reasons to finish what we started, so the innocent people won't have died in vain."

33

A BLACK RIBBON hangs from a rusty nail on the door. I knock and the door opens with a faint squeal to reveal the murky room. The windows are covered, and black drapes hang on the walls and over table and chairs. Diego and I enter, the front door snaps shut, and we stand in the dark. A rustle of cloth is heard behind us.

"Who are you? What do you want?" a ghostly, high-pitched voice asks.

Goose bumps run down my spine. Diego clutches my arm and holds onto it. He is shaking and quite audibly breaks wind. It is one of those long, drawn-out whistling efforts that turn into a staccato of explosions and never seem to have beginning or end. When the stench hits my nostrils like a soccer-boot, the ghostly voice speaks again but this time with a distinct nasal twang. So, it isn't a ghost. Ghosts don't hold their noses, do they?

"Diego, I told you not to eat the *tamales* for lunch!"

The front door is ripped open to disperse the stench. But the air in the alley, thick as it is with other foul odours, doesn't help much. The door slams shut, and a single naked light bulb is switched on. A figure dressed in a black cloak resembling a monk's habit towers over us. The face is hidden in the shadow until the hood is swept back. It is Miguel, evidently as fit as a fiddle and highly amused about our scared expressions.

"Miguel! Good to see you! How are you?" I greet him with chattering teeth.

"Just fine. Why do you ask?"

"Well, since I returned, I heard that you were close to death."

"Can I use your crapper?" mutters Diego.

"I thought you'd never ask," says Miguel and shoos him away. Turning to me, he says, "Close to death? You mustn't believe everything you hear."

"Oh, I know that," I agree. "But what's with the habit? All you need is a scythe to look like the grim reaper."

He chuckles. "Yes, that's the point. I want to look like the grim reaper. It's part of the show. I want to give the impression of having returned from death."

180

"Returned from death? So, you were…?"

"No," says Miguel and smiles. "I wasn't anywhere near death. But I had myself carried home on a stretcher pretending to be dying to bring out the fifth column in our midst."

"Fifth column? What do you mean? Traitors?"

"Yes, our workforce has been infiltrated by outsiders posing as workers."

"Goodness, but it doesn't surprise me. Is, uh, Diego…?"

"Oh no! He's a good guy and, uh, useful, you know?"

"Uh-huh… Where's Laura and the kids?"

"In a safe house. They joined the other foremen's wives and children and are guarded by six of Diego's men protecting them against the fifth column."

Waiting for Diego, Miguel brings me up to date on a few points that have me baffled. Shortly after midnight, the men, women, and children, who had been hit or grazed by rifle fire, began to die in the makeshift hospital.

The inspection of the bullets Mireilla extracted revealed that they were cyanide-tipped. Miguel cornered an unarmed commando who was searching for his wallet in the cantina and questioned him on pain of death about the bullets. The man swore on his mother's grave that the soldiers didn't know the type of ammunition they used.

The directors of the mine had supplied them with loaded magazines. The commandos had not planned to do much shooting anyway. Their orders had been to get the "subversive elements", that is, the foremen out of Tepetapa under cover of darkness, let them disappear and withdraw as quickly and quietly as they had come.

The operation was botched and both the officer in charge and the brigadier had been shot and killed by "friendly fire", the special commando assumed, the officer near his car and the brigadier at the window of the boardroom. Consequently, a sergeant major had taken command and ordered the troops not to move until the afternoon to cover up the officers' death as accidental shootings during a field exercise.

While Miguel was questioning the commando, a "worker committee" had sprung up. The men had been brought in by the military. They claimed that a strike was stupid, wanted to return to work and settle the dispute amenably. They left message at the makeshift hospital that the leader of the uprising had to surrender to the security forces. That's when Miguel decided to pretend to be mortally wounded and had himself carried home on a stretcher. He suspected that a fifth column, henchmen of the directors, had infiltrated the workforce and organised the "worker committee". Miguel wanted to drum the worms out of the woodwork.

With Laura's help, a bolt of black cloth, incense, and candles from the company store, he converted their abode into a house in mourning. It convinced the gossipy neighbours, who came around for obligatory lamentation, that Miguel, laid out on his "deathbed", was dying. Word spread quickly and after only an hour of play-acting, six guys dressed as smelter workers came by. Black rubber sneakers and manicured hands revealed that they were not part of the workforce. They wanted to take Miguel away but left him on his "deathbed" satisfied that he wouldn't see the end of the day.

Miguel knew that he had a formidable enemy in the "fifth column". The workforce had been split up and a good many men were persuaded to give up the strike. He had to come up with an idea that went beyond rhetoric, reasoning, even facts, to reunite the workforce into a strike force. He decided to play on the miners' superstitions with a disguise as the "grim reaper". Laura used all the black cloth that was left to make the cloak.

Miguel kept up the pretence of being close to death every time Diego turned up to check on him and had donned the cloak only the minute we arrived. No wonder Diego had lost control of his bowels when he saw the grim reaper that turned out to be Miguel who was suddenly up and about and fit and healthy as if cured by a miracle.

"So, what are we waiting for?" I ask.

"A taxi delivering flowers for Lucy."

"A taxi delivering flowers? That's already been here! Diego and I came here to tell you."

"It's already been here? Why didn't you say so?"

"I would have, but first there was you as the spook and then Diego…"

"Diego, are you finished?" calls Miguel. "We have to go!"

"There's no paper," comes the muffled response.

"Flush and use the brush," shouts Miguel. He grabs a roll of toilet paper from a shelf and hands it into the throne room.

182

"You better go and get changed," he says to me. "You have to wear overall, boots and helmet. All of us need to be dressed properly for the show."

Diego joins us and mutters, "Hombre, you almost scared me to death."

"Judging by the smell, I was sure you had died," says Miguel. "Listen, Diego, you have to tell the other foremen to come to the whorehouse immediately. And spread the word that every worker who is fit enough to walk must come to the plaza dressed in overall, boots and helmet. But don't say a word about my recovery. All right?"

Diego tips the peak of his helmet in a salute, nods, and leaves without another word.

I reach into my bag and take out Juanita's file. "This is for you, Miguel, from Juanita."

Miguel's face lights up. "So, the file does exist," he says and flips through it.

Excited he pulls out a document and invites me to read it. It is a bill of lading in Spanish, a shipping document for "The world's most advanced Animal Control System" from a supplier in California.

It itemises microchips suitable for injection, chip initialisation equipment, scanners, and computer software of a control system for seven thousand heads of cattle. I feel sick to my gut reading the document.

"I want to study the file a bit more," says Miguel. "You go on, Rigo, you have to get changed. I'll come by your hovel in a minute. Leave your bag with me. I'll bring it along."

He takes my smelly sneakers out of the bag, hands them to me with a disgusted look, and turns his attention to the file.

When I enter my home, I am shocked by the sight I see. My abode has been ransacked.

The bed is turned over, every plate and glass has been smashed, the little stove I never used is lying on its side and my few personal possessions are strewn over the floor. I am sure that Armandita had not gone on a rampage and left a trail of destruction in search of my wallet. There is no time to contemplate who could have done that and why. I have to get changed. I drop the sneakers, get undressed and into my overall when a hand is clamped over my face from behind.

A knee is pressed into my spine. I am arched over backwards. The blade of a knife is held to my throat. A second man in a grey overall steps in front of me and slams his fist into my gut.

"You son of a bitch!" he grunts. "Where are your identity papers? Your press pass?"

I throw up and splatter the guy in front of me with half-digested fruit, bread, and water squirting through the fingers pressed over my mouth. I collapse on the floor and curl up in a foetal position. My gut feels split wide open. I can hardly breathe, and I am kicked in the chest and the back to boot.

"Answer me, you bastard!" shouts the man in grey. "Who do you work for and where are your reports?"

My mouth full, I can't speak. I roll over, spit out the vomit and let out a tortured scream. The man with the knife squats over me and holds the tip of the gleaming blade close to my left eye ready to stab. He wears a black overall.

"I'm going to kill you and cut you to pieces, no matter if you talk or not," he growls. "But how much pain I'll inflict on you first will depend on what you say. We know you're a journalist. So, who is your employer?"

"I'm not a journalist," I yell and receive a kick in the back of my head. It rams my face into the blade that strikes the bone under my eye. It crunches when the knife is withdrawn. I clasp the wound with my hands and scream in fear of having lost an eye.

"Of course, you are!" shouts the man with the knife.

My mind is churning over at lightning speed. What can I tell these guys to spare my life? It doesn't matter. They won't believe one word. I shake my head and howl, "I'll tell you what I am."

Turning around, I sit up and have a look at the two men. I have never seen them before. They wear black sneakers identical to mine. I reach for one of my smelly rubber shoes and hold it up.

"You've just tried to kill one of your own, you dumb bastards!" I scream at the top of my lungs.

Stunned the two men stare at the stinking sneaker and turn pale. Time ticks away as they look at each other. The guy in black crouches in front of me and reaches for my shoulder.

"All right. What's the password?" he inquires.

He holds his knife to my throat when we hear the sound of dragging feet in the alley. The door to my hovel is kicked open. The hooded figure of Miguel enters. The man in black looks up

184

and lunges. His knife aims straight for Miguel's heart and gets stuck. Miguel gives the man a severe blow in the face. The man goes flying into the doorframe and tumbles out of the house. He crashes onto the uneven plates of pumice that pave the alley. The knife remains stuck in Miguel's chest. The second man pulls a knife from his sleeve and crouches down to pounce. Miguel gives him a swift kick in the crotch, punches his lights out, and throws him out into the alley. The door slams shut.

"Why are these bastards after you?" Miguel asks.

Seeing the knife stuck in his chest, I can't answer and just point at it. He looks down and pulls it out.

"I hadn't noticed," he says. "How did that get there?"

He opens his cloak and inspects the deep gash in my bag that is hanging on his chest from its strap around his neck. Juanita's thick file had absorbed the thrust of the blade and saved Miguel's life. He drops the knife into the bag and closes his monk's habit.

"Put on your boots and helmet," he says calmly while he picks up my last clean shirt, tears it to shreds, and makes a compress for the wound under my eye.

It takes me a minute to recover from the shock of the assault and Miguel's narrow escape. Still shaking, I put on boots and helmet.

When I am ready, Miguel leans heavily on me. I stagger out of the house under his weight with his arm slung around my neck.

34

THE ACT of a miner dragging a limp figure swathed in black cloth to the whorehouse has the intended impact on the crowd. My distorted and bloody face contributes to the onlookers' awe if not respect as we make our way past the cantina. Men and women step back and gawk, close ranks and follow us. Some men bend down attempting to catch a glimpse of the limp figure's face hidden in the habit's hood. Nobody dares to touch us or lend a helping hand. We climb up the stairs. The door is opened. Miguel and I enter the vestibule. The door slams shut. Seventeen foremen, Diego, Mireilla, and most of Lucy's girls and boys await us.

Miguel straightens up. He sweeps back the hood. The men and women gasp at the sight of black circles under his eyes and deep lines down his cheeks.

Vanessa, who welcomes me like an old friend with a kiss and a hug and clings to my shoulder, recognises the crude make-up that exudes the distinct smell of shoe polish. She gives it a work over with tissue paper and makes Miguel's face look gaunt and pale. Everybody applauds her fine work, and she takes a bow. Miguel hands me my bag after he has taken out the knife, two bullets, and some documents.

I go to an adjacent room where Mireilla cleans and clamps the wound under my eye. She looks ready to fall asleep, and I think that's what she does when we sit down on a sofa, and she leans against me. I hear Miguel clap his hands to get everybody's attention.

"Please, listen to me." The men and women fall silent. "The last round of our fight has begun. The media is on its way here with cameras, reporters, photographers, and journalists. Those men and women are coming here expecting a sensation. That's what they were promised, that's what we are going to deliver. But I must stress that the media types are neither on our side nor our friends. Bluntly put, they are useful idiots who will report our struggle to the nation as an aside to sensational images if, and only if they consider our show worthwhile reporting. It means that our show will have to be sensational for them to report it. You may well ask what we could possibly do the media would consider a sensation. The answer is simple. It is more than a thousand men participating in a non-violent and, uh… sensational show by doing exactly what I will do. It is crucial that every man partakes, that every man responds to what I say and follows my example. Doing the show all by myself would amount to the act of an intermission clown. A thousand men doing what I do will be the sensation! That's why you, the foremen, must admonish every man of your crew to participate! Do you have any questions?".

"Yes," says one of the foremen. "Can you guarantee that no more people will get hurt or killed?"

"No, I can't," replies Miguel forcefully. "You can! It is every man's participation in the show that will turn the television cameras on and give the media reason to report our action nationwide. That's our only guarantee to stop the guards from committing further atrocities. Not one of the guards will dare to raise his truncheon or level his gun at us while his mug is shown to millions of television viewers across Mexico."

Some grumbling is heard in response to Miguel's brash response and more men want to ask questions. But he cuts them off, claps his hands, and shouts to get going.

It is time for me to go, too. I lay Mireilla down on the sofa and put her feet up. She looks startled and asks, "What are you doing? What's the matter?"

"It's time for you to take a rest," I say. "As soon as I get back, I will tuck you in and sing you to sleep."

She gives me a doubtful look but smiles vaguely. "That's sweet of you," she mumbles with a tired voice, "but don't expect me to wait up for you."

"I won't," I assure her. While I am still stowing my bag under the sofa for safekeeping, she is already fast asleep snoring softly.

I trot after the group of foremen to the mine gate. Along the way the crowd steps back gaping at the hooded figure in black. Men and women cross themselves seeing the grim reaper rush past. It is twenty minutes to six o'clock and not a minute too late. The black car has been towed away and an even bigger red vehicle stands in its place.

Security guards are amassed behind the gate and fence, on the watchtower, and the roofs of the guardhouse and pay-office building. Heavily armed with assault rifles, handguns and riot-truncheons, the guards look ready to use each weapon for its intended purpose.

Ignoring the looming threat of firearms and truncheons, Miguel gathers the seventeen foremen and Diego at my van for a brief discussion. When the foremen and Diego leave, Miguel stands alone at the gate. He gives individual guards the heebie-jeebies by simply pointing a finger in a threatening manner at one or another. The foremen meanwhile brief their men and organise the crowd by bringing the men forward and asking the women and children to step well back.

The chains that keep the gate closed have been securely fastened. One of the directors, the reddish blonde, empty-suit Henderson, whose only distinguishing mark are his fisheyes behind metal rimmed granny glasses, has a dolly with two bottles of acetylene gas and oxygen and a cutting torch pushed to the gate. A guard fumbles with the torch and tries to light it. Henderson stares angrily at the miners and mill and smelter workers linking arms in a semi-circle from end to end of the gate.

The men began to chant, "They won't get through! They won't get through! They won't get through!"

Miguel spins around with raised hands and the crowd falls silent. He confronts Henderson and sweeps back the hood. Terrified the guard drops the cutting torch and Henderson gawks at Miguel with bulging eyes.

"You…?" is all he manages to say.

"Yes, it's me again!" bellows Miguel and holds up the knife and two bullets. "I've survived your cyanide bullets and your dumdum bullets! I've survived your knife attacks! I'm back from the dead!"

A roar of support rises from a thousand throats. It has a frightening as well as an uplifting ring to it.

"You have lost the war you wage against us!" continues Miguel. "Your reign of terror, oppression, and exploitation is over! We are willing to go back to work only on condition of you meeting our demands!"

"What demands?" Henderson asks.

Miguel holds up a legal-size sheet of paper, folds it lengthwise, and pushes it through the wire mesh of the gate. Henderson snatches the paper and mutters to the new officer of the guards who responds by shouting an order.

The guards raise their rifles and release the safety catches. Henderson looks surprised when neither Miguel nor any of the mineworkers flinch at the sight of the guns. He snaps the page open and briefly glances at it.

He folds the paper with a derisive look and says, "I can't respond to these demands. That's not within the scope of my defined activities."

Miguel shrugs as if he had expected nothing less. He points to the directors standing at the corner of the administration building and says, "You have fifteen minutes to give us your reply!"

Miguel meets with the other foremen in front of the van. He gives them instructions and they return to their crews. Banners are unfurled and chants are heard demanding fair wages, a safe workplace, and liberty. As time runs out, the tension mounts. The directors call the officer. He receives his orders and returns with the list of demands in his hand. Miguel faces the officer. The crowd falls silent.

"I have received instructions to deliver the directors' response," says the officer and laughs. He holds up the list of demands, tears it to shreds, and flings it through the wire mesh at Miguel. "This is their response, you charlatan! Now open up the gate and get that human trash out of the way or I will order my men to open fire!"

"You will have to kill every man, woman and child," responds Miguel calmly. "We are not going to move!"

"Oh yes, you will!" shouts the officer. "Just watch them run!"

On his command, the guards raise their rifles and fire over the heads of the men. None of them move. If they are frozen in fear or emboldened with courage is impossible to say. Miguel looks around, shrugs, and watches the officer shout another command. The guards level their guns at the crowd. The miners still don't move. The cars in the driveway of the mining compound are started. It is five minutes past six o'clock. Miguel looks over the crowd to his left down the road. A broad grin on his face, he opens the driver's door of the van and climbs onto the roof. Looking like a biblical figure in his black gown, he clears his throat and is ready to speak.

The first cars and trucks of the media convoy arrive at high speed. Emblazoned with television station logos and the slogans, "News Live!", "All the News - All Day!" and "News Now!" they represent several television channels and networks. Seeing what looks like a black monk on top of the van and the mining compound bristling with uniformed guards pointing assault rifles at him and the crowd, the cameramen jump out of the vehicles, video cameras rolling, and lights blazing.

"Men, women and children of Tepetapa, fellow *Jodidos*!" hollers Miguel from his raised position. "Our demand for a settlement of this dispute - it has been rejected! Our request for fairness, liberty, and justice - it is considered unreasonable! Our request for basic health care and medical treatment for families and children - it is considered outrageous! A school for our children? Denied! A playground for our children? Denied! Fair wages to feed your families and children? Denied! A safe workplace? Denied! The right to move freely within this great country, our beloved Mexico? Denied! But we will claim this right! One - for - all - and - all - for - one!"

The crowd becomes more excited every time Miguel shouts "Denied!" Men and women join him and sound like a giant chorus repeating the word and following the gestures of his arms. When his fists appear to break a chain while he shouts, "One for all and all for one," the plaza is awash in a swell of jubilation.

Hectic preparations for broadcasting live action are under way as gofers and assistants rush around and communicate via headsets with their mobile control studios.

The guards show first signs of nervousness at the sight of the media cars and trucks. Against the officer's orders, they lower their rifles when television transmission antennas are raised and a hydraulic platform on a truck slowly hoists a complete set of lights, cameras, microphones, and personnel as well as the well-known commentator Adolfo Medina and his guest, Juanita, skywards.

The guards put their guns away when a commentator from a competing network moves into position at the gate. It is Miranda Azaveda de la Hoya, the famous machine-gun-mouth with her voluminous blonde hairdo and a tight fitting, low cut black dress. Backed up by cameras aimed at the guards, Miranda demands and is denied entry to the mine for an interview with the directors. She moves back and positions herself to have Miguel on top of the van and the armed guards as a backdrop. She questions the men around her while Adolfo interviews Juanita high above the crowd.

190

Miguel observes the melee of people below him calmly. With several cameras focusing in on him, he opens his robe, smiles inscrutably, and drops the robe slowly behind him.

Clad in a miner's overall, boots, and helmet, he continues his speech.

"Men, women, and children of Tepetapa, fellow *Jodidos*! Today is the day for us to reclaim our lives! No more denials of our basic rights! No more denials of our dignity and freedom! No more hardship and misery and poverty in return for all our hard work! No more guns and truncheons and bloodshed in response to our demands for fairness! No more oppression and killing!"

"No more!" roar the men and women.

"We claim the right to receive fair wages for our work! We claim the right to a safe workplace! We claim the right to come and go as we please! We claim the right to representation of workers and community! We - claim - these - rights!"

"We - claim - these - rights!" echoes the crowd.

"We were ruled by fear to this day! The fear of death underground! The fear of your children starving to death! The fear of the directors' tyranny! The fear of the guards' brutality and corruption! The fear of losing our jobs! But I ask you - has anyone of us here lost his job? No!"

"No!" is the unified response.

"But doesn't every one of us know of a lost husband or a lost father or a lost son who was killed on the job? Yes!"

"Yes!" roars the crowd.

"The killing of husbands and fathers and sons must stop! We demand a safe workplace! We demand an end to oppression and exploitation! We demand our rights!"

"We demand our rights!" shout the men.

"But our rights are denied in Tepetapa!" continues Miguel with his voice rising slowly back to a thunderous bellow. "We will have to take our case to the people of Mexico! We will march to the city of Mexico in our quest for fairness and justice and a safe workplace! Because here we get nothing! What do we get here?"

"Nothing!" answers the crowd.

"And what do we have here?"

"Nothing!"

"And what do we own here?"

"Nothing!"

Miguel tugs at his overalls and thunders, "Do we own even these stinking overalls?"

"No!" roar the men.

"Then let us leave them right here where they belong!"

Miguel begins to unbutton his overall to the rhythm of his speech and takes it off slowly. And a thousand miners and mill and smelter workers follow suit.

"We don't need overalls - on our march to Mexico - to obtain fairness - justice - and a safe workplace! - We will show the world - what we own - and receive - in return - for our hard work! - Absolutely - nothing!"

And with that his overall goes flying over the gate and drapes itself around the head of a guard.

Miguel stands stark naked, dressed only in boots and miner's helmet, on top of my van while he raises a fist in a salute to the crowd.

A thousand miners and mill and smelter workers follow his example. A thousand overalls fly up in the air. A thousand men stand stark naked wearing only heavy boots and helmets.

A thousand men laugh and cheer to the accompaniment of shrieks and whoops of the women forming the large outer circle.

Juanita has to hold back Adolfo who almost falls off the platform gawking at all that male nudity below him.

Miranda, the assertive and loud commentator, who has never been stuck for an answer or a sharp retort, is speechless.

Standing amidst the mass of male nudity, she stares up at Miguel. She tugs down the hem of her skirt and covers her cleavage with a hand.

Laughter shakes the men as they show off their potbellies and flat bellies, square shoulders and sagging shoulders, sunken chests and broad chests, skinny legs and fat legs, dimpled arses and wrinkled arses to the cameras. And the whole range of penises and scrotums shows how similar we are in all our differences.

Miranda's eyes bulge when Felipe, the down-on-his-luck actor, takes off his helmet, covers his private parts with it, and raises both hands with the helmet staying in place. He puckers up and takes a couple of steps towards her ready for a kiss and a cuddle.

It is an amazing illusion he creates with a string of nylon cord tied around his hips to hold his helmet.

192

"Onward to Mexico!" shouts Miguel and clambers down from the van. He grabs the broomstick of a banner and gives orders to march in a formation of four men abreast.

The camera operators go stir-crazy. They flutter about taking and transmitting live pictures of a thousand stark naked men in heavy boots and safety helmets.

Adolfo demands to lower the platform. When he stands among the naked men, he can't get out a sensible word for all his excitement. He joins Miranda who is overcome by fits of hysterical laughter pointing a shaking finger at Felipe and others who follow his example.

Other reporters, earnest looking juniors, take over the broadcast until the two chief commentators regain their composure.

Miguel is swarmed and disappears among microphones on booms and cameras. He gives an impromptu press conference reiterating our demand for fair wages plus back pay, compensation for the families and dependants of all the miners killed on the job, a school for the children, and the freedom to come and go as we please. Firmly he answers the questions and assures the reporters that we would march all the way to the city of Mexico, if necessary, to draw attention to the way the gringo owners exploit Mexican miners.

The questions and answers are transmitted to the crowd by loudspeaker. The response is applause and roars of approval.

At last Miguel repeats his order of onward to the city of Mexico and the long column of naked men slowly snakes its way towards the open road.

When Felipe passes the company store, winking and blowing kisses, a couple of women faint at the sight of his helmet that is evidently suspended by virility. Lucy's girls rush to the side of the road and cheer him on with lewd comments. Ismelda is wetting herself laughing.

A radio reporter holding a microphone approaches me. Marching alongside, he describes my nakedness in lurid detail as well as my badly bruised and patched up face.

"Would you mind answering a few questions, Sir?" he asks.

"Feel free to ask," I encourage him.

"Are these terrible injuries to your face the result of a work accident, the unsafe work conditions?"

"No, they were inflicted by the security guards of this company."

"You mean to say, you've had violent confrontations?"

"Yes, indeed. In response to our demands for fairness, justice, and liberty the special forces of the Motorised Cavalry were bribed to come here. They killed hundreds of my colleagues with cyanide tipped bullets and the rest of us were roughed up by the guards who were set upon us by the gringo directors."

"Gringo directors?"

"Yes, North Americans from the USA and Canada who claim to own the mine."

"Do I understand you correctly? They claim to own the mine, in other words, they don't own it?"

"That is correct. They don't own it."

"Then who owns the mine?"

"An impoverished Mexican family owns it, a family that has been defrauded of millions of dollars through a scheme set up and agreed upon by the gringo directors and the governor of this state."

He wants to ask something else but is distracted by cars and trucks with television crews passing us. The reporter signs off and rushes to the head of the marching column where Miranda gets out of a car, marches alongside Miguel, and interviews him.

More than a dozen cameras are set up along the road and on trucks to capture the spectacle from every possible angle. In the far distance near the broken gate, a convoy of television vans blocks the road getting ready to accompany us out of the valley.

We are only couple of kilometres down the road, when four large vehicles with the directors inside drive by at high speed on the narrow strip of dirt between the mine fence and the road. It looks as if the directors are trying to get away. The convoy of television vans near the broken gate prevents their escape.

Our march comes to a standstill, and I push my way to the front. By the time I get close enough to the vehicles to hear the verbal exchange, the directors have already passed denials and false claims to the media via megaphone through a slot in the tinted side windows of the big red car. They call us extremists and anarchists who walked away from the negotiating table and caused bloody mayhem. Furthermore, the voice adds, the outrageous claim made by one miner during a radio interview that the owner of the mine is an impoverished Mexican family is a bold

194

lie. It will have severe repercussions for the miner once he has been identified.

It is impossible to see the speaker with the megaphone or the other occupants of the four cars. The windscreens are covered on the inside with sun reflectors. The side and rear windows are darkly tinted. The hidden faces make the reporters and journalists rather suspicious. It is brought to a head when Adolfo asks why the directors wouldn't speak on camera if everything they have done is clean cut and above board. After a prolonged silence, the mealy-mouthed reply cites the privacy of the directors in the first place and in the second, that the demonstration wasn't necessary to resolve the dispute. The miners need only to return to the negotiating table, come to a final agreement, and sign a contract.

Miranda and cameras turn to Miguel to capture his response.

"We have never had negotiations with the directors of this mine," says Miguel. "Our demands for fair wages and conditions were answered with the brutal use of guns and truncheons for the past four years. We, the miners, never reneged on commitments or mutually agreed arrangements. The directors did! In response to our request and their commitment to negotiate a settlement of the present dispute, the directors called in the Motorised Cavalry that maimed and killed innocent people. The directors are the anarchists and terrorists! They know our demands. They are not negotiable any longer. The directors must sign the list of demands as proof of their recognition of our legitimate claims and their agreement to meet them. We will accept nothing less!"

"Where is it then, this famous list of demands?" interjects the jarring megaphone voice and laughs triumphantly. "If you can produce it right now, we'll sign it right here!"

Before the megaphone is shut off, an exasperated shout is heard barking in English, "Are you fucking crazy?"

It is Miguel's turn to laugh. He has the directors at the point of no return where he wanted them to be all along. Unless an editor cuts the incident from the live broadcast, millions of Mexicans will have witnessed the directors' irrefutable commitment to sign the list and meet our demands.

Miguel bends down and moons the guys in the cars while he pulls several folded copies of the handwritten list of demands out of the shaft of his boot. He unfolds four sheets of paper and holds one copy flat against a window of the nearest car for the television cameras and photographers to record it. Then he passes one copy each through the slot of the windows into the four cars.

It takes more than twenty minutes to get the copies signed by all twelve directors. But time doesn't matter any longer. We have achieved what we set out to accomplish.

Unarmed and naked the mineworkers have succeeded in less than two hours where armed and violent struggles, clashes, and confrontations had failed to yield results in almost five years. Or so we think at that moment.

Upon closer examination of the list of demands, I search for the signature of Doctor Gomez. It is the only one that is familiar to me from the medical report he wrote and signed after my accident. I can't find it among the squiggles that are supposedly the directors' signatures. I point it out to Miguel and tell him that the list is useless because the gringos can claim that they didn't sign it.

Miguel is furious and pulls on a doorhandle to open the car in front of him. The door is locked, and malicious laughter can be heard from inside the vehicle. Miguel holds the four copies of our demands up to TV-cameras and explains that the squiggles are not the directors' signatures. Then he shreds the papers to the great bewilderment of the men around him. He explains to them once more what he told on camera and rage takes over.

Diego and others knock on the windows of the cars and try to break them with their bare fists. Their demand to come out of the vehicles is ignored by the directors who roar the cars' engines in response thus indicating that they still try to get away.

Hector and several guys of his crew gather around the cars. Some of them climb up on the hoods. They urinate into every air intake they can find and douse the cars. The air conditioning and ventilation systems going at full tilt fill the cars with the fusty smell of kidney-filtered coffee, beer, and tequila. When that doesn't force the coughing, choking, and cursing directors out into the open, the utterly frustrated and angry Francisco, the old guy from Coahuila, picks up a rock and smashes a side window of the red utility vehicle. That gets the directors going. As if on command they jump out of the cars and run along the fence trying to get away on foot.

Some of the younger, fit miners and smelter workers catch them before they even reach the media vans. They are dragged

196

back and offered to Miranda, Adolfo, and all the other reporters for impromptu interviews. The attempts to get a statement out of them, reveals to the viewing public that only two of them speak Spanish. The investigation of their identity papers shows that all of them are illegal aliens.

Triumphantly we march them back to an uproarious welcome on the plaza of Tepetapa. We lock them up in a basement room of the administration building and will keep them for all intents and purposes as prisoners until all papers have been signed, every miner, mill and smelter worker has been paid, the compensation demanded for the families of the killed miners has been received, and the continuing operation of the mine is assured.

Disarming the guards and the men of the fifth column and chasing them out of town and valley takes another couple of hours, but all in all our struggle is over in less than five hours.

Our victory celebration lasts a little while longer.

35

THE FOLLOWING DAY our celebratory mood is stopped dead in its tracks when we learn that Lucy passed away in the hour of our greatest triumph. The ricochet bullet I had removed from her thigh was cyanide tipped. A trace of the poison had been enough to kill her slowly.

She is given a grand funeral. Everybody chips in to buy a casket and a funeral service to embalms her remains. During the wake a couple of days later a colourful congregation passes by her coffin that is covered with flowers to celebrate the memory of her.

Everything would have been well and fitting for Lucy's final farewell if the resident priest had not refused to say Mass for Lucy and wouldn't even bless her soul. That is reason for the remarkable event of stripping him of his cassock and chasing him in his pink boxer shorts down the road and out of the valley.

We search every village and town in a fifty-kilometre radius until we find a young cleric in the village of Cañas who is happy to perform the funeral Mass. He refers to Lucy simply as "mother of Tepetapa". Either he had misunderstood us or is loath to call her a madam. It doesn't bother us in the least. On the contrary, it suits everyone who had known her just fine. Lucy had been a mother figure to her "girls and boys" and to more than one of us. Upon the young cleric's suggestion her coffin is placed in the sepulchre next to the remains of the two clergymen who passed away so many years ago.

After the funeral and once it sinks in that he is alone in this world, Juanita has a nervous breakdown. The whole community is concerned and wants to help him since he contributed crucially to the success of our uprising. We celebrate him and cheer him as our saviour, but nothing can soothe his mind and a week later he is carried off in a straitjacket to be hospitalised in a sanatorium. That rings in the end of the whorehouse. The girls and the one remaining boy, Armandita, are leaving Tepetapa.

In the meantime, we have a problem with the directors. They refuse to budge, sign an agreement, and hand over the funds we demand. It is a complicated situation because we can't find the records of their financial transactions. The computer broke down in the deluge of the sprinkler system and most of the administrative staff who could have helped us have quit and won't come back to work. Whatever cash reserves we find in the various offices and safes, is barely enough to pay everyone their newly agreed wages for two weeks. Not even Arbuckle's funds that Laura hands back to the company coffers are sufficient to pay for a computer repair to get the machine back into operation and give us access to the financial records.

Benigno, the explosives expert, has an idea to keep the directors' noses to the grindstone. We are more than a little wary of his plan to "persuade" them to return the company profits from offshore bank accounts. It sounds almost as explosive as the charges he placed underground in the mine. But before we know it, he has wired up the directors' cars with sticks of dynamite. Quite "unintentionally" he leaves the door to their basement room unlocked to see what they would do. As expected, they sneak outside where foul-mouth Blaskiewicz sees their cars lined up behind the building. He has his last laugh when he spots the ignition keys in the lock, starts a car, and blows himself to smithereens. The remaining eleven directors return in haste to the basement room yet are still unwilling to cooperate with us.

As a final measure Benigno has a bundle of sticks of dynamite with a remote-controlled timer dangling from the ceiling to keep the directors focused. The flashing red digits of the timer show precisely how much time they have left to meet our deadlines.

In less than twenty-four hours we receive signed agreements and detailed instructions for the transfer of millions of dollars from accounts in the Cayman Islands, British Virgin Islands, and Panama to a company account we open with a bank in Mexico.

As soon as we can lay our hands on the money, we call some computer technicians to have a look at the system. They see right away that most of the hardware is busted and deliver and install needed replacements.

Felipe, stage actor with the wonderful ability of using his impressive vocabulary to formulate remarkably convoluted, meaningless, and often contradictory phrases, is instrumental in "motivating" the remaining administrative employees to reactivate the electronic files and records. After a haircut, shave, and manicure in Ismelda's salon and the selection of a suit, shirt, tie, and squeaky shoes from the whorehouse stockroom, he looks and sounds like a greased government inspector strutting around like a peacock. He has the paper-shufflers and bean counters work overtime by simply issuing the thinly veiled threat of auditing their personal tax records if they don't comply.

Within three days the computer system is up and running again and provides the information we need to calculate the operating costs of the mine and the money owed to each employee and the families of miners killed on the job.

The computer records also help to untangle the control system. We inform the Californian supplier of "The World's most advanced Animal Control System" of the misuse of their hardware. They sent a team of medics to remove the microchips from the necks of thousands of men, women, and children.

Finally, it is time to contemplate what to do with the directors. We could hand them over to the authorities as illegal aliens, but the majority of mine workers votes in favour of shunting the gringos into Texas. We dress them up in the style of Mexican farm labourers, stuff them bound and gagged into the luggage compartment of a company bus and cart them to the banks of the Rio Grande west of Piedras Negras. There we chase them across the river without any identity papers. The last we see of them is their arrest by border guards. On the way back to Tepetapa it causes us endless amusement to figure out what these bedraggled gringos might have told the guards and what their reaction could have been. But we really don't care. We have got rid of a pest and it feels good.

Everybody receives a big pay cheque, and we could return to work. But so many of our colleagues are damaged from the years of maltreatment and abuse in Tepetapa that they prefer to leave with their pay and try to build a new life somewhere else. After a few days only a skeleton crew is left, barely enough to dig for ore on two levels and keep the mill and smelter running.

It is also the appropriate time for me to think of leaving this forsaken place. I ask Vicente the machinist and mechanic to do me the personal favour of repairing my van. He agrees and overhauls engine, transmission, exhaust system, brakes, and alignment. After I take the car for a spin, I am convinced that it runs better than the day I drove it out of the showroom. That means I can pack it in and leave but the question is where I should

200

go. My parents passed away some years ago and there is nobody waiting for me anywhere. I don't have a place to call home any more. I intend to think about my future over a lunchtime meal in the cantina.

I settle down with a beer when I see Mireilla walk by. She gives me a furtive glance, seems to hesitate for a moment, and then hurries away.

She has quit her job and it is time for her to leave as well. Perhaps she wanted to say good-bye and is hesitant to talk to me. I know she is quite miffed because I had left her to sleep for eighteen hours straight on a sofa in a whorehouse. She avoids me also because I was getting along too well with Vanessa and some of the other girls in that establishment. But they have left already. So, what is Mireilla's problem? I should make a move and talk to her. But after all, I am a burnt child and the last thing I need in my life is to be rejected by a woman I have come to like and respect. I am quite prepared to cut my losses and leave this place alone.

These thoughts are circling in my mind while I am tucking into my meal of burritos. I am still wondering what I should do when Laura turns up, sits down at my table, and stares at me.

"Do you remember," she begins quietly, "some time ago I said that one day you will meet a woman who deserves you?"

"Yes," I answer with an accommodating grin.

"Well, I have changed my mind," she says very sharply. "I don't think you would deserve her! You wouldn't recognise her if she bit you in the arse!"

She gets up angrily, slams the chair under the table, and struts away. Stunned I look after her. What was that all about?

When I turn my head, Mireilla stands a little distance away, sad and abandoned, and draws lines in the dirt with the tip of her shoe. I get up slowly and walk towards her with wobbling knees.

And the rest, as the saying goes, is history.

36

THE SHADY PORCH on the first floor of the old house in Irapuato is my favourite place to relax, to think, and to work. It is a quiet and peaceful spot. Occasionally I hear my wife Mireilla pottering in the kitchen making one of her tasty and wonderful meals for us as well as our guests we have ever so often. Also, the sporadic squeals of our son Juan Miguel remind me that I have a proper family now.

After only two days of courtship in Tepetapa, Mireilla and I decided to throw our lot together and leave for greener pastures. When we arrived in Guanajuato, her hometown and state of the same name, she was informed by her family lawyer that she had inherited the house in Irapuato from an uncle who had recently passed away. It took a lot of elbow grease and a horde of craftsmen to renovate it and make it inhabitable. Now it is the oasis we had imagined it to be when we first saw it.

Irapuato is a small and very picturesque town but there is practically no work to be had for a copywriter. Consequently, I took a course for industrial design at the local college and started to create "*Utensilios para nuevos chilangos*" - that are "Useful utensils for newly arrived residents in the City of Mexico". "*Chilango*" is the nickname for residents of our capital city and the butt of jokes in the rest of the country.

The first "useful" item I designed was a coffee mug with the handle on the inside. It was followed by a teapot with the spout above the handle on the same side and a pair of boots with the heel at the front. I have these articles manufactured in Irapuato and they are sold all over the country to be given as gifts to anyone leaving his community to seek his fortune in the metropolis. We are doing all right on my income, but Mireilla still took on the part time job of community nurse. It fulfils her, gets her out of the house, and makes our family a really contributing factor to the inhabitants of our town.

While I am sitting in my favourite spot and think of other crazy utensils to design, I look down into the garden. I see the gnarled apricot tree and wonder if its branches are strong enough to hold a swing for our son. That should be investigated seriously, I decide and get up when suddenly I hear the all too familiar sound of a basso profundo voice extending greetings to Mireilla downstairs.

I rush downstairs to welcome Miguel, Laura, and their kids Gabriel, Pilar, and Benito. They have come to visit us on their way to Nocupétaro, a small mountain village in Michoacán, where they will settle in accordance with Laura's wishes.

Coincidentally, Nocupétaro is the birthplace of Miguel's ancestor, General Juan Nepomuceno Almonte.

How's that for coming full circle?

The idea of putting a swing into the apricot tree has to be realised now. We can't expect the three kids to sit still in the house while the adults reminisce.

With Miguel's help a strong enough branch is found and in no time a swing is installed. Miguel and I retire to my favourite spot to watch the kids play in the garden and listen to Mireilla and Laura chatting and laughing while they prepare dinner in the kitchen.

Miguel tells me about the developments in Tepetapa. The "fifteen minutes of fame" had lasted less than a week. Gorier, sexier, more outrageous events pushed us off the television screens and front pages when the miners didn't strut around in the buff any longer and wouldn't take off their overalls in public. Titillation is the media's keyword by which it lives and survives. Substance means nothing and "powerful image" means everything. The television cameras and reporters were long gone by the time the dispute had been settled.

Today, just over a year after the event, the Tepetapa incident is all but forgotten and the mine has essentially ceased to exist. Miguel and his family were some of the last people to leave after an earth tremor caused the collapse of three levels, opened huge sinkholes, and swallowed half the administration building. Sadly, there were also the deaths of another forty miners to mourn. It was time to wind down the business and get out while it was still possible.

Miguel had escaped certain death because he had quit his job for health reasons a few days before the disaster struck. He suffers from 'white hand', the dreaded affliction of numbness and loss of feeling due to ruptured capillaries from the constant vibration of the eighty-kilogram drill he handled for years.

Out of the blue, I put a question to Miguel that had been in the back of my mind since our uprising.

"Whatever gave you the idea, Miguel, to have a thousand men strip off their overalls in public and march naked down the road?"

His initial response is a smile and a chuckle that seems to pose the question, 'What took you so long to ask?' He looks into the distance for a moment before he launches into a monologue, one of his all-encompassing explanations that are so familiar to me.

During his chat in the whorehouse after the battle with the special commandos, Miguel got to know Ismelda and Juanita as quite normal people who struggled for survival just like anybody else. The difference had been their upbringing.

His childhood, despite the material shortcomings of a low-income working-class home, had been a time of love and encouragement for him. In contrast, it had been living hell for Ismelda and Juanita who had to flee the depravity and raw brutality of their relatives at a young age and ended up on the streets in the clutches of prostitution.

Miguel spent his formative years learning to be a miner while Ismelda and Juanita learned to live with hypocrisy, lies, and deceit. As a result, their views of society were naturally quite different. While Miguel fought for respect and recognition, these aspects never even entered Ismelda and Juanita's fight for survival. They had been used and abused by the same people who publicly disparaged them as human garbage. They had learned to take advantage of the disparity of their clients' public outcries and private behaviour. They knew their clients' biggest fear was the public exposure to ridicule, a most powerful weapon.

Miguel listened attentively to Ismelda and Juanita and came to appreciate their very simple but always quirky points of view. Ultimately, it came as no surprise, and he knew what was implied when Juanita suggested that the mineworkers had to show the world that they had nothing to lose - absolutely nothing - and thus expose the mine's directors to public ridicule!

Although Miguel liked the idea, he had his qualms about persuading a thousand men to strip down to boots and helmets and face heavily armed guards in the nude, utterly vulnerable and without defences. He asked if ridicule could be so powerful and defensive to protect them against bullets and pernicious riot truncheons. Juanita assured him that ridicule is indeed as powerful

204

if not more so than violent uprisings when it is displayed publicly on nationwide TV on as many channels and networks as possible. He convinced Miguel further that he could blackmail the media into coming to Tepetapa and broadcast the nude uprising nationwide when he mentioned the names of his former clients, publicly known media types and politicians. But it was Juanita's question of what Miguel and the mineworkers had to lose that tipped the scales. And so, the action had taken its course.

The fortunate outcome of our uprising, which hadn't been certain at any time, gives us pause to reminisce. In an emotional trip down memory lane, Miguel and I recall the names of the people and the events that left indelible impressions on our minds.

Miguel tells me that Juanita needed almost a year to recover and adds that Juanita and Armandita recently opened a little hotel near Acapulco appropriately called "Mariposa", the "Butterfly". It is the jocular nickname for gays and lesbians in Mexico. They cater to the gay community flocking south from California and Texas and make a mint in the process. Good for them.

Hector, Benigno, Felipe, Vicente and many other colleagues and friends slowly drifted away from Tepetapa once they had received their big pay-off.

We have no idea where Hector ended up or if he is still alive. He was an old man who had the dream of finding a woman to marry and have a family once he had enough money. Knowing his penchant for tequila it remained in all likelihood a dream. I can just imagine him sitting soused to the eyeballs in some dingy bar, asking any old woman to marry him, and getting the advice that the nearest brothel is just around the corner.

Benigno has joined a controlled destruction company in Toluca that allows him to blow up old buildings to his heart's content and make room for new developments.

Felipe returned to his calling of being an actor. A few months ago, his repertory company staged a play here in Irapuato. I congratulated him on a wonderful performance in the role of the poet Ruben Darío. He thanked me but confessed that no matter what part he would play, he would always consider the role of government inspector in Tepetapa the performance of his lifetime.

Vicente and I had stayed in touch and eventually he decided to move to Irapuato. I helped him to set up a workshop here and we are partners in his new venture.

So many other miners and mill and smelter workers, women and children, yes, practically everybody contributed in some way to the success of our action. We stood together, we were a brotherhood, and we helped each other through a difficult period. It was this rapport that made Tepetapa such an unforgettable experience, not the dirt and grime, dust and stench, darkness and danger, pain and suffering. We had at last recognised that unity is strength and fought as one for a common goal.

My most vivid memory of Tepetapa is that fateful day of my accident when Miguel saved my life and then simply turned and went back to work as if nothing special had happened. I wanted to express my gratitude to Miguel for his act of bravery but to him it had been only part of his job. He did what needed to be done and then carried on with the work he had been hired to do. His decisive action set him apart from lesser men, me included.

Miguel is a man I can never be. I may try to aspire to his greatness. I may have my own defining moment of greatness, but I will never be his equal. Only very few men can jump into action, do what needs to be done, and once they have done it get on with life without fuss or grand gestures. His action that day stood for everything he personified: leadership, courage, and unselfish action. And I know, notwithstanding the visual proof he had slammed in my face, that Miguel was an *"hombre con cojones"*, a man with balls, a man better not to be underestimated by anyone.

I ask him what he intends to do in future. He tells me that Laura insists to give underground mining a break. Yet, he doesn't know what other job he can do having been a miner all his working life. He is certain that something will come along while he will build a house for his family, he says quite optimistically.

I suggest that with his oratory skills and persuasiveness he should go into politics. He laughs at first but then seems to give it some thought.

Time will tell if he will take my suggestion seriously and follow up on it.

A Final Note

The events described in this work are fiction except for the miners' final act of defiance. Many years ago, in the state of Puebla, south of the City of Mexico, miners took the action of walking naked to the capital in protest of their demands for fair wages and safe work conditions having been ignored. The Mexican mine management caved in after two days when the event was publicised in the national and international press. The miners' demands were met in full. Besides that event, the rest of the novel is fiction but to what extent is not known.

Many American and Canadian mine managers, who were held responsible for mine accidents and the death of hundreds of miners in the USA and Canada, preferred not to face justice and took off to warmer climes in Latin America, mostly to Mexico where hundreds of illegal mines are still in operation.

And life also has a tendency to overtake fiction. On the very day the first draft of this novel was completed, the Canadian media reported a factory accident in Mexico that reflected an altogether eerie resemblance to the attitude of the managers depicted in this story.

A fire had broken out in a foreign owned electronics assembly factory in the city of Guadalajara. Management escaped to safety while the workers were under strict orders, on pain of getting fired without compensation, to stay put. Over 120 factory employees suffered severe poisoning from the inhalation of lead and zinc laden smoke. Several women and men died in consequence and most of the survivors are incapacitated for life and will never work again.

As of this day, the managers, expatriate North Americans have not been called to account for the death and suffering they caused. There also has been no uprising of the surviving Mexican workers or the victims' families to demand justice and compensation, or at least to chase these unscrupulous gringos out of the country.

Alas, in that respect this novel will remain fiction.